Jerry of the Islands

Jerry of the Islands
Jack London

MINT EDITIONS

Jerry of the Islands was first published in 1917.

This edition published by Mint Editions 2021.

ISBN 9781513270234 | E-ISBN 9781513275239

Published by Mint Editions®

MINT
EDITIONS

minteditionbooks.com

Publishing Director: Jennifer Newens
Design & Production: Rachel Lopez Metzger
Typesetting: Westchester Publishing Services

Contents

I

Not until *Mister* Haggin abruptly picked him up under one arm and stepped into the sternsheets of the waiting whaleboat, did Jerry dream that anything untoward was to happen to him. *Mister* Haggin was Jerry's beloved master, and had been his beloved master for the six months of Jerry's life. Jerry did not know *Mister* Haggin as "master," for "master" had no place in Jerry's vocabulary, Jerry being a smooth-coated, golden-sorrel Irish terrier.

But in Jerry's vocabulary, "*Mister* Haggin" possessed all the definiteness of sound and meaning that the word "master" possesses in the vocabularies of humans in relation to their dogs. "*Mister* Haggin" was the sound Jerry had always heard uttered by Bob, the clerk, and by Derby, the foreman on the plantation, when they addressed his master. Also, Jerry had always heard the rare visiting two-legged man-creatures such as came on the *Arangi*, address his master as *Mister* Haggin.

But dogs being dogs, in their dim, inarticulate, brilliant, and heroic-worshipping ways misappraising humans, dogs think of their masters, and love their masters, more than the facts warrant. "Master" means to them, as "*Mister*" Haggin meant to Jerry, a deal more, and a great deal more, than it means to humans. The human considers himself as "master" to his dog, but the dog considers his master "God."

Now "God" was no word in Jerry's vocabulary, despite the fact that he already possessed a definite and fairly large vocabulary. "*Mister* Haggin" was the sound that meant "God." In Jerry's heart and head, in the mysterious centre of all his activities that is called consciousness, the sound, "*Mister* Haggin," occupied the same place that "God" occupies in human consciousness. By word and sound, to Jerry, "*Mister* Haggin" had the same connotation that "God" has to God-worshipping humans. In short, *Mister* Haggin was Jerry's God.

And so, when *Mister* Haggin, or God, or call it what one will with the limitations of language, picked Jerry up with imperative abruptness, tucked him under his arm, and stepped into the whaleboat, whose black crew immediately bent to the oars, Jerry was instantly and nervously aware that the unusual had begun to happen. Never before had he gone out on board the *Arangi*, which he could see growing larger and closer to each lip-hissing stroke of the oars of the blacks.

Only an hour before, Jerry had come down from the plantation house to the beach to see the *Arangi* depart. Twice before, in his half-year of life, had he had this delectable experience. Delectable it truly was, running up and down the white beach of sand-pounded coral, and, under the wise guidance of Biddy and Terrence, taking part in the excitement of the beach and even adding to it.

There was the nigger-chasing. Jerry had been born to hate niggers. His first experiences in the world as a puling puppy, had taught him that Biddy, his mother, and his father Terrence, hated niggers. A nigger was something to be snarled at. A nigger, unless he were a house-boy, was something to be attacked and bitten and torn if he invaded the compound. Biddy did it. Terrence did it. In doing it, they served their God—*Mister* Haggin. Niggers were two-legged lesser creatures who toiled and slaved for their two-legged white lords, who lived in the labour barracks afar off, and who were so much lesser and lower that they must not dare come near the habitation of their lords.

And nigger-chasing was adventure. Not long after he had learned to sprawl, Jerry had learned that. One took his chances. As long as *Mister* Haggin, or Derby, or Bob, was about, the niggers took their chasing. But there were times when the white lords were not about. Then it was "'Ware niggers!" One must dare to chase only with due precaution. Because then, beyond the white lord's eyes, the niggers had a way, not merely of scowling and muttering, but of attacking four-legged dogs with stones and clubs. Jerry had seen his mother so mishandled, and, ere he had learned discretion, alone in the high grass had been himself club-mauled by Godarmy, the black who wore a china door-knob suspended on his chest from his neck on a string of sennit braided from cocoanut fibre. More. Jerry remembered another high-grass adventure, when he and his brother Michael had fought Owmi, another black distinguishable for the cogged wheels of an alarm clock on his chest. Michael had been so severely struck on his head that for ever after his left ear had remained sore and had withered into a peculiar wilted and twisted upward cock.

Still more. There had been his brother Patsy, and his sister Kathleen, who had disappeared two months before, who had ceased and no longer were. The great god, *Mister* Haggin, had raged up and down the plantation. The bush had been searched. Half a dozen niggers had been whipped. And *Mister* Haggin had failed to solve the mystery of Patsy's and Kathleen's disappearance. But Biddy and Terrence knew. So did

Michael and Jerry. The four-months' old Patsy and Kathleen had gone into the cooking-pot at the barracks, and their puppy-soft skins had been destroyed in the fire. Jerry knew this, as did his father and mother and brother, for they had smelled the unmistakable burnt-meat smell, and Terrence, in his rage of knowledge, had even attacked Mogom the house-boy, and been reprimanded and cuffed by *Mister* Haggin, who had not smelled and did not understand, and who had always to impress discipline on all creatures under his roof-tree.

But on the beach, when the blacks, whose terms of service were up came down with their trade-boxes on their heads to depart on the *Arangi*, was the time when nigger-chasing was not dangerous. Old scores could be settled, and it was the last chance, for the blacks who departed on the *Arangi* never came back. As an instance, this very morning Biddy, remembering a secret mauling at the hands of Lerumie, laid teeth into his naked calf and threw him sprawling into the water, trade-box, earthly possessions and all, and then laughed at him, sure in the protection of *Mister* Haggin who grinned at the episode.

Then, too, there was usually at least one bush-dog on the *Arangi* at which Jerry and Michael, from the beach, could bark their heads off. Once, Terrence, who was nearly as large as an Airedale and fully as lion-hearted—Terrence the Magnificent, as Tom Haggin called him— had caught such a bush-dog trespassing on the beach and given him a delightful thrashing, in which Jerry and Michael, and Patsy and Kathleen, who were at the time alive, had joined with many shrill yelps and sharp nips. Jerry had never forgotten the ecstasy of the hair, unmistakably doggy in scent, which had filled his mouth at his one successful nip. Bush-dogs were dogs—he recognized them as his kind; but they were somehow different from his own lordly breed, different and lesser, just as the blacks were compared with *Mister* Haggin, Derby, and Bob.

But Jerry did not continue to gaze at the nearing *Arangi*. Biddy, wise with previous bitter bereavements, had sat down on the edge of the sand, her fore-feet in the water, and was mouthing her woe. That this concerned him, Jerry knew, for her grief tore sharply, albeit vaguely, at his sensitive, passionate heart. What it presaged he knew not, save that it was disaster and catastrophe connected with him. As he looked back at her, rough-coated and grief-stricken, he could see Terrence hovering solicitously near her. He, too, was rough-coated, as was Michael, and as Patsy and Kathleen had been, Jerry being the one smooth-coated member of the family.

Further, although Jerry did not know it and Tom Haggin did, Terrence was a royal lover and a devoted spouse. Jerry, from his earliest impressions, could remember the way Terrence had of running with Biddy, miles and miles along the beaches or through the avenues of cocoanuts, side by side with her, both with laughing mouths of sheer delight. As these were the only dogs, besides his brothers and sisters and the several eruptions of strange bush-dogs that Jerry knew, it did not enter his head otherwise than that this was the way of dogs, male and female, wedded and faithful. But Tom Haggin knew its unusualness. "Proper affinities," he declared, and repeatedly declared, with warm voice and moist eyes of appreciation. "A gentleman, that Terrence, and a four-legged proper man. A man-dog, if there ever was one, four-square as the legs on the four corners of him. And prepotent! My word! His blood'd breed true for a thousand generations, and the cool head and the kindly brave heart of him."

Terrence did not voice his sorrow, if sorrow he had; but his hovering about Biddy tokened his anxiety for her. Michael, however, yielding to the contagion, sat beside his mother and barked angrily out across the increasing stretch of water as he would have barked at any danger that crept and rustled in the jungle. This, too, sank to Jerry's heart, adding weight to his sure intuition that dire fate, he knew not what, was upon him.

For his six months of life, Jerry knew a great deal and knew very little. He knew, without thinking about it, without knowing that he knew, why Biddy, the wise as well as the brave, did not act upon all the message that her heart voiced to him, and spring into the water and swim after him. She had protected him like a lioness when the big *puarka* (which, in Jerry's vocabulary, along with grunts and squeals, was the combination of sound, or word, for "pig") had tried to devour him where he was cornered under the high-piled plantation house. Like a lioness, when the cook-boy had struck him with a stick to drive him out of the kitchen, had Biddy sprung upon the black, receiving without wince or whimper one straight blow from the stick, and then downing him and mauling him among his pots and pans until dragged (for the first time snarling) away by the unchiding *Mister* Haggin, who; however, administered sharp words to the cook-boy for daring to lift hand against a four-legged dog belonging to a god.

Jerry knew why his mother did not plunge into the water after him. The salt sea, as well as the lagoons that led out of the salt sea, were taboo. "Taboo," as word or sound, had no place in Jerry's vocabulary. But its definition, or significance, was there in the quickest part of his consciousness. He possessed a dim, vague, imperative knowingness that it was not merely not good, but supremely disastrous, leading to the mistily glimpsed sense of utter endingness for a dog, for any dog, to go into the water where slipped and slid and noiselessly paddled, sometimes on top, sometimes emerging from the depths, great scaly monsters, huge-jawed and horribly-toothed, that snapped down and engulfed a dog in an instant just as the fowls of *Mister* Haggin snapped and engulfed grains of corn.

Often he had heard his father and mother, on the safety of the sand, bark and rage their hatred of those terrible sea-dwellers, when, close to the beach, they appeared on the surface like logs awash. "Crocodile" was no word in Jerry's vocabulary. It was an image, an image of a log awash that was different from any log in that it was alive. Jerry, who heard, registered, and recognized many words that were as truly tools of thought to him as they were to humans, but who, by inarticulateness of birth and breed, could not utter these many words, nevertheless in his mental processes, used images just as articulate men use words in their own mental processes. And after all, articulate men, in the act of thinking, willy nilly use images that correspond to words and that amplify words.

Perhaps, in Jerry's brain, the rising into the foreground of consciousness of an image of a log awash connoted more intimate and fuller comprehension of the thing being thought about, than did the word "crocodile," and its accompanying image, in the foreground of a human's consciousness. For Jerry really did know more about crocodiles than the average human. He could smell a crocodile farther off and more differentiatingly than could any man, than could even a salt-water black or a bushman smell one. He could tell when a crocodile, hauled up from the lagoon, lay without sound or movement, and perhaps asleep, a hundred feet away on the floor mat of jungle.

He knew more of the language of crocodiles than did any man. He had better means and opportunities of knowing. He knew their many noises that were as grunts and slubbers. He knew their anger noises, their fear noises, their food noises, their love noises. And these noises were as definitely words in his vocabulary as are words in a human's vocabulary. And these crocodile noises were tools of thought. By them he weighed and judged and determined his own consequent courses of action, just like any human; or, just like any human, lazily resolved upon no course of action, but merely noted and registered a clear comprehension of something that was going on about him that did not require a correspondence of action on his part.

And yet, what Jerry did not know was very much. He did not know the size of the world. He did not know that this Meringe Lagoon, backed by high, forested mountains and fronted and sheltered by the off-shore coral islets, was anything else than the entire world. He did not know that it was a mere fractional part of the great island of Ysabel, that was again one island of a thousand, many of them greater, that composed the Solomon Islands that men marked on charts as a group of specks in the vastitude of the far-western South Pacific.

It was true, there was a somewhere else or a something beyond of which he was dimly aware. But whatever it was, it was mystery. Out of it, things that had not been, suddenly were. Chickens and puarkas and cats, that he had never seen before, had a way of abruptly appearing on Meringe Plantation. Once, even, had there been an eruption of strange four-legged, horned and hairy creatures, the images of which, registered in his brain, would have been identifiable in the brains of humans with what humans worded "goats."

It was the same way with the blacks. Out of the unknown, from the somewhere and something else, too unconditional for him to know any of the conditions, instantly they appeared, full-statured, walking about Meringe Plantation with loin-cloths about their middles and bone bodkins through their noses, and being put to work by *Mister* Haggin, Derby, and Bob. That their appearance was coincidental with the arrival of the *Arangi* was an association that occurred as a matter of course in Jerry's brain. Further, he did not bother, save that there was a companion association, namely, that their occasional disappearances into the beyond was likewise coincidental with the *Arangi's* departure.

Jerry did not query these appearances and disappearances. It never entered his golden-sorrel head to be curious about the affair or to attempt to solve it. He accepted it in much the way he accepted the wetness of water and the heat of the sun. It was the way of life and of the world he knew. His hazy awareness was no more than an awareness of something—which, by the way, corresponds very fairly with the hazy awareness of the average human of the mysteries of birth and death and of the beyondness about which they have no definiteness of comprehension.

For all that any man may gainsay, the ketch *Arangi*, trader and blackbirder in the Solomon Islands, may have signified in Jerry's mind as much the mysterious boat that traffics between the two worlds, as, at one time, the boat that Charon sculled across the Styx signified to the human mind. Out of the nothingness men came. Into the nothingness they went. And they came and went always on the *Arangi*.

And to the *Arangi*, this hot-white tropic morning, Jerry went on the whaleboat under the arm of his *Mister* Haggin, while on the beach Biddy moaned her woe, and Michael, not sophisticated, barked the eternal challenge of youth to the Unknown.

II

From the whaleboat, up the low side of the *Arangi*, and over her six-inch rail of teak to her teak deck, was but a step, and Tom Haggin made it easily with Jerry still under his arm. The deck was cluttered with an exciting crowd. Exciting the crowd would have been to untravelled humans of civilization, and exciting it was to Jerry; although to Tom Haggin and Captain Van Horn it was a mere commonplace of everyday life.

The deck was small because the *Arangi* was small. Originally a teak-built, gentleman's yacht, brass-fitted, copper-fastened, angle-ironed, sheathed in man-of-war copper and with a fin-keel of bronze, she had been sold into the Solomon Islands' trade for the purpose of blackbirding or nigger-running. Under the law, however, this traffic was dignified by being called "recruiting."

The *Arangi* was a labour-recruit ship that carried the new-caught, cannibal blacks from remote islands to labour on the new plantations where white men turned dank and pestilential swamp and jungle into rich and stately cocoanut groves. The *Arangi's* two masts were of Oregon cedar, so scraped and hot-paraffined that they shone like tan opals in the glare of sun. Her excessive sail plan enabled her to sail like a witch, and, on occasion, gave Captain Van Horn, his white mate, and his fifteen black boat's crew as much as they could handle. She was sixty feet over all, and the cross beams of her crown deck had not been weakened by deck-houses. The only breaks—and no beams had been cut for them—were the main cabin skylight and companionway, the booby hatch for'ard over the tiny forecastle, and the small hatch aft that let down into the store-room.

And on this small deck, in addition to the crew, were the "return" niggers from three far-flung plantations. By "return" was meant that their three years of contract labour was up, and that, according to contract, they were being returned to their home villages on the wild island of Malaita. Twenty of them—familiar, all, to Jerry—were from Meringe; thirty of them came from the Bay of a Thousand Ships, in the Russell Isles; and the remaining twelve were from Pennduffryn on the east coast of Guadalcanar. In addition to these—and they were all on deck, chattering and piping in queer, almost elfish, falsetto voices—were the two white men, Captain Van Horn and his Danish mate, Borckman, making a total of seventy-nine souls.

"Thought your heart'd failed you at the last moment," was Captain Van Horn's greeting, a quick pleasure light glowing into his eyes as they noted Jerry.

"It was sure near to doin' it," Tom Haggin answered. "It's only for you I'd a done it, annyways. Jerry's the best of the litter, barrin' Michael, of course, the two of them bein' all that's left and no better than them that was lost. Now that Kathleen was a sweet dog, the spit of Biddy if she'd lived.—Here, take 'm."

With a jerk of abruptness, he deposited Jerry in Van Horn's arms and turned away along the deck.

"An' if bad luck comes to him I'll never forgive you, Skipper," he flung roughly over his shoulder.

"They'll have to take my head first," the skipper chuckled.

"An' not unlikely, my brave laddy buck," Haggin growled. "Meringe owes Somo four heads, three from the dysentery, an' another wan from a tree fallin' on him the last fortnight. He was the son of a chief at that."

"Yes, and there's two heads more that the *Arangi* owes Somo," Van Horn nodded. "You recollect, down to the south'ard last year, a chap named Hawkins was lost in his whaleboat running the Arli Passage?" Haggin, returning along the deck, nodded. "Two of his boat's crew were Somo boys. I'd recruited them for Ugi Plantation. With your boys, that makes six heads the *Arangi* owes. But what of it? There's one salt-water village, acrost on the weather coast, where the *Arangi* owes eighteen. I recruited them for Aolo, and being salt-water men they put them on the *Sandfly* that was lost on the way to the Santa Cruz. They've got a jack-pot over there on the weather coast—my word, the boy that could get my head would be a second Carnegie! A hundred and fifty pigs and shell money no end the village's collected for the chap that gets me and delivers."

"And they ain't—yet," Haggin snorted.

"No fear," was the cheerful retort.

"You talk like Arbuckle used to talk," Haggin censured. "Manny's the time I've heard him string it off. Poor old Arbuckle. The most sure and most precautious chap that ever handled niggers. He never went to sleep without spreadin' a box of tacks on the floor, and when it wasn't them it was crumpled newspapers. I remember me well, bein' under the same roof at the time on Florida, when a big tomcat chased a cockroach into the papers. And it was blim, blam, blim, six times an' twice over, with his two big horse-pistols, an' the house perforated like a cullender.

Likewise there was a dead tom-cat. He could shoot in the dark with never an aim, pullin' trigger with the second finger and pointing with the first finger laid straight along the barrel.

"No, sir, my laddy buck. He was the bully boy with the glass eye. The nigger didn't live that'd lift his head. But they got 'm. They got 'm. He lasted fourteen years, too. It was his cook-boy. Hatcheted 'm before breakfast. An' it's well I remember our second trip into the bush after what was left of 'm."

"I saw his head after you'd turned it over to the Commissioner at Tulagi," Van Horn supplemented.

"An' the peaceful, quiet, everyday face of him on it, with almost the same old smile I'd seen a thousand times. It dried on 'm that way over the smokin' fire. But they got 'm, if it did take fourteen years. There's manny's the head that goes to Malaita, manny's the time untooken; but, like the old pitcher, it's tooken in the end."

"But I've got their goat," the captain insisted. "When trouble's hatching, I go straight to them and tell them what. They can't get the hang of it. Think I've got some powerful devil-devil medicine."

Tom Haggin thrust out his hand in abrupt good-bye, resolutely keeping his eyes from dropping to Jerry in the other's arms.

"Keep your eye on my return boys," he cautioned, as he went over the side, "till you land the last mother's son of 'm. They've got no cause to love Jerry or his breed, an' I'd hate ill to happen 'm at a nigger's hands. An' in the dark of the night 'tis like as not he can do a fare-you-well overside. Don't take your eye off 'm till you're quit of the last of 'm."

At sight of big *Mister* Haggin deserting him and being pulled away in the whaleboat, Jerry wriggled and voiced his anxiety in a low, whimpering whine. Captain Van Horn snuggled him closer in his arm with a caress of his free hand.

"Don't forget the agreement," Tom Haggin called back across the widening water. "If aught happens you, Jerry's to come back to me."

"I'll make a paper to that same and put it with the ship's articles," was Van Horn's reply.

Among the many words possessed by Jerry was his own name; and in the talk of the two men he had recognised it repeatedly, and he was aware, vaguely, that the talk was related to the vague and unguessably terrible thing that was happening to him. He wriggled more determinedly, and Van Horn set him down on the deck. He sprang to the rail with more quickness than was to be expected of an awkward puppy of six months, and not the quick attempt of Van Horn to cheek him would have succeeded. But Jerry recoiled from the open water lapping the *Arangi's* side. The taboo was upon him. It was the image of the log awash that was not a log but that was alive, luminous in his brain, that checked him. It was not reason on his part, but inhibition which had become habit.

He plumped down on his bob tail, lifted golden muzzle skyward, and emitted a long puppy-wail of dismay and grief.

"It's all right, Jerry, old man, brace up and be a man-dog," Van Horn soothed him.

But Jerry was not to be reconciled. While this indubitably was a white-skinned god, it was not his god. *Mister* Haggin was his god, and a superior god at that. Even he, without thinking about it at all, recognized that. His *Mister* Haggin wore pants and shoes. This god on the deck beside him was more like a black. Not only did he not wear pants, and was barefooted and barelegged, but about his middle, just like any black, he wore a brilliant-coloured loin-cloth, that, like a kilt, fell nearly to his sunburnt knees.

Captain Van Horn was a handsome man and a striking man, although Jerry did not know it. If ever a Holland Dutchman stepped out of a Rembrandt frame, Captain Van Horn was that one, despite the fact that he was New York born, as had been his knickerbocker ancestors before him clear back to the time when New York was not New York but New Amsterdam. To complete his costume, a floppy felt hat, distinctly Rembrandtish in effect, perched half on his head and mostly over one ear; a sixpenny, white cotton undershirt covered his torso; and from a belt about his middle dangled a tobacco pouch, a sheath-knife, filled clips of cartridges, and a huge automatic pistol in a leather holster.

On the beach, Biddy, who had hushed her grief, lifted it again when she heard Jerry's wail. And Jerry, desisting a moment to listen, heard Michael beside her, barking his challenge, and saw, without being conscious of it, Michael's withered ear with its persistent upward cock. Again, while Captain Van Horn and the mate, Borckman, gave orders, and while the *Arangi's* mainsail and spanker began to rise up the masts, Jerry loosed all his heart of woe in what Bob told Derby on the beach was the "grandest vocal effort" he had ever heard from any dog, and that, except for being a bit thin, Caruso didn't have anything on Jerry. But the song was too much for Haggin, who, as soon as he had landed, whistled Biddy to him and strode rapidly away from the beach.

At sight of her disappearing, Jerry was guilty of even more Caruso-like effects, which gave great joy to a Pennduffryn return boy who stood beside him. He laughed and jeered at Jerry with falsetto chucklings that were more like the jungle-noises of tree-dwelling creatures, half-bird and half-man, than of a man, all man, and therefore a god. This served as an excellent counter-irritant. Indignation that a mere black should laugh at him mastered Jerry, and the next moment his puppy teeth, sharp-pointed as needles, had scored the astonished black's naked calf in long parallel scratches from each of which leaped the instant blood. The black sprang away in trepidation, but the blood of Terrence the Magnificent was true in Jerry, and, like his father before him, he followed up, slashing the black's other calf into a ruddy pattern.

At this moment, anchor broken out and headsails running up, Captain Van Horn, whose quick eye had missed no detail of the incident, with an order to the black helmsman turned to applaud Jerry.

"Go to it, Jerry!" he encouraged. "Get him! Shake him down! Sick him! Get him! Get him!"

The black, in defence, aimed a kick at Jerry, who, leaping in instead of away—another inheritance from Terrence—avoided the bare foot and printed a further red series of parallel lines on the dark leg. This was too much, and the black, afraid more of Van Horn than of Jerry, turned and fled for'ard, leaping to safety on top of the eight Lee-Enfield rifles that lay on top of the cabin skylight and that were guarded by one member of the boat's crew. About the skylight Jerry stormed, leaping up and falling back, until Captain Van Horn called him off.

"Some nigger-chaser, that pup, *some* nigger-chaser!" Van Horn confided to Borckman, as he bent to pat Jerry and give him due reward of praise.

And Jerry, under this caressing hand of a god, albeit it did not wear pants, forgot for a moment longer the fate that was upon him.

"He's a lion-dog—more like an Airedale than an Irish terrier," Van Horn went on to his mate, still petting. "Look at the size of him already. Look at the bone of him. Some chest that. He's got the endurance. And he'll be some dog when he grows up to those feet of his."

Jerry had just remembered his grief and was starting a rush across the deck to the rail to gaze at Meringe growing smaller every second in the distance, when a gust of the South-east Trade smote the sails and pressed the *Arangi* down. And down the deck, slanted for the moment to forty-five degrees, Jerry slipped and slid, vainly clawing at the smooth surface for a hold. He fetched up against the foot of the mizzenmast, while Captain Van Horn, with the sailor's eye for the coral patch under his bow, gave the order "Hard a-lee!"

Borckman and the black steersman echoed his words, and, as the wheel spun down, the *Arangi*, with the swiftness of a witch, rounded into the wind and attained a momentary even keel to the flapping of her headsails and a shifting of headsheets.

Jerry, still intent on Meringe, took advantage of the level footing to recover himself and scramble toward the rail. But he was deflected by the crash of the mainsheet blocks on the stout deck-traveller, as the mainsail, emptied of the wind and feeling the wind on the other side, swung crazily across above him. He cleared the danger of the mainsheet with a wild leap (although no less wild had been Van Horn's leap to rescue him), and found himself directly under the mainboom with the huge sail looming above him as if about to fall upon him and crush him.

It was Jerry's first experience with sails of any sort. He did not know the beasts, much less the way of them, but, in his vivid recollection, when he had been a tiny puppy, burned the memory of the hawk, in the middle of the compound, that had dropped down upon him from out of the sky. Under that colossal threatened impact he crouched down to the deck. Above him, falling upon him like a bolt from the blue, was a winged hawk unthinkably vaster than the one he had encountered. But in his crouch was no hint of cower. His crouch was a gathering together, an assembling of all the parts of him under the rule of the spirit of him, for the spring upward to meet in mid career this monstrous, menacing thing.

But, the succeeding fraction of a moment, so that Jerry, leaping, missed even the shadow of it, the mainsail, with a second crash of blocks on traveller, had swung across and filled on the other tack.

Van Horn had missed nothing of it. Before, in his time, he had seen young dogs frightened into genuine fits by their first encounters with heaven-filling, sky-obscuring, down-impending sails. This was the first dog he had seen leap with bared teeth, undismayed, to grapple with the huge unknown.

With spontaneity of admiration, Van Horn swept Jerry from the deck and gathered him into his arms.

III

Jerry quite forgot Meringe for the time being. As he well remembered, the hawk had been sharp of beak and claw. This air-flapping, thunder-crashing monster needed watching. And Jerry, crouching for the spring and ever struggling to maintain his footing on the slippery, heeling deck, kept his eyes on the mainsail and uttered low growls at any display of movement on its part.

The *Arangi* was beating out between the coral patches of the narrow channel into the teeth of the brisk trade wind. This necessitated frequent tacks, so that, overhead, the mainsail was ever swooping across from port tack to starboard tack and back again, making air-noises like the swish of wings, sharply rat-tat-tatting its reef points and loudly crashing its mainsheet gear along the traveller. Half a dozen times, as it swooped overhead, Jerry leaped for it, mouth open to grip, lips writhed clear of the clean puppy teeth that shone in the sun like gems of ivory.

Failing in every leap, Jerry achieved a judgment. In passing, it must be noted that this judgment was only arrived at by a definite act of reasoning. Out of a series of observations of the thing, in which it had threatened, always in the same way, a series of attacks, he had found that it had not hurt him nor come in contact with him at all. Therefore—although he did not stop to think that he was thinking—it was not the dangerous, destroying thing he had first deemed it. It might be well to be wary of it, though already it had taken its place in his classification of things that appeared terrible but were not terrible. Thus, he had learned not to fear the roar of the wind among the palms when he lay snug on the plantation-house veranda, nor the onslaught of the waves, hissing and rumbling into harmless foam on the beach at his feet.

Many times, in the course of the day, alertly and nonchalantly, almost with a quizzical knowingness, Jerry cocked his head at the mainsail when it made sudden swooping movements or slacked and tautened its crashing sheet-gear. But he no longer crouched to spring for it. That had been the first lesson, and quickly mastered.

Having settled the mainsail, Jerry returned in mind to Meringe. But there was no Meringe, no Biddy and Terrence and Michael on the beach; no *Mister* Haggin and Derby and Bob; no beach: no land with the palm-trees near and the mountains afar off everlastingly lifting their green peaks into the sky. Always, to starboard or to port, at the bow or over the stern, when he stood up resting his fore-feet on the six-inch rail and gazing, he saw only the ocean, broken-faced and turbulent, yet orderly marching its white-crested seas before the drive of the trade.

Had he had the eyes of a man, nearly two yards higher than his own from the deck, and had they been the trained eyes of a man, sailor-man at that, Jerry could have seen the low blur of Ysabel to the north and the blur of Florida to the south, ever taking on definiteness of detail as the *Arangi* sagged close-hauled, with a good full, port-tacked to the south-east trade. And had he had the advantage of the marine glasses with which Captain Van Horn elongated the range of his eyes, he could have seen, to the east, the far peaks of Malaita lifting life-shadowed pink cloud-puffs above the sea-rim.

But the present was very immediate with Jerry. He had early learned the iron law of the immediate, and to accept what *was* when it was, rather than to strain after far other things. The sea was. The land no longer was. The *Arangi* certainly was, along with the life that cluttered her deck. And he proceeded to get acquainted with what was—in short, to know and to adjust himself to his new environment.

His first discovery was delightful—a wild-dog puppy from the Ysabel bush, being taken back to Malaita by one of the Meringe return boys. In age they were the same, but their breeding was different. The wild-dog was what he was, a wild-dog, cringing and sneaking, his ears for ever down, his tail for ever between his legs, for ever apprehending fresh misfortune and ill-treatment to fall on him, for ever fearing and resentful, fending off threatened hurt with lips curling malignantly from his puppy fangs, cringing under a blow, squalling his fear and his pain, and ready always for a treacherous slash if luck and safety favoured.

The wild-dog was maturer than Jerry, larger-bodied, and wiser in wickedness; but Jerry was blue-blooded, right-selected, and valiant. The wild-dog had come out of a selection equally rigid; but it was a different sort of selection. The bush ancestors from whom he had descended had survived by being fear-selected. They had never voluntarily fought against odds. In the open they had never attacked save when the prey was weak or defenceless. In place of courage, they had lived by creeping, and slinking, and hiding from danger. They had been selected blindly by nature, in a cruel and ignoble environment, where the prize of living was to be gained, in the main, by the cunning of cowardice, and, on occasion, by desperateness of defence when in a corner.

But Jerry had been love-selected and courage-selected. His ancestors had been deliberately and consciously chosen by men, who, somewhere in the forgotten past, had taken the wild-dog and made it into the thing they visioned and admired and desired it to be. It must never fight like a rat in a corner, because it must never be rat-like and slink into a corner. Retreat must be unthinkable. The dogs in the past who retreated had been rejected by men. They had not become Jerry's ancestors. The dogs selected for Jerry's ancestors had been the brave ones, the up-standing and out-dashing ones, who flew into the face of danger and battled and died, but who never gave ground. And, since it is the way of kind to beget kind, Jerry was what Terrence was before him, and what Terrence's forefathers had been for a long way back.

So it was that Jerry, when he chanced upon the wild-dog stowed shrewdly away from the wind in the lee-corner made by the mainmast and the cabin skylight, did not stop to consider whether the creature was bigger or fiercer than he. All he knew was that it was the ancient enemy—the wild-dog that had not come in to the fires of man. With a wild paean of joy that attracted Captain Van Horn's all-hearing ears and all-seeing eyes, Jerry sprang to the attack. The wild puppy gained his feet in full retreat with incredible swiftness, but was caught by the rush of Jerry's body and rolled over and over on the sloping deck. And as he rolled, and felt sharp teeth pricking him, he snapped and snarled, alternating snarls with whimperings and squallings of terror, pain, and abject humility.

And Jerry was a gentleman, which is to say he was a gentle dog. He had been so selected. Because the thing did not fight back, because it was abject and whining, because it was helpless under him, he abandoned the attack, disengaging himself from the top of the tangle into which he had slid in the lee scuppers. He did not think about it. He did it because he was so made. He stood up on the reeling deck, feeling excellently satisfied with the delicious, wild-doggy smell of hair in his mouth and consciousness, and in his ears and consciousness the praising cry of Captain Van Horn: "Good boy, Jerry! You're the goods, Jerry! Some dog, eh! *Some* dog!"

As he stalked away, it must be admitted that Jerry displayed pride in himself, his gait being a trifle stiff-legged, the cocking of his head back over his shoulder at the whining wild-dog having all the articulateness of: "Well, I guess I gave you enough this time. You'll keep out of my way after this."

Jerry continued the exploration of his new and tiny world that was never at rest, for ever lifting, heeling, and lunging on the rolling face of the sea. There were the Meringe return boys. He made it a point to identify all of them, receiving, while he did so, scowls and mutterings, and reciprocating with cocky bullyings and threatenings. Being so trained, he walked on his four legs superior to them, two-legged though they were; for he had moved and lived always under the aegis of the great two-legged and be-trousered god, *Mister* Haggin.

Then there were the strange return boys, from Pennduffryn and the Bay of a Thousand Ships. He insisted on knowing them all. He might need to know them in some future time. He did not think this. He merely equipped himself with knowledge of his environment without any awareness of provision or without bothering about the future.

In his own way of acquiring knowledge, he quickly discovered, just as on the plantation house-boys were different from field-boys, that on the *Arangi* there was a classification of boys different from the return boys. This was the boat's crew. The fifteen blacks who composed it were closer than the others to Captain Van Horn. They seemed more directly to belong to the *Arangi* and to him. They laboured under him at word of command, steering at the wheel, pulling and hauling on ropes, healing water upon the deck from overside and scrubbing with brooms.

Just as Jerry had learned from *Mister* Haggin that he must be more tolerant of the house-boys than of the field-boys if they trespassed on the compound, so, from Captain Van Horn, he learned that he must be more tolerant of the boat's crew than of the return boys. He had less license with them, more license with the others. As long as Captain Van Horn did not want his boat's crew chased, it was Jerry's duty not to chase. On the other hand he never forgot that he was a white-god's dog. While he might not chase these particular blacks, he declined familiarity with them. He kept his eye on them. He had seen blacks as tolerated as these, lined up and whipped by *Mister* Haggin. They occupied an intermediate place in the scheme of things, and they were to be watched in case they did not keep their place. He accorded them room, but he did not accord them equality. At the best, he could be stand-offishly considerate of them.

He made thorough examination of the galley, a rude affair, open on the open deck, exposed to wind and rain and storm, a small stove that was not even a ship's stove, on which somehow, aided by strings and wedges, commingled with much smoke, two blacks managed to cook the food for the four-score persons on board.

Next, he was interested by a strange proceeding on the part of the boat's crew. Upright pipes, serving as stanchions, were being screwed into the top of the *Arangi's* rail so that they served to support three strands of barbed wire that ran completely around the vessel, being broken only at the gangway for a narrow space of fifteen inches. That this was a precaution against danger, Jerry sensed without a passing thought to it. All his life, from his first impressions of life, had been passed in the heart of danger, ever-impending, from the blacks. In the plantation house at Meringe, always the several white men had looked askance at the many blacks who toiled for them and belonged to them. In the living-room, where were the eating-table, the billiard-table, and the phonograph, stood stands of rifles, and in each bedroom, beside each bed, ready to hand, had been revolvers and rifles. As well, *Mister* Haggin and Derby and Bob had always carried revolvers in their belts when they left the house to go among their blacks.

Jerry knew these noise-making things for what they were— instruments of destruction and death. He had seen live things destroyed by them, such as puarkas, goats, birds, and crocodiles. By means of such things the white-gods by their will crossed space without crossing it with their bodies, and destroyed live things. Now he, in order to damage anything, had to cross space with his body to get to it. He was different. He was limited. All impossible things were possible to the unlimited, two-legged white-gods. In a way, this ability of theirs to destroy across space was an elongation of claw and fang. Without pondering it, or being conscious of it, he accepted it as he accepted the rest of the mysterious world about him.

Once, even, had Jerry seen his *Mister* Haggin deal death at a distance in another noise-way. From the veranda he had seen him fling sticks of exploding dynamite into a screeching mass of blacks who had come raiding from the Beyond in the long war canoes, beaked and black, carved and inlaid with mother-of-pearl, which they had left hauled up on the beach at the door of Meringe.

Many precautions by the white-gods had Jerry been aware of, and so, sensing it almost in intangible ways, as a matter of course he accepted this barbed-wire fence on the floating world as a mark of the persistence of danger. Disaster and death hovered close about, waiting the chance to leap upon life and drag it down. Life had to be very alive in order to live was the law Jerry had learned from the little of life he knew.

Watching the rigging up of the barbed wire, Jerry's next adventure was an encounter with Lerumie, the return boy from Meringe, who, only that morning, on the beach embarking, had been rolled by Biddy, along with his possessions into the surf. The encounter occurred on the starboard side of the skylight, alongside of which Lerumie was standing as he gazed into a cheap trade-mirror and combed his kinky hair with a hand-carved comb of wood.

Jerry, scarcely aware of Lerumie's presence, was trotting past on his way aft to where Borckman, the mate, was superintending the stringing of the barbed wire to the stanchions. And Lerumie, with a side-long look to see if the deed meditated for his foot was screened from observation, aimed a kick at the son of his four-legged enemy. His bare foot caught Jerry on the sensitive end of his recently bobbed tail, and Jerry, outraged, with the sense of sacrilege committed upon him, went instantly wild.

Captain Van Horn, standing aft on the port quarter, gauging the slant of the wind on the sails and the inadequate steering of the black at the wheel, had not seen Jerry because of the intervening skylight. But his eyes had taken in the shoulder movement of Lerumie that advertised the balancing on one foot while the other foot had kicked. And from what followed, he divined what had already occurred.

Jerry's outcry, as he sprawled, whirled, sprang, and slashed, was a veritable puppy-scream of indignation. He slashed ankle and foot as he received the second kick in mid-air; and, although he slid clear down the slope of deck into the scuppers, he left on the black skin the red tracery of his puppy-needle teeth. Still screaming his indignation, he clawed his way back up the steep wooden hill.

Lerumie, with another side-long look, knew that he was observed and that he dare not go to extremes. He fled along the skylight to escape down the companionway, but was caught by Jerry's sharp teeth in his calf. Jerry, attacking blindly, got in the way of the black's feet. A long, stumbling fall, accelerated by a sudden increase of wind in the sails, ensued, and Lerumie, vainly trying to catch his footing, fetched up against the three strands of barbed wire on the lee rail.

The deck-full of blacks shrieked their merriment, and Jerry, his rage undiminished, his immediate antagonist out of the battle, mistaking himself as the object of the laughter of the blacks, turned upon them, charging and slashing the many legs that fled before him. They dropped down the cabin and forecastle companionways, ran out the bowsprit, and sprang into the rigging till they were perched everywhere in the air like monstrous birds. In the end, the deck belonged to Jerry, save for the boat's crew; for he had already learned to differentiate. Captain Van Horn was hilariously vocal of his praise, calling Jerry to him and giving him man-thumps of joyful admiration. Next, the captain turned to his many passengers and orated in *beche-de-mer* English.

"Hey! You fella boy! I make 'm big fella talk. This fella dog he belong along me. One fella boy hurt 'm that fella dog—my word!—me cross too much along that fella boy. I knock 'm seven bells outa that fella boy. You take 'm care leg belong you. I take 'm care dog belong me. Savve?"

And the passengers, still perched in the air, with gleaming black eyes and with querulerus chirpings one to another, accepted the white man's law. Even Lerumie, variously lacerated by the barbed wire, did not scowl nor mutter threats. Instead, and bringing a roar of laughter from his fellows and a twinkle into the skipper's eyes, he rubbed questing fingers over his scratches and murmured: "My word! Some big fella dog that fella!"

It was not that Jerry was unkindly. Like Biddy and Terrence, he was fierce and unafraid; which attributes were wrapped up in his heredity. And, like Biddy and Terrence, he delighted in nigger-chasing, which, in turn, was a matter of training. From his earliest puppyhood he had been so trained. Niggers were niggers, but white men were gods, and it was the white-gods who had trained him to chase niggers and keep them in their proper lesser place in the world. All the world was held in the hollow of the white man's hands. The niggers—well, had not he seen them always compelled to remain in their lesser place? Had he not seen them, on occasion, triced up to the palm-trees of the Meringe compound and their backs lashed to ribbons by the white-gods? Small wonder that a high-born Irish terrier, in the arms of love of the white-god, should look at niggers through white-god's eyes, and act toward niggers in the way that earned the white-god's reward of praise.

It was a busy day for Jerry. Everything about the *Arangi* was new and strange, and so crowded was she that exciting things were continually happening. He had another encounter with the wild-dog, who treacherously attacked him in flank from ambuscade. Trade boxes belonging to the blacks had been irregularly piled so that a small space was left between two boxes in the lower tier. From this hole, as Jerry trotted past in response to a call from the skipper, the wild-dog sprang, scratched his sharp puppy-teeth into Jerry's yellow-velvet hide, and scuttled back into his lair.

Again Jerry's feelings were outraged. He could understand flank attack. Often he and Michael had played at that, although it had only been playing. But to retreat without fighting from a fight once started was alien to Jerry's ways and nature. With righteous wrath he charged into the hole after his enemy. But this was where the wild-dog fought to best advantage—in a corner. When Jerry sprang up in the confined space he bumped his head on the box above, and the next moment felt the snarling impact of the other's teeth against his own teeth and jaw.

There was no getting at the wild-dog, no chance to rush against him whole heartedly, with generous full weight in the attack. All Jerry could do was to crawl and squirm and belly forward, and always he was met by a snarling mouthful of teeth. Even so, he would have got the wild-dog in the end, had not Borckman, in passing, reached in and dragged Jerry out by a hind-leg. Again came Captain Van Horn's call, and Jerry, obedient, trotted on aft.

A meal was being served on deck in the shade of the spanker, and Jerry, sitting between the two men received his share. Already he had made the generalization that of the two, the captain was the superior god, giving many orders that the mate obeyed. The mate, on the other hand, gave orders to the blacks, but never did he give orders to the captain. Furthermore, Jerry was developing a liking for the captain, so he snuggled close to him. When he put his nose into the captain's plate, he was gently reprimanded. But once, when he merely sniffed at the mate's steaming tea-cup, her received a snub on the nose from the mate's grimy forefinger. Also, the mate did not offer him food.

Captain Van Horn gave him, first of all, a pannikin of oatmeal mush, generously flooded with condensed cream and sweetened with a heaping spoonful of sugar. After that, on occasion, he gave him morsels of buttered bread and slivers of fried fish from which he first carefully picked the tiny bones.

His beloved *Mister* Haggin had never fed him from the table at meal time, and Jerry was beside himself with the joy of this delightful experience. And, being young, he allowed his eagerness to take possession of him, so that soon he was unduly urging the captain for more pieces of fish and of bread and butter. Once, he even barked his demand. This put the idea into the captain's head, who began immediately to teach him to "speak."

At the end of five minutes he had learned to speak softly, and to speak only once—a low, mellow, bell-like bark of a single syllable. Also, in this first five minutes, he had learned to "sit down," as distinctly different from "lie down"; and that he must sit down whenever he spoke, and that he must speak without jumping or moving from the sitting position, and then must wait until the piece of food was passed to him.

Further, he had added three words to his vocabulary. For ever after, "speak" would mean to him "speak," and "sit down" would mean "sit down" and would not mean "lie down." The third addition to his vocabulary was "Skipper." That was the name he had heard the mate repeatedly call Captain Van Horn. And just as Jerry knew that when a human called "Michael," that the call referred to Michael and not to Biddy, or Terrence, or himself, so he knew that *Skipper* was the name of the two-legged white master of this new floating world.

"That isn't just a dog," was Van Horn's conclusion to the mate. "There's a sure enough human brain there behind those brown eyes. He's six months old. Any boy of six years would be an infant phenomenon to learn in five minutes all that he's just learned. Why, Gott-fer-dang, a dog's brain has to be like a man's. If he does things like a man, he's got to think like a man."

IV

The companionway into the main cabin was a steep ladder, and down this, after his meal, Jerry was carried by the captain. The cabin was a long room, extending for the full width of the *Arangi* from a lazarette aft to a tiny room for'ard. For'ard of this room, separated by a tight bulkhead, was the forecastle where lived the boat's crew. The tiny room was shared between Van Horn and Borckman, while the main cabin was occupied by the three-score and odd return boys. They squatted about and lay everywhere on the floor and on the long low bunks that ran the full length of the cabin along either side.

In the little stateroom the captain tossed a blanket on the floor in a corner, and he did not find it difficult to get Jerry to understand that that was his bed. Nor did Jerry, with a full stomach and weary from so much excitement, find it difficult to fall immediately asleep.

An hour later he was awakened by the entrance of Borckman. When he wagged his stub of a tail and smiled friendly with his eyes, the mate scowled at him and muttered angrily in his throat. Jerry made no further overtures, but lay quietly watching. The mate had come to take a drink. In truth, he was stealing the drink from Van Horn's supply. Jerry did not know this. Often, on the plantation, he had seen the white men take drinks. But there was something somehow different in the manner of Borckman's taking a drink. Jerry was aware, vaguely, that there was something surreptitious about it. What was wrong he did not know, yet he sensed the wrongness and watched suspiciously.

After the mate departed, Jerry would have slept again had not the carelessly latched door swung open with a bang. Opening his eyes, prepared for any hostile invasion from the unknown, he fell to watching a large cockroach crawling down the wall. When he got to his feet and warily stalked toward it, the cockroach scuttled away with a slight rustling noise and disappeared into a crack. Jerry had been acquainted with cockroaches all his life, but he was destined to learn new things about them from the particular breed that dwelt on the *Arangi*.

After a cursory examination of the stateroom he wandered out into the cabin. The blacks, sprawled about everywhere, but, conceiving it to be his duty to his *Skipper*, Jerry made it a point to identify each one. They scowled and uttered low threatening noises when he sniffed close to them. One dared to menace him with a blow, but Jerry, instead of slinking away, showed his teeth and prepared to spring. The black hastily dropped the offending hand to his side and made soothing, penitent noises, while others chuckled; and Jerry passed on his way. It was nothing new. Always a blow was to be expected from blacks when white men were not around. Both the mate and the captain were on deck, and Jerry, though unafraid, continued his investigations cautiously.

But at the doorless entrance to the lazarette aft, he threw caution to the winds and darted in in pursuit of the new scent that came to his nostrils. A strange person was in the low, dark space whom he had never smelled. Clad in a single shift and lying on a coarse grass-mat spread upon a pile of tobacco cases and fifty-pound tins of flour, was a young black girl.

There was something furtive and lurking about her that Jerry did not fail to sense, and he had long since learned that something was wrong when any black lurked or skulked. She cried out with fear as he barked an alarm and pounced upon her. Even though his teeth scratched her bare arm, she did not strike at him. Not did she cry out again. She cowered down and trembled and did not fight back. Keeping his teeth locked in the hold he had got on her flimsy shift, he shook and dragged at her, all the while growling and scolding for her benefit and yelping a high clamour to bring Skipper or the mate.

In the course of the struggle the girl over-balanced on the boxes and tins and the entire heap collapsed. This caused Jerry to yelp a more frenzied alarm, while the blacks, peering in from the cabin, laughed with cruel enjoyment.

When Skipper arrived, Jerry wagged his stump tail and, with ears laid back, dragged and tugged harder than ever at the thin cotton of the girl's garment. He expected praise for what he had done, but when Skipper merely told him to let go, he obeyed with the realization that this lurking, fear-struck creature was somehow different, and must be treated differently, from other lurking creatures.

Fear-struck she was, as it is given to few humans to be and still live. Van Horn called her his parcel of trouble, and he was anxious to be rid of the parcel, without, however, the utter annihilation of the parcel. It was this annihilation which he had saved her from when he bought her in even exchange for a fat pig.

Stupid, worthless, spiritless, sick, not more than a dozen years old, no delight in the eyes of the young men of her village, she had been consigned by her disappointed parents to the cooking-pot. When

Captain Van Horn first encountered her had been when she was the central figure in a lugubrious procession on the banks of the Balebuli River.

Anything but a beauty—had been his appraisal when he halted the procession for a pow-wow. Lean from sickness, her skin mangy with the dry scales of the disease called *bukua*, she was tied hand and foot and, like a pig, slung from a stout pole that rested on the shoulders of the bearers, who intended to dine off of her. Too hopeless to expect mercy, she made no appeal for help, though the horrible fear that possessed her was eloquent in her wild-staring eyes.

In the universal beche-de-mer English, Captain Van Horn had learned that she was not regarded with relish by her companions, and that they were on their way to stake her out up to her neck in the running water of the Balebuli. But first, before they staked her, their plan was to dislocate her joints and break the big bones of the arms and legs. This was no religious rite, no placation of the brutish jungle gods. Merely was it a matter of gastronomy. Living meat, so treated, was made tender and tasty, and, as her companions pointed out, she certainly needed to be put through such a process. Two days in the water, they told the captain, ought to do the business. Then they would kill her, build the fire, and invite in a few friends.

After half an hour of bargaining, during which Captain Van Horn had insisted on the worthlessness of the parcel, he had bought a fat pig worth five dollars and exchanged it for her. Thus, since he had paid for the pig in trade goods, and since trade goods were rated at a hundred per cent. profit, the girl had actually cost him two dollars and fifty cents.

And then Captain Van Horn's troubles had begun. He could not get rid of the girl. Too well he knew the natives of Malaita to turn her over to them anywhere on the island. Chief Ishikola of Su'u had offered five twenties of drinking coconuts for her, and Bau, a bush chief, had offered two chickens on the beach at Malu. But this last offer had been accompanied by a sneer, and had tokened the old rascal's scorn of the girl's scrawniness. Failing to connect with the missionary brig, the *Western Cross*, on which she would not have been eaten, Captain Van Horn had been compelled to keep her in the cramped quarters of the *Arangi* against a problematical future time when he would be able to turn her over to the missionaries.

But toward him the girl had no heart of gratitude because she had no brain of understanding. She, who had been sold for a fat pig, considered her pitiful role in the world to be unchanged. Eatee she had been. Eatee she remained. Her destination merely had been changed, and this big fella white marster of the *Arangi* would undoubtedly be her destination when she had sufficiently fattened. His designs on her had been transparent from the first, when he had tried to feed her up. And she had outwitted him by resolutely eating no more than would barely keep her alive.

As a result, she, who had lived in the bush all her days and never so much as set foot in a canoe, rocked and rolled unendingly over the broad ocean in a perpetual nightmare of fear. In the beche-de-mer that was current among the blacks of a thousand islands and ten thousand dialects, the *Arangi's* procession of passengers assured her of her fate. "My word, you fella Mary," one would say to her, "short time little bit that big fella white marster kai-kai along you." Or, another: "Big fella white marster kai-kai along you, my word, belly belong him walk about too much."

Kai-kai was the beche-de-mer for "eat." Even Jerry knew that. "Eat" did not obtain in his vocabulary; but kai-kai did, and it meant all and more than "eat," for it served for both noun and verb.

But the girl never replied to the jeering of the blacks. For that matter, she never spoke at all, not even to Captain Van Horn, who did not so much as know her name.

It was late afternoon, after discovering the girl in the lazarette, when Jerry again came on deck. Scarcely had Skipper, who had carried him up the steep ladder, dropped him on deck than Jerry made a new discovery—land. He did not see it, but he smelled it. His nose went up in the air and quested to windward along the wind that brought the message, and he read the air with his nose as a man might read a newspaper—the salt smells of the seashore and of the dank muck of mangrove swamps at low tide, the spicy fragrances of tropic vegetation, and the faint, most faint, acrid tingle of smoke from smudgy fires.

The trade, which had laid the *Arangi* well up under the lee of this outjutting point of Malaita, was now failing, so that she began to roll in the easy swells with crashings of sheets and tackles and thunderous flappings of her sails. Jerry no more than cocked a contemptuous quizzical eye at the mainsail anticking above him. He knew already the empty windiness of its threats, but he was careful of the mainsheet blocks, and walked around the traveller instead of over it.

While Captain Van Horn, taking advantage of the calm to exercise the boat's crew with the fire-arms and to limber up the weapons, was passing out the Lee-Enfields from their place on top the cabin skylight, Jerry suddenly crouched and began to stalk stiff-legged. But the wild-dog, three feet from his lair under the trade-boxes, was not unobservant. He watched and snarled threateningly. It was not a nice snarl. In fact, it was as nasty and savage a snarl as all his life had been nasty and savage. Most small creatures were afraid of that snarl, but it had no deterrent effect on Jerry, who continued his steady stalking. When the wild-dog sprang for the hole under the boxes, Jerry sprang after, missing his enemy by inches. Tossing overboard bits of wood, bottles and empty tins, Captain Van Horn ordered the eight eager boat's crew with rifles to turn loose. Jerry was excited and delighted with the fusillade, and added his puppy yelpings to the noise. As the empty brass cartridges were ejected, the return boys scrambled on the deck for them, esteeming them as very precious objects and thrusting them, still warm, into the empty holes in their ears. Their ears were perforated with many of these holes, the smallest capable of receiving a cartridge, while the larger ones contained-clay pipes, sticks of tobacco, and even boxes of matches. Some of the holes in the ear-lobes were so huge that they were plugged with carved wooden cylinders three inches in diameter.

Mate and captain carried automatics in their belts, and with these they turned loose, shooting away clip after clip to the breathless admiration of the blacks for such marvellous rapidity of fire. The boat's crew were not even fair shots, but Van Horn, like every captain in the Solomons, knew that the bush natives and salt-water men were so much worse shots, and knew that the shooting of his boat's crew could be depended upon—if the boat's crew itself did not turn against the ship in a pinch.

At first, Borckman's automatic jammed, and he received a caution from Van Horn for his carelessness in not keeping it clean and thin-oiled. Also, Borckman was twittingly asked how many drinks he had taken, and if that was what accounted for his shooting being under his average. Borckman explained that he had a touch of fever, and Van Horn deferred stating his doubts until a few minutes later, squatting in the shade of the spanker with Jerry in his arms, he told Jerry all about it.

"The trouble with him is the schnapps, Jerry," he explained. "Gott-fer-dang, it makes me keep all my watches and half of his. And he says it's the fever. Never believe it, Jerry. It's the schnapps—just the plain s-c-h-n-a-p-p-s schnapps. An' he's a good sailor-man, Jerry, when he's sober. But when he's schnappy he's sheer lunatic. Then his noddle goes pinwheeling and he's a blighted fool, and he'd snore in a gale and suffer for sleep in a dead calm.—Jerry, you're just beginning to pad those four little soft feet of yours into the world, so take the advice of one who knows and leave the schnapps alone. Believe me, Jerry, boy—listen to your father—schnapps will never buy you anything."

Whereupon, leaving Jerry on deck to stalk the wild-dog, Captain Van Horn went below into the tiny stateroom and took a long drink from the very bottle from which Borckman was stealing.

The stalking of the wild-dog became a game, at least to Jerry, who was so made that his heart bore no malice, and who hugely enjoyed it. Also, it gave him a delightful consciousness of his own mastery, for the wild-dog always fled from him. At least so far as dogs were concerned, Jerry was cock of the deck of the *Arangi*. It did not enter his head to query how his conduct affected the wild-dog, though, in truth, he led that individual a wretched existence. Never, except when Jerry was below, did the wild one dare venture more than several feet from his retreat, and he went about in fear and trembling of the fat roly-poly puppy who was unafraid of his snarl.

In the late afternoon, Jerry trotted aft, after having administered another lesson to the wild-dog, and found Skipper seated on the deck, back against the low rail, knees drawn up, and gazing absently off to leeward. Jerry sniffed his bare calf—not that he needed to identify it, but just because he liked to, and in a sort of friendly greeting. But Van Horn took no notice, continuing to stare out across the sea. Nor was he aware of the puppy's presence.

Jerry rested the length of his chin on Skipper's knee and gazed long and earnestly into Skipper's face. This time Skipper knew, and was pleasantly thrilled; but still he gave no sign. Jerry tried a new tack. Skipper's hand drooped idly, half open, from where the forearm rested on the other knee. Into the part-open hand Jerry thrust his soft golden muzzle to the eyes and remained quite still. Had he been situated to see, he would have seen a twinkle in Skipper's eyes, which had been withdrawn from the sea and were looking down upon him. But Jerry could not see. He kept quiet a little longer, and then gave a prodigious sniff.

This was too much for Skipper, who laughed with such genial heartiness as to lay Jerry's silky ears back and down in self-deprecation of affection and pleadingness to bask in the sunshine of the god's smile. Also, Skipper's laughter set Jerry's tail wildly bobbing. The half-open hand closed in a firm grip that gathered in the slack of the skin of one side of Jerry's head and jowl. Then the hand began to shake him back and forth with such good will that he was compelled to balance back and forth on all his four feet.

It was bliss to Jerry. Nay, more, it was ecstasy. For Jerry knew there was neither anger nor danger in the roughness of the shake, and that it was play of the sort that he and Michael had indulged in. On occasion, he had so played with Biddy and lovingly mauled her about. And, on very rare occasion, *Mister* Haggin had lovingly mauled him about. It was speech to Jerry, full of unmistakable meaning.

As the shake grew rougher, Jerry emitted his most ferocious growl, which grew more ferocious with the increasing violence of the shaking. But that, too, was play, a making believe to hurt the one he liked too well to hurt. He strained and tugged at the grip, trying to twist his jowl in the slack of skin so as to reach a bite.

When Skipper, with a quick thrust, released him and shoved him clear, he came back, all teeth and growl, to be again caught and shaken. The play continued, with rising excitement to Jerry. Once, too quick for Skipper, he caught his hand between teeth; but he did not bring them together. They pressed lovingly, denting the skin, but there was no bite in them.

The play grew rougher, and Jerry lost himself in the play. Still playing, he grew so excited that all that had been feigned became actual. This was battle a struggle against the hand that seized and shook him and thrust him away. The make-believe of ferocity passed out of his growls; the ferocity in them became real. Also, in the moments when he was shoved away and was springing back to the attack, he yelped in high-pitched puppy hysteria. And Captain Van Horn, realizing, suddenly, instead of clutching, extended his hand wide open in the peace sign that is as ancient as the human hand. At the same time his voice rang out the single word, "Jerry!" In it was all the imperativeness of reproof and command and all the solicitous insistence of love.

Jerry knew and was checked back to himself. He was instantly contrite, all soft humility, ears laid back with pleadingness for forgiveness and protestation of a warm throbbing heart of love. Instantly, from an open-mouthed, fang-bristling dog in full career of attack, he melted into a bundle of softness and silkiness, that trotted to the open hand and kissed it with a tongue that flashed out between white gleaming teeth like a rose-red jewel. And the next moment he was in Skipper's arms, jowl against cheek, and the tongue was again flashing out in all the articulateness possible for a creature denied speech. It was a veritable love-feast, as dear to one as to the other.

"Gott-fer-dang!" Captain Van Horn crooned. "You're nothing but a bunch of high-strung sensitiveness, with a golden heart in the middle and a golden coat wrapped all around. Gott-fer-dang, Jerry, you're gold, pure gold, inside and out, and no dog was ever minted like you in all the world. You're heart of gold, you golden dog, and be good to me and love me as I shall always be good to you and love you for ever and for ever."

And Captain Van Horn, who ruled the *Arangi* in bare legs, a loin cloth, and a sixpenny under-shirt, and ran cannibal blacks back and forth in the blackbird trade with an automatic strapped to his body waking and sleeping and with his head forfeit in scores of salt-water villages and bush strongholds, and who was esteemed the toughest skipper in the Solomons where only men who are tough may continue to live and esteem toughness, blinked with sudden moisture in his eyes, and could not see for the moment the puppy that quivered all its body of love in his arms and kissed away the salty softness of his eyes.

V

A nd swift tropic night smote the *Arangi*, as she alternately rolled in calms and heeled and plunged ahead in squalls under the lee of the cannibal island of Malaita. It was a stoppage of the south-east trade wind that made for variable weather, and that made cooking on the exposed deck galley a misery and sent the return boys, who had nothing to wet but their skins, scuttling below.

The first watch, from eight to twelve, was the mate's; and Captain Van Horn, forced below by the driving wet of a heavy rain squall, took Jerry with him to sleep in the tiny stateroom. Jerry was weary from the manifold excitements of the most exciting day in his life; and he was asleep and kicking and growling in his sleep, ere Skipper, with a last look at him and a grin as he turned the lamp low, muttered aloud: "It's that wild-dog, Jerry. Get him. Shake him. Shake him hard."

So soundly did Jerry sleep, that when the rain, having robbed the atmosphere of its last breath of wind, ceased and left the stateroom a steaming, suffocating furnace, he did not know when Skipper, panting for air, his loin cloth and undershirt soaked with sweat, arose, tucked blanket and pillow under his arm, and went on deck.

Jerry only awakened when a huge three-inch cockroach nibbled at the sensitive and hairless skin between his toes. He awoke kicking the offended foot, and gazed at the cockroach that did not scuttle, but that walked dignifiedly away. He watched it join other cockroaches that paraded the floor. Never had he seen so many gathered together at one time, and never had he seen such large ones. They were all of a size, and they were everywhere. Long lines of them poured out of cracks in the walls and descended to join their fellows on the floor.

The thing was indecent—at least, in Jerry's mind, it was not to be tolerated. *Mister* Haggin, Derby, and Bob had never tolerated cockroaches, and their rules were his rules. The cockroach was the eternal tropic enemy. He sprang at the nearest, pouncing to crush it to the floor under his paws. But the thing did what he had never known a cockroach to do. It arose in the air strong-flighted as a bird. And as if at a signal, all the multitude of cockroaches took wings of flight and filled the room with their flutterings and circlings.

He attacked the winged host, leaping into the air, snapping at the flying vermin, trying to knock them down with his paws. Occasionally he succeeded and destroyed one; nor did the combat cease until all the cockroaches, as if at another signal, disappeared into the many cracks, leaving the room to him.

Quickly, his next thought was: Where is Skipper? He knew he was not in the room, though he stood up on his hind-legs and investigated the low bunk, his keen little nose quivering delightedly while he made little sniffs of delight as he smelled the recent presence of Skipper. And what made his nose quiver and sniff, likewise made his stump of a tail bob back and forth.

But where was Skipper? It was a thought in his brain that was as sharp and definite as a similar thought would be in a human brain. And it similarly preceded action. The door had been left hooked open, and Jerry trotted out into the cabin where half a hundred blacks made queer sleep-moanings, and sighings, and snorings. They were packed closely together, covering the floor as well as the long sweep of bunks, so that he was compelled to crawl over their naked legs. And there was no white god about to protect him. He knew it, but was unafraid.

Having made sure that Skipper was not in the cabin, Jerry prepared for the perilous ascent of the steep steps that were almost a ladder, then recollected the lazarette. In he trotted and sniffed at the sleeping girl in the cotton shift who believed that Van Horn was going to eat her if he could succeed in fattening her.

Back at the ladder-steps, he looked up and waited in the hope that Skipper might appear from above and carry him up. Skipper had passed that way, he knew, and he knew for two reasons. It was the only way he could have passed, and Jerry's nose told him that he had passed. His first attempt to climb the steps began well. Not until a third of the way up, as the *Arangi* rolled in a sea and recovered with a jerk, did he slip and fall. Two or three boys awoke and watched him while they prepared and chewed betel nut and lime wrapped in green leaves.

Twice, barely started, Jerry slipped back, and more boys, awakened by their fellows, sat up and enjoyed his plight. In the fourth attempt he managed to gain half way up before he fell, coming down heavily on his side. This was hailed with low laughter and querulous chirpings that might well have come from the throats of huge birds. He regained his feet, absurdly bristled the hair on his shoulders and absurdly growled his high disdain of these lesser, two-legged things that came and went and obeyed the wills of great, white-skinned, two-legged gods such as Skipper and Mister Haggin.

Undeterred by his heavy fall, Jerry essayed the ladder again. A temporary easement of the *Arangi's* rolling gave him his opportunity, so that his forefeet were over the high combing of the companion when the next big roll came. He held on by main strength of his bent forelegs, then scrambled over and out on deck.

Amidships, squatting on the deck near the sky-light, he investigated several of the boat's crew and Lerumie. He identified them circumspectly, going suddenly stiff-legged as Lerumie made a low, hissing, menacing noise. Aft, at the wheel, he found a black steering, and, near him, the mate keeping the watch. Just as the mate spoke to him and stooped to pat him, Jerry whiffed Skipper somewhere near at hand. With a conciliating, apologetic bob of his tail, he trotted on up wind and came upon Skipper on his back, rolled in a blanket so that only his head stuck out, and sound asleep.

First of all Jerry needs must joyfully sniff him and joyfully wag his tail. But Skipper did not awake and a fine spray of rain, almost as thin as mist, made Jerry curl up and press closely into the angle formed by Skipper's head and shoulder. This did awake him, for he uttered "Jerry" in a low, crooning voice, and Jerry responded with a touch of his cold damp nose to the other's cheek. And then Skipper went to sleep again. But not Jerry. He lifted the edge of the blanket with his nose and crawled across the shoulder until he was altogether inside. This roused Skipper, who, half-asleep, helped him to curl up.

Still Jerry was not satisfied, and he squirmed around until he lay in the hollow of Skipper's arm, his head resting on Skipper's shoulder, when, with a profound sigh of content, he fell asleep.

Several times the noises made by the boat's crew in trimming the sheets to the shifting draught of air roused Van Horn, and each time, remembering the puppy, he pressed him caressingly with his hollowed arm. And each time, in his sleep, Jerry stirred responsively and snuggled cosily to him.

For all that he was a remarkable puppy, Jerry had his limitations, and he could never know the effect produced on the hard-bitten captain by the soft warm contact of his velvet body. But it made the captain remember back across the years to his own girl babe asleep on his arm. And so poignantly did he remember, that he became wide awake, and many pictures, beginning, with the girl babe, burned their torment in his brain. No white man in the Solomons knew what he carried about with him, waking and often sleeping; and it was because of these pictures that he had come to the Solomons in a vain effort to erase them.

First, memory-prodded by the soft puppy in his arm, he saw the girl and the mother in the little Harlem flat. Small, it was true, but tight-packed with the happiness of three that made it heaven.

He saw the girl's flaxen-yellow hair darken to her mother's gold as it lengthened into curls and ringlets until finally it became two thick long braids. From striving not to see these many pictures he came even to dwelling upon them in the effort so to fill his consciousness as to keep out the one picture he did not want to see.

He remembered his work, the wrecking car, and the wrecking crew that had toiled under him, and he wondered what had become of Clancey, his right-hand man. Came the long day, when, routed from bed at three in the morning to dig a surface car out of the wrecked show windows of a drug store and get it back on the track, they had laboured all day clearing up a half-dozen smash-ups and arrived at the car house at nine at night just as another call came in.

"Glory be!" said Clancey, who lived in the next block from him. He could see him saying it and wiping the sweat from his grimy face. "Glory be, 'tis a small matter at most, an' right in our neighbourhood—not a dozen blocks away. Soon as it's done we can beat it for home an' let the down-town boys take the car back to the shop."

"We've only to jack her up for a moment," he had answered.

"What is it?" Billy Jaffers, another of the crew, asked.

"Somebody run over—can't get them out," he said, as they swung on board the wrecking-car and started.

He saw again all the incidents of the long run, not omitting the delay caused by hose-carts and a hook-and-ladder running to a cross-town fire, during which time he and Clancey had joked Jaffers over the dates with various fictitious damsels out of which he had been cheated by the night's extra work.

Came the long line of stalled street-cars, the crowd, the police holding it back, the two ambulances drawn up and waiting their freight, and the young policeman, whose beat it was, white and shaken, greeting him with: "It's horrible, man. It's fair sickening. Two of them. We can't get them out. I tried. One was still living, I think."

But he, strong man and hearty, used to such work, weary with the hard day and with a pleasant picture of the bright little flat waiting him a dozen blocks away when the job was done, spoke cheerfully, confidently, saying that he'd have them out in a jiffy, as he stooped and crawled under the car on hands and knees.

Again he saw himself as he pressed the switch of his electric torch and looked. Again he saw the twin braids of heavy golden hair ere his thumb relaxed from the switch, leaving him in darkness.

"Is the one alive yet?" the shaken policeman asked.

And the question was repeated, while he struggled for will power sufficient to press on the light.

He heard himself reply, "I'll tell you in a minute."

Again he saw himself look. For a long minute he looked.

"Both dead," he answered quietly. "Clancey, pass in a number three jack, and get under yourself with another at the other end of the truck."

He lay on his back, staring straight up at one single star that rocked mistily through a thinning of cloud-stuff overhead. The old ache was in his throat, the old harsh dryness in mouth and eyes. And he knew—what no other man knew—why he was in the Solomons, skipper of the teak-built yacht *Arangi*, running niggers, risking his head, and drinking more Scotch whiskey than was good for any man.

Not since that night had he looked with warm eyes on any woman. And he had been noted by other whites as notoriously cold toward pickanninnies white or black.

But, having visioned the ultimate horror of memory, Van Horn was soon able to fall asleep again, delightfully aware, as he drowsed off, of Jerry's head on his shoulder. Once, when Jerry, dreaming of the beach at Meringe and of *Mister* Haggin, Biddy, Terrence, and Michael, set up a low whimpering, Van Horn roused sufficiently to soothe him closer to him, and to mutter ominously: "Any nigger that'd hurt that pup. . ."

At midnight when the mate touched him on the shoulder, in the moment of awakening and before he was awake Van Horn did two things automatically and swiftly. He darted his right hand down to the pistol at his hip, and muttered: "Any nigger that'd hurt that pup. . ."

"That'll be Kopo Point abreast," Borckman explained, as both men stared to windward at the high loom of the land. "She hasn't made more than ten miles, and no promise of anything steady."

"There's plenty of stuff making up there, if it'll ever come down," Van Horn said, as both men transferred their gaze to the clouds drifting with many breaks across the dim stars.

Scarcely had the mate fetched a blanket from below and turned in on deck, than a brisk steady breeze sprang up from off the land, sending the *Arangi* through the smooth water at a nine-knot clip. For a time Jerry tried to stand the watch with Skipper, but he soon curled up and dozed off, partly on the deck and partly on Skipper's bare feet.

When Skipper carried him to the blanket and rolled him in, he was quickly asleep again; and he was quickly awake, out of the blanket, and padding after along the deck as Skipper paced up and down. Here began another lesson, and in five minutes Jerry learned it was the will of Skipper that he should remain in the blanket, that everything was all right, and that Skipper would be up and down and near him all the time.

At four the mate took charge of the deck.

"Reeled off thirty miles," Van Horn told him. "But now it is baffling again. Keep an eye for squalls under the land. Better throw the halyards down on deck and make the watch stand by. Of course they'll sleep, but make them sleep on the halyards and sheets."

Jerry roused to Skipper's entrance under the blanket, and, quite as if it were a long-established custom, curled in between his arm and side, and, after one happy sniff and one kiss of his cool little tongue, as Skipper pressed his cheek against him caressingly, dozed off to sleep.

Half an hour later, to all intents and purposes, so far as Jerry could or could not comprehend, the world might well have seemed suddenly coming to an end. What awoke him was the flying leap of Skipper that sent the blanket one way and Jerry the other. The deck of the *Arangi* had become a wall, down which Jerry slipped through the roaring dark. Every rope and shroud was thrumming and screeching in resistance to the fierce weight of the squall.

"Stand by main halyards!—Jump!" he could hear Skipper shouting loudly; also he heard the high note of the mainsheet screaming across the sheaves as Van Horn, bending braces in the dark, was swiftly slacking the sheet through his scorching palms with a single turn on the cleat.

While all this, along with many other noises, squealings of boat-boys and shouts of Borckman, was impacting on Jerry's ear-drums, he was still sliding down the steep deck of his new and unstable world. But he did not bring up against the rail where his fragile ribs might well have been broken. Instead, the warm ocean water, pouring inboard across the buried rail in a flood of pale phosphorescent fire, cushioned his fall. A raffle of trailing ropes entangled him as he struck out to swim.

And he swam, not to save his life, not with the fear of death upon him. There was but one idea in his mind. *Where was Skipper?* Not that he had any thought of trying to save Skipper, nor that he might be of assistance to him. It was the heart of love that drives one always toward the beloved. As the mother in catastrophe tries to gain her babe, as the Greek who, dying, remembered sweet Argos, as soldiers on a stricken field pass with the names of their women upon their lips, so Jerry, in this wreck of a world, yearned toward Skipper.

The squall ceased as abruptly as it had struck. The *Arangi* righted with a jerk to an even keel, leaving Jerry stranded in the starboard scuppers. He trotted across the level deck to Skipper, who, standing erect on wide-spread legs, the bight of the mainsheet still in his hand, was exclaiming:

"Gott-fer-dang! Wind he go! Rain he no come!"

He felt Jerry's cool nose against his bare calf, heard his joyous sniff, and bent and caressed him. In the darkness he could not see, but his heart warmed with knowledge that Jerry's tail was surely bobbing.

Many of the frightened return boys had crowded on deck, and their plaintive, querulous voices sounded like the sleepy noises of a roost of birds. Borckman came and stood by Van Horn's shoulder, and both men, strung to their tones in the tenseness of apprehension, strove to penetrate the surrounding blackness with their eyes, while they listened with all their ears for any message of the elements from sea and air.

"Where's the rain?" Borckman demanded peevishly. "Always wind first, the rain follows and kills the wind. There is no rain."

Van Horn still stared and listened, and made no answer.

The anxiety of the two men was sensed by Jerry, who, too, was on his toes. He pressed his cool nose to Skipper's leg, and the rose-kiss of his tongue brought him the salt taste of sea-water.

Skipper bent suddenly, rolled Jerry with quick toughness into the blanket, and deposited him in the hollow between two sacks of yams lashed on deck aft of the mizzenmast. As an afterthought, he fastened the blanket with a piece of rope yarn, so that Jerry was as if tied in a sack.

Scarcely was this finished when the spanker smashed across overhead, the headsails thundered with a sudden filling, and the great mainsail, with all the scope in the boom-tackle caused by Van Horn's giving of the sheet, came across and fetched up to tautness on the tackle with a crash that shook the vessel and heeled her violently to port. This second knock-down had come from the opposite direction, and it was mightier than the first.

Jerry heard Skipper's voice ring out, first, to the mate: "Stand by main-halyards! Throw off the turns! I'll take care of the tackle!"; and, next, to some of the boat's crew: "Batto! you fella slack spanker tackle quick fella! Ranga! you fella let go spanker sheet!"

Here Van Horn was swept off his legs by an avalanche of return boys who had cluttered the deck with the first squall. The squirming mass, of which he was part, slid down into the barbed wire of the port rail beneath the surface of the sea.

Jerry was so secure in his nook that he did not roll away. But when he heard Skipper's commands cease, and, seconds later, heard his cursings in the barbed wire, he set up a shrill yelping and clawed and scratched frantically at the blanket to get out. Something had happened to Skipper. He knew that. It was all that he knew, for he had no thought of himself in the chaos of the ruining world.

But he ceased his yelping to listen to a new noise—a thunderous slatting of canvas accompanied by shouts and cries. He sensed, and sensed wrongly, that it boded ill, for he did not know that it was the mainsail being lowered on the run after Skipper had slashed the boom-tackle across with his sheath-knife.

As the pandemonium grew, he added his own yelping to it until he felt a fumbling hand without the blanket. He stilled and sniffed. No, it was not Skipper. He sniffed again and recognized the person. It was Lerumie, the black whom he had seen rolled on the beach by Biddy only the previous morning, who, still were recently, had kicked him on his stub of a tail, and who not more than a week before he had seen throw a rock at Terrence.

The rope yarn had been parted, and Lerumie's fingers were feeling inside the blanket for him. Jerry snarled his wickedest. The thing was sacrilege. He, as a white man's dog, was taboo to all blacks. He had early learned the law that no nigger must ever touch a white-god's dog. Yet Lerumie, who was all of evil, at this moment when the world crashed about their ears, was daring to touch him.

And when the fingers touched him, his teeth closed upon them. Next, he was clouted by the black's free hand with such force as to tear his clenched teeth down the fingers through skin and flesh until the fingers went clear.

Raging like a tiny fiend, Jerry found himself picked up by the neck, half-throttled, and flung through the air. And while flying through the air, he continued to squall his rage. He fell into the sea and went under, gulping a mouthful of salt water into his lungs, and came up strangling but swimming. Swimming was one of the things he did not have to think about. He had never had to learn to swim, any more than he had had to learn to breathe. In fact, he had been compelled to learn to walk; but he swam as a matter of course.

The wind screamed about him. Flying froth, driven on the wind's breath, filled his mouth and nostrils and beat into his eyes, stinging and blinding him. In the struggle to breathe he, all unlearned in the ways of the sea, lifted his muzzle high in the air to get out of the suffocating welter. As a result, off the horizontal, the churning of his legs no longer sustained him, and he went down and under perpendicularly. Again he emerged, strangling with more salt water in his windpipe. This time, without reasoning it out, merely moving along the line of least resistance, which was to him the line of greatest comfort, he straightened out in the sea and continued so to swim as to remain straightened out.

Through the darkness, as the squall spent itself, came the slatting of the half-lowered mainsail, the shrill voices of the boat's crew, a curse of Borckman's, and, dominating all, Skipper's voice, shouting:

"Grab the leech, you fella boys! Hang on! Drag down strong fella! Come in mainsheet two blocks! Jump, damn you, jump!"

VI

At recognition of Skipper's voice, Jerry, floundering in the stiff and crisping sea that sprang up with the easement of the wind, yelped eagerly and yearningly, all his love for his new-found beloved eloquent in his throat. But quickly all sounds died away as the *Arangi* drifted from him. And then, in the loneliness of the dark, on the heaving breast of the sea that he recognized as one more of the eternal enemies, he began to whimper and cry plaintively like a lost child.

Further, by the dim, shadowy ways of intuition, he knew his weakness in that merciless sea with no heart of warmth, that threatened the unknowable thing, vaguely but terribly guessed, namely, death. As regarded himself, he did not comprehend death. He, who had never known the time when he was not alive, could not conceive of the time when he would cease to be alive.

Yet it was there, shouting its message of warning through every tissue cell, every nerve quickness and brain sensitivity of him—a totality of sensation that foreboded the ultimate catastrophe of life about which he knew nothing at all, but which, nevertheless, he *felt* to be the conclusive supreme disaster. Although he did not comprehend it, he apprehended it no less poignantly than do men who know and generalize far more deeply and widely than mere four-legged dogs.

As a man struggles in the throes of nightmare, so Jerry struggled in the vexed, salt-suffocating sea. And so he whimpered and cried, lost child, lost puppy-dog that he was, only half a year existent in the fair world sharp with joy and suffering. And he *wanted Skipper*. Skipper was a god.

ON BOARD THE *ARANGI*, RELIEVED by the lowering of her mainsail, as the fierceness went out of the wind and the cloudburst of tropic rain began to fall, Van Horn and Borckman lurched toward each other in the blackness.

"A double squall," said Van Horn. "Hit us to starboard and to port."

"Must a-split in half just before she hit us," the mate concurred.

"And kept all the rain in the second half—"

Van Horn broke off with an oath.

"Hey! What's the matter along you fella boy?" he shouted to the man at the wheel.

For the ketch, under her spanker which had just then been flat-hauled, had come into the wind, emptying her after-sail and permitting her headsails to fill on the other tack. The *Arangi* was beginning to work back approximately over the course she had just traversed. And this meant that she was going back toward Jerry floundering in the sea. Thus, the balance, on which his life titubated, was inclined in his favour by the blunder of a black steersman.

Keeping the *Arangi* on the new tack, Van Horn set Borckman clearing the mess of ropes on deck, himself, squatting in the rain, undertaking to long-splice the tackle he had cut. As the rain thinned, so that the crackle of it on deck became less noisy, he was attracted by a sound from out over the water. He suspended the work of his hands to listen, and, when he recognized Jerry's wailing, sprang to his feet, galvanized into action.

"The pup's overboard!" he shouted to Borckman. "Back your jib to wind'ard!"

He sprang aft, scattering a cluster of return boys right and left.

"Hey! You fella boat's crew! Come in spanker sheet! Flatten her down good fella!"

He darted a look into the binnacle and took a hurried compass bearing of the sounds Jerry was making.

"Hard down your wheel!" he ordered the helmsman, then leaped to the wheel and put it down himself, repeating over and over aloud, "Nor'east by east a quarter, nor'east by east a quarter."

Back and peering into the binnacle, he listened vainly for another wail from Jerry in the hope of verifying his first hasty bearing. But not long he waited. Despite the fact that by his manoeuvre the *Arangi* had been hove to, he knew that windage and sea-driftage would quickly send her away from the swimming puppy. He shouted Borckman to come aft and haul in the whaleboat, while he hurried below for his electric torch and a boat compass.

The ketch was so small that she was compelled to tow her one whaleboat astern on long double painters, and by the time the mate had it hauled in under the stern, Van Horn was back. He was undeterred by the barbed wire, lifting boy after boy of the boat's crew over it and dropping them sprawling into the boat, following himself, as the last, by swinging over on the spanker boom, and calling his last instructions as the painters were cast off.

"Get a riding light on deck, Borckman. Keep her hove to. Don't hoist the mainsail. Clean up the decks and bend the watch tackle on the main boom."

He took the steering-sweep and encouraged the rowers with: "Washee-washee, good fella, washee-washee!"—which is the beche-de-mer for "row hard."

As he steered, he kept flashing the torch on the boat compass so that he could keep headed north-east by east a quarter east. Then he remembered that the boat compass, on such course, deviated two whole points from the *Arangi's* compass, and altered his own course accordingly.

Occasionally he bade the rowers cease, while he listened and called for Jerry. He had them row in circles, and work back and forth, up to windward and down to leeward, over the area of dark sea that he reasoned must contain the puppy.

"Now you fella boy listen ear belong you," he said, toward the first. "Maybe one fella boy hear 'm pickaninny dog sing out, I give 'm that fella boy five fathom calico, two ten sticks tobacco."

At the end of half an hour he was offering "Two ten fathoms calico and ten ten sticks tobacco" to the boy who first heard "pickaninny dog sing out."

JERRY WAS IN BAD SHAPE. Not accustomed to swimming, strangled by the salt water that lapped into his open mouth, he was getting loggy when first he chanced to see the flash of the captain's torch. This, however, he did not connect with Skipper, and so took no more notice of it than he did of the first stars showing in the sky. It never entered his mind that it might be a star nor even that it might not be a star. He continued to wail and to strangle with more salt water. But when he at length heard Skipper's voice he went immediately wild. He attempted to stand up and to rest his forepaws on Skipper's voice coming out of the darkness, as he would have rested his forepaws on Skipper's leg had he been near. The result was disastrous. Out of the horizontal, he sank down and under, coming up with a new spasm of strangling.

This lasted for a short time, during which the strangling prevented him from answering Skipper's cry, which continued to reach him. But when he could answer he burst forth in a joyous yelp. Skipper was coming to take him out of the stinging, biting sea that blinded his eyes and hurt him to breathe. Skipper was truly a god, his god, with a god's power to save.

Soon he heard the rhythmic clack of the oars on the thole-pins, and the joy in his own yelp was duplicated by the joy in Skipper's voice, which kept up a running encouragement, broken by objurgations to the rowers.

"All right, Jerry, old man. All right, Jerry. All right.—Washee-washee, you fella boy!—Coming, Jerry, coming. Stick it out, old man. Stay with it.—Washee-washee like hell!—Here we are, Jerry. Stay with it. Hang on, old boy, we'll get you.—Easy. . . easy. 'Vast washee."

And then, with amazing abruptness, Jerry saw the whaleboat dimly emerge from the gloom close upon him, was blinded by the stab of the torch full in his eyes, and, even as he yelped his joy, felt and recognized Skipper's hand clutching him by the slack of the neck and lifting him into the air.

He landed wet and soppily against Skipper's rain-wet chest, his tail bobbing frantically against Skipper's containing arm, his body wriggling, his tongue dabbing madly all over Skipper's chin and mouth and cheeks and nose. And Skipper did not know that he was himself wet, and that he was in the first shock of recurrent malaria precipitated by the wet and the excitement. He knew only that the puppy-dog, given him only the previous morning, was safe back in his arms.

While the boat's crew bent to the oars, he steered with the sweep between his arm and his side in order that he might hold Jerry with the other arm.

"You little son of a gun," he crooned, and continued to croon, over and over. "You little son of a gun."

And Jerry responded with tongue-kisses, whimpering and crying as is the way of lost children immediately after they are found. Also, he shivered violently. But it was not from the cold. Rather was it due to his over-strung, sensitive nerves.

Again on board, Van Horn stated his reasoning to the mate.

"The pup didn't just calmly walk overboard. Nor was he washed overboard. I had him fast and triced in the blanket with a rope yarn."

He walked over, the centre of the boat's crew and of the three-score return boys who were all on deck, and flashed his torch on the blanket still lying on the yams.

"That proves it. The rope-yarn's cut. The knot's still in it. Now what nigger is responsible?"

He looked about at the circle of dark faces, flashing the light on them, and such was the accusation and anger in his eyes, that all eyes fell before his or looked away.

"If only the pup could speak," he complained. "He'd tell who it was."

He bent suddenly down to Jerry, who was standing as close against his legs as he could, so close that his wet forepaws rested on Skipper's bare feet.

"You know 'm, Jerry, you known the black fella boy," he said, his words quick and exciting, his hand moving in questing circles toward the blacks.

Jerry was all alive on the instant, jumping about, barking with short yelps of eagerness.

"I do believe the dog could lead me to him," Van Horn confided to the mate. "Come on, Jerry, find 'm, sick 'm, shake 'm down. Where is he, Jerry? Find 'm. Find 'm."

All that Jerry knew was that Skipper wanted something. He must find something that Skipper wanted, and he was eager to serve. He pranced about aimlessly and willingly for a space, while Skipper's urging cries increased his excitement. Then he was struck by an idea, and a most definite idea it was. The circle of boys broke to let him through as he raced for'ard along the starboard side to the tight-lashed heap of trade-boxes. He put his nose into the opening where the wild-dog laired, and sniffed. Yes, the wild-dog was inside. Not only did he smell him, but he heard the menace of his snarl.

He looked up to Skipper questioningly. Was it that Skipper wanted him to go in after the wild-dog? But Skipper laughed and waved his hand to show that he wanted him to search in other places for something else.

He leaped away, sniffing in likely places where experience had taught him cockroaches and rats might be. Yet it quickly dawned on him that it was not such things Skipper was after. His heart was wild with desire to serve, and, without clear purpose, he began sniffing legs of black boys.

This brought livelier urgings and encouragements from Skipper, and made him almost frantic. That was it. He must identify the boat's crew and the return boys by their legs. He hurried the task, passing swiftly from boy to boy, until he came to Lerumie.

And then he forgot that Skipper wanted him to do something. All he knew was that it was Lerumie who had broken the taboo of his sacred person by laying hands on him, and that it was Lerumie who had thrown him overboard.

With a cry of rage, a flash of white teeth, and a bristle of short neck-hair, he sprang for the black. Lerumie fled down the deck, and Jerry pursued amid the laughter of all the blacks. Several times, in making the circuit of the deck, he managed to scratch the flying calves with his teeth. Then Lerumie took to the main rigging, leaving Jerry impotently to rage on the deck beneath him.

About this point the blacks grouped in a semi-circle at a respectful distance, with Van Horn to the fore beside Jerry. Van Horn centred his electric torch on the black in the rigging, and saw the long parallel scratches on the fingers of the hand that had invaded Jerry's blanket. He pointed them out significantly to Borckman, who stood outside the circle so that no black should be able to come at his back.

Skipper picked Jerry up and soothed his anger with:

"Good boy, Jerry. You marked and sealed him. Some dog, you, some big man-dog."

He turned back to Lerumie, illuminating him as he clung in the rigging, and his voice was harsh and cold as he addressed him.

"What name belong along you fella boy?" he demanded.

"Me fella Lerumie," came the chirping, quavering answer.

"You come along Pennduffryn?"

"Me come along Meringe."

Captain Van Horn debated the while he fondled the puppy in his arms. After all, it was a return boy. In a day, in two days at most, he would have him landed and be quit of him.

"My word," he harangued, "me angry along you. Me angry big fella too much along you. Me angry along you any amount. What name you fella boy make 'm pickaninny dog belong along me walk about along water?"

Lerumie was unable to answer. He rolled his eyes helplessly, resigned to receive a whipping such as he had long since bitterly learned white masters were wont to administer.

Captain Van Horn repeated the question, and the black repeated the helpless rolling of his eyes.

"For two sticks tobacco I knock 'm seven bells outa you," the skipper bullied. "Now me give you strong fella talk too much. You look 'm eye belong you one time along this fella dog belong me, I knock 'm seven bells and whole starboard watch outa you. Savve?"

"Me savve," Lerumie, plaintively replied; and the episode was closed.

The return boys went below to sleep in the cabin. Borckman and the boat's crew hoisted the mainsail and put the *Arangi* on her course. And Skipper, under a dry blanket from below, lay down to sleep with Jerry, head on his shoulder, in the hollow of his arm.

VII

At seven in the morning, when Skipper rolled him out of the blanket and got up, Jerry celebrated the new day by chasing the wild-dog back into his hole and by drawing a snicker from the blacks on deck, when, with a growl and a flash of teeth, he made Lerumie side-step half a dozen feet and yield the deck to him.

He shared breakfast with Skipper, who, instead of eating, washed down with a cup of coffee fifty grains of quinine wrapped in a cigarette paper, and who complained to the mate that he would have to get under the blankets and sweat out the fever that was attacking him. Despite his chill, and despite his teeth that were already beginning to chatter while the burning sun extracted the moisture in curling mist-wreaths from the deck planking, Van Horn cuddled Jerry in his arms and called him princeling, and prince, and a king, and a son of kings.

For Van Horn had often listened to the recitals of Jerry's pedigree by Tom Haggin, over Scotch-and-sodas, when it was too pestilentially hot to go to bed. And the pedigree was as royal-blooded as was possible for an Irish terrier to possess, whose breed, beginning with the ancient Irish wolf-hound, had been moulded and established by man in less than two generations of men.

There was Terrence the Magnificent—descended, as Van Horn remembered, from the American-bred Milton Droleen, out of the Queen of County Antrim, Breda Muddler, which royal bitch, as every one who is familiar with the stud book knows, goes back as far as the almost mythical Spuds, with along the way no primrose dallyings with black-and-tan Killeney Boys and Welsh nondescripts. And did not Biddy trace to Erin, mother and star of the breed, through a long descendant out of Breda Mixer, herself an ancestress of Breda Muddler? Nor could be omitted from the purple record the later ancestress, Moya Doolen.

So Jerry knew the ecstasy of loving and of being loved in the arms of his love-god, although little he knew of such phrases as "king's son" and "son of kings," save that they connoted love for him in the same way that Lerumie's hissing noises connoted hate. One thing Jerry knew without knowing that he knew, namely, that in the few hours he had been with Skipper he loved him more than he had loved Derby and Bob, who, with the exception of Mister Haggin, were the only other white-gods he had ever known. He was not conscious of this. He merely loved, merely acted on the prompting of his heart, or head, or whatever organic or anatomical part of him that developed the mysterious, delicious, and insatiable hunger called "love."

Skipper went below. He went all unheeding of Jerry, who padded softly at his heels until the companionway was reached. Skipper was unheeding of Jerry because of the fever that wrenched his flesh and chilled his bones, that made his head seem to swell monstrously, that glazed the world to his swimming eyes and made him walk feebly and totteringly like a drunken man or a man very aged. And Jerry sensed that something was wrong with Skipper.

Skipper, beginning the babblings of delirium which alternated with silent moments of control in order to get below and under blankets, descended the ladder-like stairs, and Jerry, all-yearning, controlled himself in silence and watched the slow descent with the hope that when Skipper reached the bottom he would raise his arms and lift him down. But Skipper was too far gone to remember that Jerry existed. He staggered, with wide-spread arms to keep from falling, along the cabin floor for'ard to the bunk in the tiny stateroom.

Jerry was truly of a kingly line. He wanted to call out and beg to be taken down. But he did not. He controlled himself, he knew not why, save that he was possessed by a nebulous awareness that Skipper must be considered as a god should be considered, and that this was no time to obtrude himself on Skipper. His heart was torn with desire, although he made no sound, and he continued only to yearn over the companion combing and to listen to the faint sounds of Skipper's progress for'ard.

But even kings and their descendants have their limitations, and at the end of a quarter of an hour Jerry was ripe to cease from his silence. With the going below of Skipper, evidently in great trouble, the light had gone out of the day for Jerry. He might have stalked the wild-dog, but no inducement lay there. Lerumie passed by unnoticed, although he knew he could bully him and make him give deck space. The myriad scents of the land entered his keen nostrils, but he made no note of them. Not even the flopping, bellying mainsail overhead, as the *Arangi* rolled becalmed, could draw a glance of quizzical regard from him.

Just as it was tremblingly imperative that Jerry must suddenly squat down, point his nose at the zenith, and vocalize his heart-rending woe, an idea came to him. There is no explaining how this idea came. No more can it be explained than can a human explain why, at luncheon to-day, he selects green peas and rejects string beans, when only yesterday he elected to choose string beans and to reject green peas. No more can it be explained than can a human judge, sentencing a convicted criminal and imposing eight years imprisonment instead of the five or nine years that also at the same time floated upward in his brain, explain why he categorically determined on eight years as the just, adequate punishment. Since not even humans, who are almost half-gods, can fathom the mystery of the genesis of ideas and the dictates of choice, appearing in their consciousness as ideas, it is not to be expected of a more dog to know the why of the ideas that animate it to definite acts toward definite ends.

And so Jerry. Just as he must immediately howl, he was aware that the idea, an entirely different idea, was there, in the innermost centre of the quick-thinkingness of him, with all its compulsion. He obeyed the idea as a marionette obeys the strings, and started forthwith down the deck aft in quest of the mate.

He had an appeal to make to Borckman. Borckman was also a two-legged white-god. Easily could Borckman lift him down the precipitous ladder, which was to him, unaided, a taboo, the violation of which was pregnant with disaster. But Borckman had in him little of the heart of love, which is understanding. Also, Borckman was busy. Besides overseeing the continuous adjustment, by trimming of sails and orders to the helmsman, of the *Arangi* to her way on the sea, and overseeing the boat's crew at its task of washing deck and polishing brasswork, he was engaged in steadily nipping from a stolen bottle of his captain's whiskey which he had stowed away in the hollow between the two sacks of yams lashed on deck aft the mizzenmast.

Borckman was on his way for another nip, after having thickly threatened to knock seven bells and the ten commandments out of the black at the wheel for faulty steering, when Jerry appeared before him and blocked the way to his desire. But Jerry did not block him as he would have blocked Lerumie, for instance. There was no showing of teeth, no bristling of neck hair. Instead, Jerry was all placation and appeal, all softness of pleading in a body denied speech that nevertheless was articulate, from wagging tail and wriggling sides to flat-laid ears and eyes that almost spoke, to any human sensitive of understanding.

But Borckman saw in his way only a four-legged creature of the brute world, which, in his arrogant brutalness he esteemed more brute than himself. All the pretty picture of the soft puppy, instinct with communicativeness, bursting with tenderness of petition, was veiled to his vision. What he saw was merely a four-legged animal to be thrust aside while he continued his lordly two-legged progress toward the bottle that could set maggots crawling in his brain and make him dream dreams that he was prince, not peasant, that he was a master of matter rather than a slave of matter.

And thrust aside Jerry was, by a rough and naked foot, as harsh and unfeeling in its impact as an inanimate breaking sea on a beach-jut of insensate rock. He half-sprawled on the slippery deck, regained his balance, and stood still and looked at the white-god who had treated him so cavalierly. The meanness and unfairness had brought from Jerry no snarling threat of retaliation, such as he would have offered Lerumie or any other black. Nor in his brain was any thought of retaliation. This was no Lerumie. This was a superior god, two-legged, white-skinned, like Skipper, like Mister Haggin and the couple of other superior gods he had known. Only did he know hurt, such as any child knows under the blow of a thoughtless or unloving mother.

In the hurt was mingled a resentment. He was keenly aware that there were two sorts of roughness. There was the kindly roughness of love, such as when Skipper gripped him by the jowl, shook him till his teeth rattled, and thrust him away with an unmistakable invitation to come back and be so shaken again. Such roughness, to Jerry, was heaven. In it was the intimacy of contact with a beloved god who in such manner elected to express a reciprocal love.

But this roughness of Borckman was different. It was the other kind of roughness in which resided no warm affection, no heart-touch of love. Jerry did not quite understand, but he sensed the difference and resented, without expressing in action, the wrongness and unfairness of it. So he stood, after regaining balance, and soberly regarded, in a vain effort to understand, the mate with a bottle-bottom inverted skyward, the mouth to his lips, the while his throat made gulping contractions and noises. And soberly he continued to regard the mate when he went aft and threatened to knock the "Song of Songs" and the rest of the Old Testament out of the black helmsman whose smile of teeth was as humbly gentle and placating as Jerry's had been when he made his appeal.

Leaving this god as a god unliked and not understood, Jerry sadly trotted back to the companionway and yearned his head over the combing in the direction in which he had seen Skipper disappear. What bit at his consciousness and was a painful incitement in it, was his desire to be with Skipper who was not right, and who was in trouble. He wanted Skipper. He wanted to be with him, first and sharply, because he loved him, and, second and dimly, because he might serve him. And, wanting Skipper, in his helplessness and youngness in experience of the world, he whimpered and cried his heart out across the companion combing, and was too clean and direct in his sorrow to be deflected by an outburst of anger against the niggers, on deck and below, who chuckled at him and derided him.

From the crest of the combing to the cabin floor was seven feet. He had, only a few hours before, climbed the precipitous stairway; but it was impossible, and he knew it, to descend the stairway. And yet, at the last, he dared it. So compulsive was the prod of his heart to gain to Skipper at any cost, so clear was his comprehension that he could not climb down the ladder head first, with no grippingness of legs and feet and muscles such as were possible in the ascent, that he did not attempt it. He launched outward and down, in one magnificent and love-heroic leap. He knew that he was violating a taboo of life, just as he knew he was violating a taboo if he sprang into Meringe Lagoon where swam the dreadful crocodiles. Great love is always capable of expressing itself in sacrifice and self-immolation. And only for love, and for no lesser reason, could Jerry have made the leap.

He struck on his side and head. The one impact knocked the breath out of him; the other stunned him. Even in his unconsciousness, lying on his side and quivering, he made rapid, spasmodic movements of his legs as if running for'ard to Skipper. The boys looked on and laughed, and when he no longer quivered and churned his legs they continued to laugh. Born in savagery, having lived in savagery all their lives and known naught else, their sense of humour was correspondingly savage. To them, the sight of a stunned and possibly dead puppy was a side-splitting, ludicrous event.

Not until the fourth minute ticked off did returning consciousness enable Jerry to crawl to his feet and with wide-spread legs and swimming eyes adjust himself to the *Arangi's* roll. Yet with the first glimmerings of consciousness persisted the one idea that he must gain to Skipper. Blacks? In his anxiety and solicitude and love they did not count. He ignored the chuckling, grinning, girding black boys, who, but for the fact that he was under the terrible aegis of the big fella white marster, would have delighted to kill and eat the puppy who, in the process of training, was proving a most capable nigger-chaser. Without a turn of head or roll of eye, aristocratically positing their non-existingness to their faces, he trotted for'ard along the cabin floor and into the stateroom where Skipper babbled maniacally in the bunk.

Jerry, who had never had malaria, did not understand. But in his heart he knew great trouble in that Skipper was in trouble. Skipper did not recognize him, even when he sprang into the bunk, walked across Skipper's heaving chest, and licked the acrid sweat of fever from Skipper's face. Instead, Skipper's wildly-thrashing arms brushed him away and flung him violently against the side of the bunk.

This was roughness that was not love-roughness. Nor was it the roughness of Borckman spurning him away with his foot. It was part of Skipper's trouble. Jerry did not reason this conclusion. But, and to the point, he acted upon it as if he had reasoned it. In truth, through inadequacy of one of the most adequate languages in the world, it can only be said that Jerry *sensed* the new difference of this roughness.

He sat up, just out of range of one restless, beating arm, yearned to come closer and lick again the face of the god who knew him not, and who, he knew, loved him well, and palpitatingly shared and suffered all Skipper's trouble.

"Eh, Clancey," Skipper babbled. "It's a fine job this day, and no better crew to clean up after the dubs of motormen... Number three jack, Clancey. Get under the for'ard end." And, as the spectres of his nightmare metamorphosed: "Hush, darling, talking to your dad like that, telling him the combing of your sweet and golden hair. As if I couldn't, that have combed it these seven years—better than your mother, darling, better than your mother. I'm the one gold-medal prize-winner in the combing of his lovely daughter's lovely hair... She's broken out! Give her the wheel aft there! Jib and fore-topsail halyards! Full and by, there! A good full! ... Ah, she takes it like the beauty fairy boat that she is upon the sea... I'll just lift that—sure, the limit. Blackey, when you pay as much to see my cards as I'm going to pay to see yours, you're going to see some cards, believe me!"

And so the farrago of unrelated memories continued to rise vocal on Skipper's lips to the heave of his body and the beat of his arms, while Jerry, crouched against the side of the bunk mourned and mourned his grief and inability to be of help. All that was occurring was beyond him. He knew no more of poker hands than did he know of getting ships under way, of clearing up surface car wrecks in New York, or of combing the long yellow hair of a loved daughter in a Harlem flat.

"Both dead," Skipper said in a change of delirium. He said it quietly, as if announcing the time of day, then wailed: "But, oh, the bonnie, bonnie braids of all the golden hair of her!"

He lay motionlessly for a space and sobbed out a breaking heart. This was Jerry's chance. He crept inside the arm that tossed, snuggled against Skipper's side, laid his head on Skipper's shoulder, his cool nose barely touching Skipper's cheek, and felt the arm curl about him and press him closer. The hand bent from the wrist and caressed him protectingly, and the warm contact of his velvet body put a change in Skipper's sick dreams, for he began to mutter in cold and bitter ominousness: "Any nigger that as much as bats an eye at that puppy. . ."

VIII

When, in half an hour, Van Horn's sweat culminated in profusion, it marked the breaking of the malarial attack. Great physical relief was his, and the last mists of delirium ebbed from his brain. But he was left limply weak, and, after tossing off the blankets and recognizing Jerry, he fell into a refreshing natural sleep.

Not till two hours later did he awake and start to go on deck. Halfway up the companion, he deposited Jerry on deck and went back to the stateroom for a forgotten bottle of quinine. But he did not immediately return to Jerry. The long drawer under Borckman's bunk caught his eye. The wooden button that held it shut was gone, and it was far out and hanging at an angle that jammed it and prevented it from falling to the floor. The matter was serious. There was little doubt in his mind, had the drawer, in the midst of the squall of the previous night, fallen to the floor, that no *Arangi* and no soul of the eighty souls on board would have been left. For the drawer was filled with a heterogeneous mess of dynamite sticks, boxes of fulminating caps, coils of fuses, lead sinkers, iron tools, and many boxes of rifle, revolver and pistol cartridges. He sorted and arranged the varied contents, and with a screwdriver and a longer screw reattached the button.

In the meantime, Jerry was encountering new adventure not of the pleasantest. While waiting for Skipper to return, Jerry chanced to see the wild-dog brazenly lying on deck a dozen feet from his lair in the trade-boxes. Instantly stiffly crouching, Jerry began to stalk. Success seemed assured, for the wild-dog, with closed eyes, was apparently asleep.

And at this moment the mate, two-legging it along the deck from for'ard in the direction of the bottle stored between the yam sacks, called, "Jerry," in a remarkably husky voice. Jerry flattened his filbert-shaped ears and wagged his tail in acknowledgment, but advertised his intention of continuing to stalk his enemy. And at sound of the mate's voice the wild-dog flung quick-opened eyes in Jerry's direction and flashed into his burrow, where he immediately turned around, thrust his head out with a show of teeth, and snarled triumphant defiance.

Baulked of his quarry by the inconsiderateness of the mate, Jerry trotted back to the head of the companion to wait for Skipper. But Borckman, whose brain was well a-crawl by virtue of the many nips, clung to a petty idea after the fashion of drunken men. Twice again, imperatively, he called Jerry to him, and twice again, with flattened ears of gentleness and wagging tail, Jerry good-naturedly expressed his disinclination. Next, he yearned his head over the coming and into the cabin after Skipper.

Borckman remembered his first idea and continued to the bottle, which he generously inverted skyward. But the second idea, petty as it was, persisted; and, after swaying and mumbling to himself for a time, after unseeingly making believe to study the crisp fresh breeze that filled the *Arangi's* sails and slanted her deck, and, after sillily attempting on the helmsman to portray eagle-like vigilance in his drink-swimming eyes, he lurched amidships toward Jerry.

Jerry's first intimation of Borckman's arrival was a cruel and painful clutch on his flank and groin that made him cry out in pain and whirl around. Next, as the mate had seen Skipper do in play, Jerry had his jowls seized in a tooth-clattering shake that was absolutely different from the Skipper's rough love-shake. His head and body were shaken, his teeth clattered painfully, and with the roughest of roughness he was flung part way down the slippery slope of deck.

Now Jerry was a gentleman. All the soul of courtesy was in him, for equals and superiors. After all, even in an inferior like the wild-dog, he did not consciously press an advantage very far—never extremely far. In his stalking and rushing of the wild-dog, he had been more sound and fury than an overbearing bully. But with a superior, with a two-legged white-god like Borckman, there was more a demand upon his control, restraint, and inhibition of primitive promptings. He did not want to play with the mate a game that he ecstatically played with Skipper, because he had experienced no similar liking for the mate, two-legged white-god that he was.

And still Jerry was all gentleness. He came back in a feeble imitation rush of the whole-hearted rush that he had learned to make on Skipper. He was, in truth, acting, play-acting, attempting to do what he had no heart-prompting to do. He made believe to play, and uttered simulated growls that failed of the verity of simulation.

He bobbed his tail good-naturedly and friendly, and growled ferociously and friendly; but the keenness of the drunkenness of the mate discerned the difference and aroused in him, vaguely, the intuition of difference, of play-acting, of cheating. Jerry was cheating—out of his heart of consideration. Borckman drunkenly recognized the cheating without crediting the heart of good behind it. On the instant he was antagonistic. Forgetting that he was only a brute, he posited that this was no more than a brute with which he strove to play in the genial comradely way that the Skipper played.

Red war was inevitable—not first on Jerry's part, but on Borckman's part. Borckman felt the abysmal urgings of the beast, as a beast, to prove himself master of this four-legged beast. Jerry felt his jowl and jaw clutched still more harshly and hardly, and, with increase of harshness and hardness, he was flung farther down the deck, which, on account of its growing slant due to heavier gusts of wind, had become a steep and slippery hill.

He came back, clawing frantically up the slope that gave him little footing; and he came back, no longer with poorly attempted simulation of ferocity, but impelled by the first flickerings of real ferocity. He did not know this. If he thought at all, he was under the impression that he was playing the game as he had played it with Skipper. In short, he was taking an interest in the game, although a radically different interest from what he had taken with Skipper.

This time his teeth flashed quicker and with deeper intent at the jowl-clutching hand, and, missing, he was seized and flung down the smooth incline harder and farther than before. He was growing angry, as he clawed back, though he was not conscious of it. But the mate, being a man, albeit a drunken one, sensed the change in Jerry's attack ere Jerry dreamed there was any change in it. And not only did Borckman sense it, but it served as a spur to drive him back into primitive beastliness, and to fight to master this puppy as a primitive man, under dissimilar provocation, might have fought with the members of the first litter stolen from a wolf-den among the rocks.

True, Jerry could trace as far back. His ancient ancestors had been Irish wolf-hounds, and, long before that, the ancestors of the wolf-hounds had been wolves. The note in Jerry's growls changed. The unforgotten and ineffaceable past strummed the fibres of his throat. His teeth flashed with fierce intent, in the desire of sinking as deep in the man's hand as passion could drive. For Jerry by this time was all passion. He had leaped back into the dark stark rawness of the early world almost as swiftly as had Borckman. And this time his teeth scored, ripping the tender and sensitive and flesh of all the inside of the first and second joints of Borckman's right hand. Jerry's teeth were needles that stung, and Borckman, gaining the grasp on Jerry's jaw, flung him away and down so that almost he hit the *Arangi's* tiny-rail ere his clawing feet stopped him.

And Van Horn, having finished his rearrangement and repair of the explosive-filled drawer under the mate's bunk, climbed up the companion steps, saw the battle, paused, and quietly looked on.

But he looked across a million years, at two mad creatures who had slipped the leach of the generations and who were back in the darkness of spawning life ere dawning intelligence had modified the chemistry of such life to softness of consideration. What stirred in the brain crypts of Borckman's heredity, stirred in the brain-crypts of Jerry's heredity. Time had gone backward for both. All the endeavour and achievement of the ten thousand generations was not, and, as wolf-dog and wild-man, the combat was between Jerry and the mate. Neither saw Van Horn, who was inside the companionway hatch, his eyes level with the combing.

To Jerry, Borckman was now no more a god than was he himself a mere, smooth-coated Irish terrier. Both had forgotten the million years stamped into their heredity more feebly, less eraseably, than what had been stamped in prior to the million years. Jerry did not know drunkenness, but he did know unfairness; and it was with raging indignation that he knew it. Borckman fumbled his next counter to Jerry's attack, missed, and had both hands slashed in quick succession ere he managed to send the puppy sliding.

And still Jerry came back. As any screaming creature of the jungle, he hysterically squalled his indignation. But he made no whimper. Nor did he wince or cringe to the blows. He bored straight in, striving, without avoiding a blow, to beat and meet the blow with his teeth. So hard was he flung down the last time that his side smashed painfully against the rail, and Van Horn cried out:

"Cut that out, Borckman! Leave the puppy alone!"

The mate turned in the startle of surprise at being observed. The sharp, authoritative words of Van Horn were a call across the million years. Borckman's anger-convulsed face ludicrously attempted a sheepish, deprecating grin, and he was just mumbling, "We was only playing," when Jerry arrived back, leaped in the air, and sank his teeth into the offending hand.

Borckman immediately and insanely went back across the million years. An attempted kick got his ankle scored for his pains. He gibbered his own rage and hurt, and, stooping, dealt Jerry a tremendous blow alongside the head and neck. Being in mid-leap when he received the blow Jerry was twistingly somersaulted sidewise before he struck the deck on his back. As swiftly as he could scramble to footing and charge, he returned to the attack, but was checked by Skipper's:

"Jerry! Stop it! Come here!"

He obeyed, but only by prodigious effort, his neck bristling and his lips writhing clear of his teeth as he passed the mate. For the first time there was a whimper in his throat; but it was not the whimper of fear, nor of pain, but of outrage, and of desire to continue the battle which he struggled to control at Skipper's behest.

Stepping out on deck, Skipper picked him up and patted and soothed him the while he expressed his mind to the mate.

"Borckman, you ought to be ashamed. You ought to be shot or have your block knocked off for this. A puppy, a little puppy scarcely weaned. For two cents I'd give you what-for myself. The idea of it. A little puppy, a weanling little puppy. Glad your hands are ripped. You deserved it. Hope you get blood-poisoning in them. Besides, you're drunk. Go below and turn in, and don't you dare come on deck until you're sober. Savve?"

And Jerry, far-journeyer across life and across the history of all life that goes to make the world, strugglingly mastering the abysmal slime of the prehistoric with the love that had come into existence and had become warp and woof of him in far later time, his wrath of ancientness still faintly reverberating in his throat like the rumblings of a passing thunder-storm, knew, in the wide warm ways of feeling, the augustness and righteousness of Skipper. Skipper was in truth a god who did right, who was fair, who protected, and who imperiously commanded this other and lesser god that slunk away before his anger.

IX

Jerry and Skipper shared the long afternoon-watch together, the latter being guilty of recurrent chuckles and exclamations such as: "Gott-fer-dang, Jerry, believe *me*, you're some fighter and all dog"; or, "You're a proper man's dog, you are, a lion dog. I bet the lion don't live that could get your goat."

And Jerry, understanding none of the words, with the exception of his own name, nevertheless knew that the sounds made by Skipper were broad of praise and warm of love. And when Skipper stooped and rubbed his ears, or received a rose-kiss on extended fingers, or caught him up in his arms, Jerry's heart was nigh to bursting. For what greater ecstasy can be the portion of any creature than that it be loved by a god? This was just precisely Jerry's ecstasy. This was a god, a tangible, real, three-dimensioned god, who went about and ruled his world in a loin-cloth and on two bare legs, and who loved him with crooning noises in throat and mouth and with two wide-spread arms that folded him in.

At four o'clock, measuring a glance at the afternoon sun and gauging the speed of the *Arangi* through the water in relation to the closeness of Su'u, Van Horn went below and roughly shook the mate awake. Until both returned, Jerry held the deck alone. But for the fact that the white-gods were there below and were certain to be back at any moment, not many moments would Jerry have held the deck, for every lessened mile between the return boys and Malaita contributed a rising of their spirits, and under the imminence of their old-time independence, Lerumie, as an instance of many of them, with strong gustatory sensations and a positive drooling at the mouth, regarded Jerry in terms of food and vengeance that were identical.

Flat-hauled on the crisp breeze, the *Arangi* closed in rapidly with the land. Jerry peered through the barbed wire, sniffing the air, Skipper beside him and giving orders to the mate and helmsman. The heap of trade-boxes was now unlashed, and the boys began opening and shutting them. What gave them particular delight was the ringing of the bell with which each box was equipped and which rang whenever a lid was raised. Their pleasure in the toy-like contrivance was that of children, and each went back again and again to unlock his own box and make the bell ring.

Fifteen of the boys were to be landed at Su'u and with wild gesticulations and cries they began to recognize and point out the infinitesimal details of the landfall of the only spot they had known on earth prior to the day, three years before, when they had been sold into slavery by their fathers, uncles, and chiefs.

A narrow neck of water, scarcely a hundred yards across, gave entrance to a long and tiny bay. The shore was massed with mangroves and dense, tropical vegetation. There was no sign of houses nor of human occupancy, although Van Horn, staring at the dense jungle so close at hand, knew as a matter of course that scores, and perhaps hundreds, of pairs of human eyes were looking at him.

"Smell 'm, Jerry, smell 'm," he encouraged.

And Jerry's hair bristled as he barked at the mangrove wall, for truly his keen scent informed him of lurking niggers.

"If I could smell like him," the captain said to the mate, "there wouldn't be any risk at all of my ever losing my head."

But Borckman made no reply and sullenly went about his work. There was little wind in the bay, and the *Arangi* slowly forged in and dropped anchor in thirty fathoms. So steep was the slope of the harbour bed from the beach that even in such excessive depth the *Arangi's* stern swung in within a hundred feet of the mangroves.

Van Horn continued to cast anxious glances at the wooded shore. For Su'u had an evil name. Since the schooner *Fair Hathaway*, recruiting labour for the Queensland plantations, had been captured by the natives and all hands slain fifteen years before, no vessel, with the exception of the *Arangi*, had dared to venture into Su'u. And most white men condemned Van Horn's recklessness for so venturing.

Far up the mountains, that towered many thousands of feet into the trade-wind clouds, arose many signal smokes that advertised the coming of the vessel. Far and near, the *Arangi's* presence was known; yet from the jungle so near at hand only shrieks of parrots and chatterings of cockatoos could be heard.

The whaleboat, manned with six of the boat's crew, was drawn alongside, and the fifteen Su'u boys and their boxes were loaded in. Under the canvas flaps along the thwarts, ready to hand for the rowers, were laid five of the Lee-Enfields. On deck, another of the boat's crew, rifle in hand, guarded the remaining weapons. Borckman had brought up his own rifle to be ready for instant use. Van Horn's rifle lay handy in the stern sheets where he stood near Tambi, who steered with a long sweep. Jerry raised a low whine and yearned over the rail after Skipper, who yielded and lifted him down.

The place of danger was in the boat; for there was little likelihood, at this particular time, of a rising of the return boys on the *Arangi*. Being of Somo, No-ola, Langa-Langa, and far Malu they were in wholesome fear, did they lose the protection of their white masters, of being eaten by the Su'u folk, just as the Su'u boys would have feared being eaten by the Somo and Langa-Langa and No-ola folk.

What increased the danger of the boat was the absence of a covering boat. The invariable custom of the larger recruiting vessels was to send two boats on any shore errand. While one landed on the beach, the other lay off a short distance to cover the retreat of the shore party, if trouble broke out. Too small to carry one boat on deck, the *Arangi* could not conveniently tow two astern; so Van Horn, who was the most daring of the recruiters, lacked this essential safeguard.

Tambi, under Van Horn's low-uttered commands, steered a parallel course along the shore. Where the mangroves ceased, and where high ground and a beaten runway came down to the water's edge, Van Horn motioned the rowers to back water and lay on their oars. High palms and lofty, wide-branched trees rose above the jungle at this spot, and the runway showed like the entrance of a tunnel into the dense, green wall of tropical vegetation.

Van Horn, regarding the shore for some sign of life, lighted a cigar and put one hand to the waist-line of his loin-cloth to reassure himself of the presence of the stick of dynamite that was tucked between the loin-cloth and his skin. The lighted cigar was for the purpose, if emergency arose, of igniting the fuse of the dynamite. And the fuse was so short, with its end split to accommodate the inserted head of a safety match, that between the time of touching it off with the live cigar to the time of the explosion not more than three seconds could elapse. This required quick cool work on Van Horn's part, in case need arose. In three seconds he would have to light the fuse and throw the sputtering stick with directed aim to its objective. However, he did not expect to use it, and had it ready merely as a precautionary measure.

Five minutes passed, and the silence of the shore remained profound. Jerry sniffed Skipper's bare leg as if to assure him that he was beside him no matter what threatened from the hostile silence of the land, then stood up with his forepaws on the gunwale and continued to sniff eagerly and audibly, to prick his neck hair, and to utter low growls.

"They're there, all right," Skipper confided to him; and Jerry, with a sideward glance of smiling eyes, with a bobbing of his tail and a quick love-flattening of his ears, turned his nose shoreward again and resumed his reading of the jungle tale that was wafted to him on the light fans of the stifling and almost stagnant air.

"Hey!" Van Horn suddenly shouted. "Hey, you fella boy stick'm head out belong you!"

As if in a transformation scene, the apparently tenantless jungle spawned into life. On the instant a hundred stark savages appeared. They broke forth everywhere from the vegetation. All were armed, some with Snider rifles and ancient horse pistols, others with bows and arrows, with long throwing spears, with war-clubs, and with long-handled tomahawks. In a flash, one of them leaped into the sunlight in the open space where runway and water met. Save for decorations, he was naked as Adam before the Fall. A solitary white feather uprose from his kinky, glossy, black hair. A polished bodkin of white petrified shell, with sharp-pointed ends, thrust through a hole in the partition of his nostrils, extended five inches across his face. About his neck, from a cord of twisted coconut sennit, hung an ivory-white necklace of wild-boar's tusks. A garter of white cowrie shells encircled one leg just below the knee. A flaming scarlet flower was coquettishly stuck over one ear, and through a hole in the other ear was threaded a pig's tail so recently severed that it still bled.

As this dandy of Melanesia leaped into the sunshine, the Snider rifle in his hands came into position, aimed from his hip, the generous muzzle bearing directly on Van Horn. No less quick was Van Horn. With equal speed he had snatched his rifle and brought it to bear from his hip. So they stood and faced each other, death in their finger-tips, forty feet apart. The million years between barbarism and civilization also yawned between them across that narrow gulf of forty feet. The hardest thing for modern, evolved man to do is to forget his ancient training. Easiest of all things is it for him to forget his modernity and slip back across time to the howling ages. A lie in the teeth, a blow in the face, a love-thrust of jealousy to the heart, in a fraction of an instant can turn a twentieth-century philosopher into an ape-like arborean pounding his chest, gnashing his teeth, and seeing red.

So Van Horn. But with a difference. He straddled time. He was at one and the same instant all modern, all imminently primitive, capable of fighting in redness of tooth and claw, desirous of remaining modern for as long as he could with his will master the study of ebon black of skin and dazzling white of decoration that confronted him.

A long ten seconds of silence endured. Even Jerry, he knew not why, stilled the growl in his throat. Five score of head-hunting cannibals on the fringe of the jungle, fifteen Su'u return blacks in the boat, seven black boat's crew, and a solitary white man with a cigar in his mouth, a rifle at his hip, and an Irish terrier bristling against his bare calf, kept the solemn pact of those ten seconds, and no one of them knew or guessed what the outcome would be.

One of the return boys, in the bow of the whaleboat, made the peace sign with his palm extended outward and weaponless, and began to chirp in the unknown Su'u dialect. Van Horn held his aim and waited. The dandy lowered his Snider, and breath came more easily to the chests of all who composed the picture.

"Me good fella boy," the dandy piped, half bird-like and half elf.

"You big fella fool too much," Van Horn retorted harshly, dropping his gun into the stern-sheets, motioning to rowers and steersman to turn the boat around, and puffing his cigar as carelessly casual as if, the moment before, life and death had not been the debate.

"My word," he went on with fine irritable assumption. "What name you stick 'm gun along me? Me no kai-kai (eat) along you. Me kai-kai along you, stomach belong me walk about. You kai-kai along me, stomach belong you walk about. You no like 'm kai-kai Su'u boy belong along you? Su'u boy belong you all the same brother along you. Long time before, three monsoon before, me speak 'm true speak. Me say three monsoon boy come back. My word, three monsoon finish, boy stop along me come back."

By this time the boat had swung around, reversing bow and stern, Van Horn pivoting so as to face the Snider-armed dandy. At another signal from Van Horn the rowers backed water and forced the boat, stern in, up to the solid ground of the runway. And each rower, his oar in position in case of attack, privily felt under the canvas flap to make sure of the exact location of his concealed Lee-Enfield.

"All right boy belong you walk about?" Van Horn queried of the dandy, who signified the affirmative in the Solomon Islands fashion by half-closing his eyes and nodding his head upward, in a queer, perky way;

"No kai-kai 'm Su'u fella boy suppose walk about along you?"

"No fear," the dandy answered. "Suppose 'm Su'u fella boy, all right. Suppose 'm no fella Su'u boy, my word, big trouble. Ishikola, big fella black marster along this place, him talk 'm me talk along you. Him say any amount bad fella boy stop 'm along bush. Him say big fella white marster no walk about. Him say jolly good big fella white marster stop 'm along ship."

Van Horn nodded in an off-hand way, as if the information were of little value, although he knew that for this time Su'u would furnish him no fresh recruits. One at a time, compelling the others to remain in their places, he directed the return boys astern and ashore. It was Solomon Islands tactics. Crowding was dangerous. Never could the blacks be risked to confusion in numbers. And Van Horn, smoking his cigar in lordly indifferent fashion, kept his apparently uninterested eyes glued to each boy who made his way aft, box on shoulder, and stepped out on the land. One by one they disappeared into the runway tunnel, and when the last was ashore he ordered the boat back to the ship.

"Nothing doing here this trip," he told the mate. "We'll up hook and out in the morning."

The quick tropic twilight swiftly blent day and darkness. Overhead all stars were out. No faintest breath of air moved over the water, and the humid heat beaded the faces and bodies of both men with profuse sweat. They ate their deck-spread supper languidly and ever and anon used their forearms to wipe the stinging sweat from their eyes.

"Why a man should come to the Solomons—beastly hole," the mate complained.

"Or stay on," the captain rejoined.

"I'm too rotten with fever," the mate grumbled. "I'd die if I left. Remember, I tried it two years ago. It takes the cold weather to bring out the fever. I arrived in Sydney on my back. They had to take me to hospital in an ambulance. I got worse and worse. The doctors told me the only thing to do was to head back where I got the fever. If I did I might live a long time. If I hung on in Sydney it meant a quick finish. They packed me on board in another ambulance. And that's all I saw of Australia for my holiday. I don't want to stay in the Solomons. It's plain hell. But I got to, or croak."

He rolled, at a rough estimate, thirty grains of quinine in a cigarette paper, regarded the result sourly for a moment, then swallowed it at a gulp. This reminded Van Horn, who reached for the bottle and took a similar dose.

"Better put up a covering cloth," he suggested.

Borckman directed several of the boat's crew in the rigging up of a thin tarpaulin, like a curtain along the shore side of the *Arangi*. This was a precaution against any bushwhacking bullet from the mangroves only a hundred feet away.

Van Horn sent Tambi below to bring up the small phonograph and run off the dozen or so scratchy, screechy records that had already been under the needle a thousand times. Between records, Van Horn recollected the girl, and had her haled out of her dark hole in the lazarette to listen to the music. She obeyed in fear, apprehensive that her time had come. She looked dumbly at the big fella white master, her eyes large with fright; nor did the trembling of her body cease for a long time after he had made her lie down. The phonograph meant nothing to her. She knew only fear—fear of this terrible white man that she was certain was destined to eat her.

Jerry left the caressing hand of Skipper for a moment to go over and sniff her. This was an act of duty. He was identifying her once again. No matter what happened, no matter what months or years might elapse, he would know her again and for ever know her again. He returned to the free hand of Skipper that resumed its caressing. The other hand held the cigar which he was smoking.

The wet sultry heat grew more oppressive. The air was nauseous with the dank mucky odour that cooked out of the mangrove swamp. Rowelled by the squeaky music to recollection of old-world ports and places, Borckman lay on his face on the hot planking, beat a tattoo with his naked toes, and gutturally muttered an unending monologue of curses. But Van Horn, with Jerry panting under his hand, placidly and philosophically continued to smoke, lighting a fresh cigar when the first gave out.

He roused abruptly at the faint wash of paddles which he was the first on board to hear. In fact, it was Jerry's low growl and neck-rippling of hair that had keyed Van Horn to hear. Pulling the stick of dynamite out from the twist of his loin cloth and glancing at the cigar to be certain it was alight, he rose to his feet with leisurely swiftness and with leisurely swiftness gained the rail.

"What name belong you?" was his challenge to the dark.

"Me fella Ishikola," came the answer in the quavering falsetto of age.

Van Horn, before speaking again, loosened his automatic pistol half out of its holster, and slipped the holster around from his hip till it rested on his groin conveniently close to his hand.

JACK LONDON

"How many fella boy stop along you?" he demanded.

"One fella ten-boy altogether he stop," came the aged voice.

"Come alongside then." Without turning his head, his right hand unconsciously dropping close to the butt of the automatic, Van Horn commanded: "You fella Tambi. Fetch 'm lantern. No fetch 'm this place. Fetch 'm aft along mizzen rigging and look sharp eye belong you."

Tambi obeyed, exposing the lantern twenty feet away from where his captain stood. This gave Van Horn the advantage over the approaching canoe-men, for the lantern, suspended through the barbed wire across the rail and well down, would clearly illuminate the occupants of the canoe while he was left in semi-darkness and shadow.

"Washee-washee!" he urged peremptorily, while those in the invisible canoe still hesitated.

Came the sound of paddles, and, next, emerging into the lantern's area of light, the high, black bow of a war canoe, curved like a gondola, inlaid with silvery-glistening mother-of-pearl; the long lean length of the canoe which was without outrigger; the shining eyes and the black-shining bodies of the stark blacks who knelt in the bottom and paddled; Ishikola, the old chief, squatting amidships and not paddling, an unlighted, empty-bowled, short-stemmed clay pipe upside-down between his toothless gums; and, in the stern, as coxswain, the dandy, all nakedness of blackness, all whiteness of decoration, save for the pig's tail in one ear and the scarlet hibiscus that still flamed over the other ear.

Less than ten blacks had been known to rush a blackbirder officered by no more than two white men, and Van Horn's hand closed on the butt of his automatic, although he did not pull it clear of the holster, and although, with his left hand, he directed the cigar to his mouth and puffed it lively alight.

"Hello, Ishikola, you blooming old blighter," was Van Horn's greeting to the old chief, as the dandy, with a pry of his steering-paddle against the side of the canoe and part under its bottom, brought the dug-out broadside-on to the *Arangi* so that the sides of both crafts touched.

Ishikola smiled upward in the lantern light. He smiled with his right eye, which was all he had, the left having been destroyed by an arrow in a youthful jungle-skirmish.

"My word!" he greeted back. "Long time you no stop eye belong me."

Van Horn joked him in understandable terms about the latest wives he had added to his harem and what price he had paid for them in pigs.

"My word," he concluded, "you rich fella too much together."

"Me like 'm come on board gammon along you," Ishikola meekly suggested.

"My word, night he stop," the captain objected, then added, as a concession against the known rule that visitors were not permitted aboard after nightfall: "You come on board, boy stop 'm along boat."

Van Horn gallantly helped the old man to clamber to the rail, straddle the barbed wire, and gain the deck. Ishikola was a dirty old savage. One of his tambos (tambo being beche-de-mer and Melanesian for "taboo") was that water unavoidable must never touch his skin. He who lived by the salt sea, in a land of tropic downpour, religiously shunned contact with water. He never went swimming or wading, and always fled to shelter from a shower. Not that this was true of the rest of his tribe. It was the peculiar tambo laid upon him by the devil-devil doctors. Other tribesmen the devil-devil doctors tabooed against eating shark, or handling turtle, or contacting with crocodiles or the fossil remains of crocodiles, or from ever being smirched by the profanity of a woman's touch or of a woman's shadow cast across the path.

So Ishikola, whose tambo was water, was crusted with the filth of years. He was sealed like a leper, and, weazen-faced and age-shrunken, he hobbled horribly from an ancient spear-thrust to the thigh that twisted his torso droopingly out of the vertical. But his one eye gleamed brightly and wickedly, and Van Horn knew that it observed as much as did both his own eyes.

Van Horn shook hands with him—an honour he accorded only chiefs—and motioned him to squat down on deck on his hams close to the fear-struck girl, who began trembling again at recollection of having once heard Ishikola offer five twenties of drinking coconuts for the meat of her for a dinner.

Jerry needs must sniff, for future identification purposes, this graceless, limping, naked, one-eyed old man. And, when he had sniffed and registered the particular odour, Jerry must growl intimidatingly and win a quick eye-glance of approval from Skipper.

"My word, good fella kai-kai dog," said Ishikola. "Me give 'm half-fathom shell money that fella dog."

For a mere puppy this offer was generous, because half a fathom of shell-money, strung on a thread of twisted coconut fibres, was equivalent in cash to half a sovereign in English currency, to two dollars and a half in American, or, in live-pig currency, to half of a fair-sized fat pig.

"One fathom shell-money that fella dog," Van Horn countered, in his heart knowing that he would not sell Jerry for a hundred fathoms, or for any fabulous price from any black, but in his head offering so small a price over par as not to arouse suspicion among the blacks as to how highly he really valued the golden-coated son of Biddy and Terrence.

Ishikola next averred that the girl had grown much thinner, and that he, as a practical judge of meat, did not feel justified this time in bidding more than three twenty-strings of drinking coconuts.

After these amenities, the white master and the black talked of many things, the one bluffing with the white-man's superiority of intellect and knowledge, the other feeling and guessing, primitive statesman that he was, in an effort to ascertain the balance of human and political forces that bore upon his Su'u territory, ten miles square, bounded by the sea and by landward lines of an inter-tribal warfare that was older than the oldest Su'u myth. Eternally, heads had been taken and bodies eaten, now on one side, now on the other, by the temporarily victorious tribes. The boundaries had remained the same. Ishikola, in crude beche-de-mer, tried to learn the Solomon Islands general situation in relation to Su'u, and Van Horn was not above playing the unfair diplomatic game as it is unfairly played in all the chancellories of the world powers.

"My word," Van Horn concluded; "you bad fella too much along this place. Too many heads you fella take; too much kai-kai long pig along you." (Long pig, meaning barbecued human flesh.)

"What name, long time black fella belong Su'u take'm heads, kai-kai along long pig?" Ishikola countered.

"My word," Van Horn came back, "too much along this place. Bime by, close up, big fella warship stop'm along Su'u, knock seven balls outa Su'u."

"What name him big fella warship stop'm along Solomons?" Ishikola demanded.

"Big fella *Cambrian*, him fella name belong ship," Van Horn lied, too well aware that no British cruiser had been in the Solomons for the past two years.

The conversation was becoming rather a farcical dissertation upon the relations that should obtain between states, irrespective of size, when it was broken off by a cry from Tambi, who, with another lantern hanging overside at the end of his arm had made a discovery.

"Skipper, gun he stop along canoe!" was his cry.

Van Horn, with a leap, was at the rail and peering down over the barbed wire. Ishikola, despite his twisted body, was only seconds behind him.

"What name that fella gun stop 'm along bottom?" Van Horn indignantly demanded.

The dandy, in the stern, with a careless look upward, tried with his foot to shove over the green leaves so as to cover the out-jutting butts of several rifles, but made the matter worse by exposing them more fully. He bent to rake the leaves over with his hand, but sat swiftly upright when Van Horn roared at him:

"Stand clear! Keep 'm fella hand belong you long way big bit!"

Van Horn turned on Ishikola, and simulated wrath which he did not feel against the ancient and ever-recurrent trick.

"What name you come alongside, gun he stop along canoe belong you?" he demanded.

The old salt-water chief rolled his one eye and blinked a fair simulation of stupidity and innocence.

"My word, me cross along you too much," Van Horn continued. "Ishikola, you plenty bad fella boy. You get 'm to hell overside."

The old fellow limped across the deck with more agility than he had displayed coming aboard, straddled the barbed wire without assistance, and without assistance dropped into the canoe, cleverly receiving his weight on his uninjured leg. He blinked up for forgiveness and in reassertion of innocence. Van Horn turned his face aside to hide a grin, and then grinned outright when the old rascal, showing his empty pipe, wheedled up:

"Suppose 'm five stick tobacco you give 'm along me?"

While Borckman went below for the tobacco, Van Horn orated to Ishikola on the sacred solemnity of truth and promises. Next, he leaned across the barbed wire and handed down the five sticks of tobacco.

"My word," he threatened. "Somo day, Ishikola, I finish along you altogether. You no good friend stop along salt-water. You big fool stop along bush."

When Ishikola attempted protest, he shut him off with, "My word, you gammon along me too much."

Still the canoe lingered. The dandy's toe strayed privily to feel out the butts of the Sniders under the green leaves, and Ishikola was loth to depart.

"Washee-washee!" Van Horn cried with imperative suddenness.

The paddlers, without command from chief or dandy, involuntarily obeyed, and with deep, strong strokes sent the canoe into the encircling darkness. Just as quickly Van Horn changed his position on deck to the tune of a dozen yards, so that no hazarded bullet might reach him. He crouched low and listened to the wash of paddles fade away in the distance.

"All right, you fella Tambi," he ordered quietly. "Make 'm music he fella walk about."

And while "Red Wing" screeched its cheap and pretty rhythm, he reclined elbow on deck, smoked his cigar, and gathered Jerry into caressing inclosure.

As he smoked he watched the abrupt misting of the stars by a rain-squall that made to windward or to where windward might vaguely be configured. While he gauged the minutes ere he must order Tambi below with the phonograph and records, he noted the bush-girl gazing at him in dumb fear. He nodded consent with half-closed eyes and up-tilting face, clinching his consent with a wave of hand toward the companionway. She obeyed as a beaten dog, spirit-broken, might have obeyed, dragging herself to her feet, trembling afresh, and with backward glances of her perpetual terror of the big white master that she was convinced would some day eat her. In such fashion, stabbing Van Horn to the heart because of his inability to convey his kindness to her across the abyss of the ages that separated them, she slunk away to the companionway and crawled down it feet-first like some enormous, large-headed worm.

After he had sent Tambi to follow her with the precious phonograph, Van Horn continued to smoke on while the sharp, needle-like spray of the rain impacted soothingly on his heated body.

Only for five minutes did the rain descend. Then, as the stars drifted back in the sky, the smell of steam seemed to stench forth from deck and mangrove swamp, and the suffocating heat wrapped all about.

Van Horn knew better, but ill health, save for fever, had never concerned him; so he did not bother for a blanket to shelter him.

"Yours the first watch," he told Borckman. "I'll have her under way in the morning, before I call you."

He tucked his head on the biceps of his right arm, with the hollow of the left snuggling Jerry in against his chest, and dozed off to sleep.

And thus adventuring, white men and indigenous black men from day to day lived life in the Solomons, bickering and trafficking, the whites striving to maintain their heads on their shoulders, the blacks striving, no less single-heartedly, to remove the whites' heads from their shoulders and at the same time to keep their own anatomies intact.

And Jerry, who knew only the world of Meringe Lagoon, learning that these new worlds of the ship *Arangi* and of the island of Malaita were essentially the same, regarded the perpetual game between the white and the black with some slight sort of understanding.

X

Daylight saw the *Arangi* under way, her sails drooping heavily in the dead air while the boat's crew toiled at the oars of the whaleboat to tow her out through the narrow entrance. Once, when the ketch, swerved by some vagrant current, came close to the break of the shore-surf, the blacks on board drew toward one another in apprehension akin to that of startled sheep in a fold when a wild woods marauder howls outside. Nor was there any need for Van Horn's shout to the whaleboat: "Washee-washee! Damn your hides!" The boat's crew lifted themselves clear of the thwarts as they threw all their weight into each stroke. They knew what dire fate was certain if ever the sea-washed coral rock gripped the *Arangi's* keel. And they knew fear precisely of the same sort as that of the fear-struck girl below in the lazarette. In the past more than one Langa-Langa and Somo boy had gone to make a Su'u feast day, just as Su'u boys, on occasion, had similarly served feasts at Langa-Langa and at Somo.

"My word," Tambi, at the wheel, addressed Van Horn as the period of tension passed and the *Arangi* went clear. "Brother belong my father, long time before he come boat's crew along this place. Big fella schooner brother belong my father he come along. All finish this place Su'u. Brother belong my father Su'u boys kai-kai along him altogether."

Van Horn recollected the *Fair Hathaway* of fifteen years before, looted and burned by the people of Su'u after all hands had been killed. Truly, the Solomons at this beginning of the twentieth century were savage, and truly, of the Solomons, this great island of Malaita was savagest of all.

He cast his eyes speculatively up the slopes of the island to the seaman's landmark, Mount Kolorat, green-forested to its cloud-capped summit four thousand feet in the air. Even as he looked, thin smoke-columns were rising along the slopes and lesser peaks, and more were beginning to rise.

"My word," Tambi grinned. "Plenty boy stop 'm bush lookout along you eye belong him."

Van Horn smiled understandingly. He knew, by the ancient telegraphy of smoke-signalling, the message was being conveyed from village to village and tribe to tribe that a labour-recruiter was on the leeward coast.

All morning, under a brisk beam wind which had sprung up with the rising of the sun, the *Arangi* flew north, her course continuously advertised by the increasing smoke-talk that gossiped along the green summits. At high noon, with Van Horn, ever-attended by Jerry, standing for'ard and conning, the *Arangi* headed into the wind to thread the passage between two palm-tufted islets. There was need for conning. Coral patches uprose everywhere from the turquoise depths, running the gamut of green from deepest jade to palest tourmaline, over which the sea filtered changing shades, creamed lazily, or burst into white fountains of sun-flashed spray.

The smoke columns along the heights became garrulous, and long before the *Arangi* was through the passage the entire leeward coast, from the salt-water men of the shore to the remotest bush villagers, knew that the labour recruiter was going in to Langa-Langa. As the lagoon, formed by the chain of islets lying off shore, opened out, Jerry began to smell the reef-villages. Canoes, many canoes, urged by paddles or sailed before the wind by the weight of the freshening South East trade on spread fronds of coconut palms, moved across the smooth surface of the lagoon. Jerry barked intimidatingly at those that came closest, bristling his neck and making a ferocious simulation of an efficient protector of the white god who stood beside him. And after each such warning, he would softly dab his cool damp muzzle against the sun-heated skin of Skipper's leg.

Once inside the lagoon, the *Arangi* filled away with the wind a-beam. At the end of a swift half-mile she rounded to, with head-sails trimming down and with a great flapping of main and mizzen, and dropped anchor in fifty feet of water so clear that every huge fluted clamshell was visible on the coral floor. The whaleboat was not necessary to put the Langa-Langa return boys ashore. Hundreds of canoes lay twenty deep along both sides of the *Arangi*, and each boy, with his box and bell, was clamoured for by scores of relatives and friends.

In such height of excitement, Van Horn permitted no one on board. Melanesians, unlike cattle, are as prone to stampede to attack as to retreat. Two of the boat's crew stood beside the Lee-Enfields on the skylight. Borckman, with half the boat's crew, went about the ship's work. Van Horn, Jerry at his heels, careful that no one should get at his back, superintended the departure of the Langa-Langa returns and kept a vigilant eye on the remaining half of the boat's crew that guarded the barbed-wire rails. And each Somo boy sat on his trade-box to prevent it from being tossed into the waiting canoes by some Langa-Langa boy.

In half an hour the riot departed ashore. Only several canoes lingered, and from one of these Van Horn beckoned aboard Nau-hau, the biggest chief of the stronghold of Langa-Langa. Unlike most of the big chiefs, Nau-hau was young, and, unlike most of the Melanesians, he was handsome, even beautiful.

"Hello, King o' Babylon," was Van Horn's greeting, for so he had named him because of fancied Semitic resemblance blended with the crude power that marked his visage and informed his bearing.

Born and trained to nakedness, Nau-hau trod the deck boldly and unashamed. His sole gear of clothing was a length of trunk strap buckled about his waist. Between this and his bare skin was thrust the naked blade of a ten-inch ripping knife. His sole decoration was a white China soup-plate, perforated and strung on coconut sennit, suspended from about his neck so that it rested flat on his chest and half-concealed the generous swell of muscles. It was the greatest of treasures. No man of Malaita he had ever heard of possessed an unbroken soup-plate.

Nor was he any more ridiculous because of the soup-plate than was he ludicrous because of his nakedness. He was royal. His father had been a king before him, and he had proved himself greater than his father. Life and death he bore in his hands and head. Often he had exercised it, chirping to his subjects in the tongue of Langa-Langa: "Slay here," and "Slay there"; "Thou shalt die," and "Thou shalt live." Because his father, a year abdicated, had chosen foolishly to interfere with his son's government, he had called two boys and had them twist a cord of coconut around his father's neck so that thereafter he never breathed again. Because his favourite wife, mother of his eldest born, had dared out of silliness of affection to violate one of his kingly tamboos, he had had her killed and had himself selfishly and religiously eaten the last of her even to the marrow of her cracked joints, sharing no morsel with his boonest of comrades.

Royal he was, by nature, by training, by deed. He carried himself with consciousness of royalty. He looked royal—as a magnificent stallion may look royal, as a lion on a painted tawny desert may look royal. He was as splendid a brute—an adumbration of the splendid human conquerors and rulers, higher on the ladder of evolution, who have appeared in other times and places. His pose of body, of chest, of shoulders, of head, was royal. Royal was the heavy-lidded, lazy, insolent way he looked out of his eyes.

Royal in courage was he, this moment on the *Arangi*, despite the fact that he knew he walked on dynamite. As he had long since bitterly learned, any white man was as much dynamite as was the mysterious death-dealing missile he sometimes employed. When a stripling, he had made one of the canoe force that attacked the sandalwood-cutter that had been even smaller than the *Arangi*. He had never forgotten that mystery. Two of the three white men he had seen slain and their heads removed on deck. The third, still fighting, had but the minute before fled below. Then the cutter, along with all her wealth of hoop-iron, tobacco, knives and calico, had gone up into the air and fallen back into the sea in scattered and fragmented nothingness. It had been dynamite—the *Mystery*. And he, who had been hurled uninjured through the air by a miracle of fortune, had divined that white men in themselves were truly dynamite, compounded of the same mystery as the substance with which they shot the swift-darting schools of mullet, or blow up, in extremity, themselves and the ships on which they voyaged the sea from far places. And yet on this unstable and death-terrific substance of which he was well aware Van Horn was composed, he trod heavily with his personality, daring, to the verge of detonation, to impact it with his insolence.

"My word," he began, "what name you make 'm boy belong me stop along you too much?" Which was a true and correct charge that the boys which Van Horn had just returned had been away three years and a half instead of three years.

"You talk that fella talk I get cross too much along you," Van Horn bristled back, and then added, diplomatically, dipping into a half-case of tobacco sawed across and proffering a handful of stick tobacco: "Much better you smoke 'm up and talk 'm good fella talk."

But Nau-hau grandly waved aside the gift for which he hungered.

"Plenty tobacco stop along me," he lied. "What name one fella boy go way no come back?" he demanded.

Van Horn pulled the long slender account book out of the twist of his loin-cloth, and, while he skimmed its pages, impressed Nau-hau with the dynamite of the white man's superior powers which enabled him to remember correctly inside the scrawled sheets of a book instead of inside his head.

"Sati," Van Horn read, his finger marking the place, his eyes alternating watchfully between the writing and the black chief before him, while the black chief himself speculated and studied the chance of getting behind him and, with the single knife-thrust he knew so well, of severing the other's spinal cord at the base of the neck.

"Sati," Van Horn read. "Last monsoon begin about this time, him fella Sati get 'm sick belly belong him too much; bime by him fella Sati finish altogether," he translated into beche-de-mer the written information: *Died of dysentery July 4th*, 1901.

"Plenty work him fella Sati, long time," Nau-hau drove to the point. "What come along money belong him?"

Van Horn did mental arithmetic from the account.

"Altogether him make 'm six tens pounds and two fella pounds gold money," was his translation of sixty-two pounds of wages. "I pay advance father belong him one ten pounds and five fella pounds. Him finish altogether four tens pounds and seven fella pounds."

"What name stop four tens pounds and seven fella pounds?" Nau-hau demanded, his tongue, but not his brain, encompassing so prodigious a sum.

Van Horn held up his hand.

"Too much hurry you fella Nau-hau. Him fella Sati buy 'm slop chest along plantation two tens pounds and one fella pound. Belong Sati he finish altogether two tens pounds and six fella pounds."

"What name stop two tens pounds and six fella pounds?" Nau-hau continued inflexibly.

"Stop 'm along me," the captain answered curtly.

"Give 'm me two tens pounds and six fella pounds."

"Give 'm you hell," Van Horn refused, and in the blue of his eyes the black chief sensed the impression of the dynamite out of which white men seemed made, and felt his brain quicken to the vision of the bloody day he first encountered an explosion of dynamite and was hurled through the air.

"What name that old fella boy stop 'm along canoe?" Van Horn asked, pointing to an old man in a canoe alongside. "Him father belong Sati?"

"Him father belong Sati," Nau-hau affirmed.

Van Horn motioned the old man in and on board, beckoned Borckman to take charge of the deck and of Nau-hau, and went below to get the money from his strong-box. When he returned, cavalierly ignoring the chief, he addressed himself to the old man.

"What name belong you?"

"Me fella Nino," was the quavering response. "Him fella Sati belong along me."

Van Horn glanced for verification to Nau-hau, who nodded affirmation in the reverse Solomon way; whereupon Van Horn counted twenty-six gold sovereigns into the hand of Sati's father.

Immediately thereafter Nau-hau extended his hand and received the sum. Twenty gold pieces the chief retained for himself, returning to the old man the remaining six. It was no quarrel of Van Horn's. He had fulfilled his duty and paid properly. The tyranny of a chief over a subject was none of his business.

Both masters, white and black, were fairly contented with themselves. Van Horn had paid the money where it was due; Nau-hau, by virtue of kingship, had robbed Sati's father of Sati's labour before Van Horn's eyes. But Nau-hau was not above strutting. He declined a proffered present of tobacco, bought a case of stick tobacco from Van Horn, paying him five pounds for it, and insisted on having it sawed open so that he could fill his pipe.

"Plenty good boy stop along Langa-Langa?" Van Horn, unperturbed, politely queried, in order to make conversation and advertise nonchalance.

The King o' Babylon grinned, but did not deign to reply.

"Maybe I go ashore and walk about?" Van Horn challenged with tentative emphasis.

"Maybe too much trouble along you," Nau-hau challenged back. "Maybe plenty bad fella boy kai-kai along you."

Although Van Horn did not know it, at this challenge he experienced the hair-pricking sensations in his scalp that Jerry experienced when he bristled his back.

"Hey, Borckman," he called. "Man the whaleboat."

When the whaleboat was alongside, he descended into it first, superiorly, then invited Nau-hau to accompany him.

"My word, King o' Babylon," he muttered in the chief's ears as the boat's crew bent to the oars, "one fella boy make 'm trouble, I shoot 'm hell outa you first thing. Next thing I shoot 'm hell outa Langa-Langa. All the time you me fella walk about, you walk about along me. You no like walk about along me, you finish close up altogether."

And ashore, a white man alone, attended by an Irish terrier puppy with a heart flooded with love and by a black king resentfully respectful of the dynamite of the white man, Van Horn went, swashbuckling barelegged through a stronghold of three thousand souls, while his white mate, addicted to schnapps, held the deck of the tiny craft at anchor off shore, and while his black boat's crew, oars in hands, held the whaleboat stern-on to the beach to receive the expected flying leap of the man they served but did not love, and whose head they would eagerly take any time were it not for fear of him.

Van Horn had had no intention of going ashore, and that he went ashore at the black chief's insolent challenge was merely a matter of business. For an hour he strolled about, his right hand never far from the butt of the automatic that lay along his groin, his eyes never too far from the unwilling Nau-hau beside him. For Nau-hau, in sullen volcanic rage, was ripe to erupt at the slightest opportunity. And, so strolling, Van Horn was given to see what few white men have seen, for Langa-Langa and her sister islets, beautiful beads strung along the lee coast of Malaita, were as unique as they were unexplored.

Originally these islets had been mere sand-banks and coral reefs awash in the sea or shallowly covered by the sea. Only a hunted, wretched creature, enduring incredible hardship, could have eked out a miserable existence upon them. But such hunted, wretched creatures, survivors of village massacres, escapes from the wrath of chiefs and from the long-pig fate of the cooking-pot, did come, and did endure. They, who knew only the bush, learned the salt water and developed the salt-water-man breed. They learned the ways of the fish and the shell-fish, and they invented hooks and lines, nets and fish-traps, and all the diverse cunning ways by which swimming meat can be garnered from the shifting, unstable sea.

Such refugees stole women from the mainland, and increased and multiplied. With herculean labour, under the burning sun, they conquered the sea. They walled the confines of their coral reefs and sand-banks with coral-rock stolen from the mainland on dark nights. Fine masonry, without mortar or cutting chisel, they builded to withstand the ocean surge. Likewise stolen from the mainland, as mice steal from human habitations when humans sleep, they stole canoe-loads, and millions of canoe-loads, of fat, rich soil.

Generations and centuries passed, and, behold, in place of naked sandbanks half awash were walled citadels, perforated with launching-ways for the long canoes, protected against the mainland by the lagoons that were to them their narrow seas. Coconut palms, banana trees, and lofty breadfruit trees gave food and sun-shelter. Their gardens prospered. Their long, lean war-canoes ravaged the coasts and visited vengeance for their forefathers upon the descendants of them that had persecuted and desired to eat.

Like the refugees and renegades who slunk away in the salt marshes of the Adriatic and builded the palaces of powerful Venice on her deep-sunk piles, so these wretched hunted blacks builded power until they became masters of the mainland, controlling traffic and trade-routes, compelling the bushmen for ever after to remain in the bush and never to dare attempt the salt-water.

And here, amidst the fat success and insolence of the sea-people, Van Horn swaggered his way, taking his chance, incapable of believing that he might swiftly die, knowing that he was building good future business in the matter of recruiting labour for the plantations of other adventuring white men on far islands who dared only less greatly than he.

And when, at the end of an hour, Van Horn passed Jerry into the sternsheets of the whaleboat and followed, he left on the beach a stunned and wondering royal black, who, more than ever before, was respectful of the dynamite-compounded white men who brought to him stick tobacco, calico, knives and hatchets, and inexorably extracted from such trade a profit.

XI

B ack on board, Van Horn immediately hove short, hoisted sail, broke out the anchor, and filled away for the ten-mile beat up the lagoon to windward that would fetch Somo. On the way, he stopped at Binu to greet Chief Johnny and land a few Binu returns. Then it was on to Somo, and to the end of voyaging for ever of the *Arangi* and of many that were aboard of her.

Quite the opposite to his treatment at Langa-Langa was that accorded Van Horn at Somo. Once the return boys were put ashore, and this was accomplished no later than three-thirty in the afternoon, he invited Chief Bashti on board. And Chief Bashti came, very nimble and active despite his great age, and very good-natured—so good-natured, in fact, that he insisted on bringing three of his elderly wives on board with him. This was unprecedented. Never had he permitted any of his wives to appear before a white man, and Van Horn felt so honoured that he presented each of them with a gay clay pipe and a dozen sticks of tobacco.

Late as the afternoon was, trade was brisk, and Bashti, who had taken the lion's share of the wages due to the fathers of two boys who had died, bought liberally of the *Arangi's* stock. When Bashti promised plenty of fresh recruits, Van Horn, used to the changeableness of the savage mind, urged signing them up right away. Bashti demurred, and suggested next day. Van Horn insisted that there was no time like the present, and so well did he insist that the old chief sent a canoe ashore to round up the boys who had been selected to go away to the plantations.

"Now, what do you think?" Van Horn asked of Borckman, whose eyes were remarkably fishy. "I never saw the old rascal so friendly. Has he got something up his sleeve?"

The mate stared at the many canoes alongside, noted the numbers of women in them, and shook his head.

"When they're starting anything they always send the Marys into the bush," he said.

"You never can tell about these niggers," the captain grumbled. "They may be short on imagination, but once in a while they do figure out something new. Now Bashti's the smartest old nigger I've ever seen. What's to prevent his figuring out that very bet and playing it in reverse? Just because they've never had their women around when trouble was on the carpet is no reason that they will always keep that practice."

"Not even Bashti's got the savvee to pull a trick like that," Borckman objected. "He's just feeling good and liberal. Why, he's bought forty pounds of goods from you already. That's why he wants to sign on a new batch of boys with us, and I'll bet he's hoping half of them die so's he can have the spending of their wages."

All of which was most reasonable. Nevertheless, Van Horn shook his head.

"All the same keep your eyes sharp on everything," he cautioned. "And remember, the two of us mustn't ever be below at the same time. And no more schnapps, mind, until we're clear of the whole kit and caboodle."

Bashti was incredibly lean and prodigiously old. He did not know how old he was himself, although he did know that no person in his tribe had been alive when he was a young boy in the village. He remembered the days when some of the old men, still alive, had been born; and, unlike him, they were now decrepit, shaken with palsy, blear-eyed, toothless of mouth, deaf of ear, or paralysed. All his own faculties remained unimpaired. He even boasted a dozen worn fangs of teeth, gum-level, on which he could still chew. Although he no longer had the physical endurance of youth, his thinking was as original and clear as it had always been. It was due to his thinking that he found his tribe stronger than when he had first come to rule it. In his small way he had been a Melanesian Napoleon. As a warrior, the play of his mind had enabled him to beat back the bushmen's boundaries. The scars on his withered body attested that he had fought to the fore. As a Law-giver, he had encouraged and achieved strength and efficiency within his tribe. As a statesman, he had always kept one thought ahead of the thoughts of the neighbouring chiefs in the making of treaties and the granting of concessions.

And with his mind, still keenly alive, he had but just evolved a scheme whereby he might outwit Van Horn and get the better of the vast British Empire about which he guessed little and know less.

For Somo had a history. It was that queer anomaly, a salt-water tribe that lived on the lagoon mainland where only bushmen were supposed to live. Far back into the darkness of time, the folk-lore of Somo cast a glimmering light. On a day, so far back that there was no way of estimating its distance, one, Somo, son of Loti, who was the chief of the island fortress of Umbo, had quarrelled with his father and fled from his wrath along with a dozen canoe-loads of young men. For two monsoons they had engaged in an odyssey. It was in the myth that they circumnavigated Malaita twice, and forayed as far as Ugi and San Cristobal across the wide seas.

Women they had inevitably stolen after successful combats, and, in the end, being burdened with women and progeny, Somo had descended upon the mainland shore, driven the bushmen back, and established the salt-water fortress of Somo. Built it was, on its sea-front, like any island fortress, with walled coral-rock to oppose the sea and chance marauders from the sea, and with launching ways through the walls for the long canoes. To the rear, where it encroached on the jungle, it was like any scattered bush village. But Somo, the wide-seeing father of the new tribe, had established his boundaries far up in the bush on the shoulders of the lesser mountains, and on each shoulder had planted a village. Only the greatly daring that fled to him had Somo permitted to join the new tribe. The weaklings and cowards they had promptly eaten, and the unbelievable tale of their many heads adorning the canoe-houses was part of the myth.

And this tribe, territory, and stronghold, at the latter end of time, Bashti had inherited, and he had bettered his inheritance. Nor was he above continuing to better it. For a long time he had reasoned closely and carefully in maturing the plan that itched in his brain for fulfilment. Three years before, the tribe of Ano Ano, miles down the coast, had captured a recruiter, destroyed her and all hands, and gained a fabulous store of tobacco, calico, beads, and all manner of trade goods, rifles and ammunition.

Little enough had happened in the way of price that was paid. Half a year after, a war vessel had poked her nose into the lagoon, shelled Ano Ano, and sent its inhabitants scurrying into the bush. The landing-party that followed had futilely pursued along the jungle runways. In the end it had contented itself with killing forty fat pigs and chopping down a hundred coconut trees. Scarcely had the war vessel passed out to open sea, when the people of Ano Ano were back from the bush to the village. Shell fire on flimsy grass houses is not especially destructive. A few hours' labour of the women put that little matter right. As for the forty dead pigs, the entire tribe fell upon the carcasses, roasted them under the ground with hot stones, and feasted. The tender tips of the fallen palms were likewise eaten, while the thousands of coconuts were husked and split and sun-dried and smoke-cured into copra to be sold to the next passing trader.

Thus, the penalty exacted had proved a picnic and a feast—all of which appealed to the thrifty, calculating brain of Bashti. And what was good for Ano Ano, in his judgment was surely good for Somo. Since such were white men's ways who sailed under the British flag and killed pigs and cut down coconuts in cancellation of blood-debts and headtakings, Bashti saw no valid reason why he should not profit as Ano Ano had profited. The price to be paid at some possible future time was absurdly disproportionate to the immediate wealth to be gained. Besides, it had been over two years since the last British war vessel had appeared in the Solomons.

And thus, Bashti, with a fine fresh idea inside his head, bowed his chief's head in consent that his people could flock aboard and trade. Very few of them knew what his idea was or that he even had an idea.

Trade grew still brisker as more canoes came alongside and black men and women thronged the deck. Then came the recruits, new-caught, young, savage things, timid as deer, yet yielding to stern parental and tribal law and going down into the *Arangi's* cabin, one by one, their fathers and mothers and relatives accompanying them in family groups, to confront the big fella white marster, who wrote their names down in a mysterious book, had them ratify the three years' contract of their labour by a touch of the right hand to the pen with which he wrote, and who paid the first year's advance in trade goods to the heads of their respective families.

Old Bashti sat near, taking his customary heavy tithes out of each advance, his three old wives squatting humbly at his feet and by their mere presence giving confidence to Van Horn, who was elated by the stroke of business. At such rate his cruise on Malaita would be a short one, when he would sail away with a full ship.

On deck, where Borckman kept a sharp eye out against danger, Jerry prowled about, sniffing the many legs of the many blacks he had never encountered before. The wild-dog had gone ashore with the return boys, and of the return boys only one had come back. It was Lerumie, past whom Jerry repeatedly and stiff-leggedly bristled without gaining response of recognition. Lerumie coolly ignored him, went down below once and purchased a trade hand-mirror, and, with a look of the eyes, assured old Bashti that all was ready and ripe to break at the first favourable moment.

On deck, Borckman gave this favourable moment. Nor would he have so given it had he not been guilty of carelessness and of disobedience to his captain's orders. He did not leave the schnapps alone. Be did not sense what was impending all about him. Aft, where he stood, the deck was almost deserted. Amidships and for'ard, gamming with the boat's crew, the deck was crowded with blacks of both sexes. He made his way to the yam sacks lashed abaft the mizzenmast and got his bottle. Just before he drank, with a shred of caution, he cast a glance behind him. Near him stood a harmless Mary, middle-aged, fat, squat, asymmetrical, unlovely, a sucking child of two years astride her hip and taking nourishment. Surely no harm was to be apprehended there. Furthermore, she was patently a weaponless Mary, for she wore no stitch of clothing that otherwise might have concealed a weapon. Over against the rail, ten feet to one side, stood Lerumie, smirking into the trade mirror he had just bought.

It was in the trade mirror that Lerumie saw Borckman bend to the yam-sacks, return to the erect, throw his head back, the mouth of the bottle glued to his lips, the bottom elevated skyward. Lerumie lifted his right hand in signal to a woman in a canoe alongside. She bent swiftly for something that she tossed to Lerumie. It was a long-handled tomahawk, the head of it an ordinary shingler's hatchet, the haft of it, native-made, a black and polished piece of hard wood, inlaid in rude designs with mother-of-pearl and wrapped with coconut sennit to make a hand grip. The blade of the hatchet had been ground to razor-edge.

As the tomahawk flew noiselessly through the air to Lerumie's hand, just as noiselessly, the next instant, it flew through the air from his hand into the hand of the fat Mary with the nursing child who stood behind the mate. She clutched the handle with both hands, while the child, astride her hip, held on to her with both small arms part way about her.

Still she waited the stroke, for with Borckman's head thrown back was no time to strive to sever the spinal cord at the neck. Many eyes beheld the impending tragedy. Jerry saw, but did not understand. With all his hostility to niggers he had not divined the attack from the air. Tambi, who chanced to be near the skylight, saw, and, seeing, reached for a Lee-Enfield. Lerumie saw Tambi's action and hissed haste to the Mary.

Borckman, as unaware of this, his last second of life, as he had been of his first second of birth, lowered the bottle and straightened forward his head. The keen edge sank home. What, in that flash of instant when his brain was severed from the rest of his body, Borckman may have felt or thought, if he felt or thought at all, is a mystery unsolvable to living man. No man, his spinal cord so severed, has ever given one word or whisper of testimony as to what were his sensations and impressions. No less swift than the hatchet stroke was the limp placidity into which Borckman's body melted to the deck. He did not reel or pitch. He *melted*, as a sack of wind suddenly emptied, as a bladder of air suddenly punctured. The bottle fell from his dead hand upon the yams without breaking, although the remnant of its contents gurgled gently out upon the deck.

So quick was the occurrence of action, that the first shot from Tambi's musket missed the Mary ere Borckman had quite melted to the deck. There was no time for a second shot, for the Mary, dropping the tomahawk, holding her child in both her hands and plunging to the rail, was in the air and overboard, her fall capsizing the canoe which chanced to be beneath her.

Scores of actions were simultaneous. From the canoes on both sides uprose a glittering, glistening rain of mother-of-pearl-handled tomahawks that descended into the waiting hands of the Somo men on deck, while the Marys on deck crouched down and scrambled out of the fray. At the same time that the Mary who had killed Borckman leapt the rail, Lerumie bent for the tomahawk she had dropped, and Jerry, aware of red war, slashed the hand that reached for the tomahawk. Lerumie stood upright and loosed loudly, in a howl, all the pent rage and hatred, of months which he had cherished against the puppy. Also, as he gained the perpendicular and as Jerry flew at his legs, he launched a kick with all his might that caught and lifted Jerry squarely under the middle.

And in the next second, or fraction of second, as Jerry lifted and soared through the air, over the barbed wire of the rail and overboard, while Sniders were being passed up overside from the canoes, Tambi fired his next hasty shot. And Lerumie, the foot with which he had kicked not yet returned to the deck as again he was in mid-action of stooping to pick up the tomahawk, received the bullet squarely in the heart and pitched down to melt with Borckman into the softness of death.

Ere Jerry struck the water, the glory of Tambi's marvellously lucky shot was over for Tambi; for, at the moment he pressed trigger to the successful shot, a tomahawk bit across his skull at the base of the brain and darkened from his eyes for ever the bright vision of the sea-washed, sun-blazoned tropic world. As swiftly, all occurring almost simultaneously, did the rest of the boat's crew pass and the deck became a shambles.

It was to the reports of the Sniders and the noises of the death scuffle that Jerry's head emerged from the water. A man's hand reached over a canoe-side and dragged him in by the scruff of the neck, and, although he snarled and struggled to bite his rescuer, he was not so much enraged as was he torn by the wildest solicitude for Skipper. He knew, without thinking about it, that the *Arangi* had been boarded by the hazily sensed supreme disaster of life that all life intuitively apprehends and that only man knows and calls by the name of "death." Borckman he had seen struck down. Lerumie he had heard struck down. And now he was hearing the explosions of rifles and the yells and screeches of triumph and fear.

So it was, helpless, suspended in the air by the nape of the neck, that he bawled and squalled and choked and coughed till the black, disgusted, flung him down roughly in the canoe's bottom. He scrambled to his feet and made two leaps: one upon the gunwale of the canoe; the next, despairing and hopeless, without consideration of self, for the rail of the *Arangi*.

His forefeet missed the rail by a yard, and he plunged down into the sea. He came up, swimming frantically, swallowing and strangling salt water because he still yelped and wailed and barked his yearning to be on board with Skipper.

But a boy of twelve, in another canoe, having witnessed the first black's adventure with Jerry, treated him without ceremony, laying, first the flat, and next the edge, of a paddle upon his head while he still swam. And the darkness of unconsciousness welled over his bright little love-suffering brain, so that it was a limp and motionless puppy that the black boy dragged into his canoe.

In the meantime, down below in the *Arangi's* cabin, ere ever Jerry hit the water from Lerumie's kick, even while he was in the air, Van Horn, in one great flashing profound fraction of an instant, had known his death. Not for nothing had old Bashti lived longest of any living man in his tribe, and ruled wisest of all the long line of rulers since Somo's time. Had he been placed more generously in earth space and time, he might well have proved an Alexander, a Napoleon, or a swarthy Kahehameha. As it was, he performed well, and splendidly well, in his limited little kingdom on the leeward coast of the dark cannibal island of Malaita.

And such a performance! In cool good nature in rigid maintenance of his chiefship rights, he had smiled at Van Horn, given royal permission to his young men to sign on for three years of plantation slavery, and exacted his share of each year's advance. Aora, who might be described as his prime minister and treasurer, had received the tithes as fast as they were paid over, and filled them into large, fine-netted bags of coconut sennit. At Bashti's back, squatting on the bunk-boards, a slim and smooth-skinned maid of thirteen had flapped the flies away from his royal head with the royal fly-flapper. At his feet had squatted his three old wives, the oldest of them, toothless and somewhat palsied, ever presenting to his hand, at his head nod, a basket rough-woven of pandanus leaf.

And Bashti, his keen old ears pitched for the first untoward sound from on deck, had continually nodded his head and dipped his hand into the proffered basket—now for betel-nut, and lime-box, and the invariable green leaf with which to wrap the mouthful; now for tobacco with which to fill his short clay pipe; and, again, for matches with which to light the pipe which seemed not to draw well and which frequently went out.

Toward the last the basket had hovered constantly close to his hand, and, at the last, he made one final dip. It was at the moment when the Mary's axe, on deck, had struck Borckman down and when Tambi loosed the first shot at her from his Lee-Enfield. And Bashti's withered ancient hand, the back of it netted with a complex of large up-standing veins from which the flesh had shrunk away, dipped out a huge pistol of such remote vintage that one of Cromwell's round-heads might well have carried it or that it might well have voyaged with Quiros or La Perouse. It was a flint-lock, as long as a man's forearm, and it had been loaded that afternoon by no less a person than Bashti himself.

Quick as Bashti had been, Van Horn was almost as quick, but not quite quick enough. Even as his hand leapt to the modern automatic lying out of it's holster and loose on his knees, the pistol of the centuries went off. Loaded with two slugs and a round bullet, its effect was that of a sawed-off shotgun. And Van Horn knew the blaze and the black of death, even as "Gott fer dang!" died unuttered on his lips and as his fingers relaxed from the part-lifted automatic, dropping it to the floor.

Surcharged with black powder, the ancient weapon had other effect. It burst in Bashti's hand. While Aora, with a knife produced apparently from nowhere, proceeded to hack off the white master's head, Bashti looked quizzically at his right forefinger dangling by a strip of skin. He seized it with his left hand, with a quick pull and twist wrenched it off, and grinningly tossed it, as a joke, into the pandanus basket which still his wife with one hand held before him while with the other she clutched her forehead bleeding from a flying fragment of pistol.

Collaterally with this, three of the young recruits, joined by their fathers and uncles, had downed, and were finishing off the only one of the boat's crew that was below. Bashti, who had lived so long that he was a philosopher who minded pain little and the loss of a finger less, chuckled and chirped his satisfaction and pride of achievement in the outcome, while his three old wives, who lived only at the nod of his head, fawned under him on the floor in the abjectness of servile congratulation and worship. Long had they lived, and they had lived long only by his kingly whim. They floundered and gibbered and mowed at his feet, lord of life and death that he was, infinitely wise as he had so often proved himself, as he had this time proved himself again.

And the lean, fear-stricken girl, like a frightened rabbit in the mouth of its burrow, on hands and knees peered forth upon the scene from the lazarette and knew that the cooking-pot and the end of time had come for her.

XII

What happened aboard the *Arangi* Jerry never knew. He did know that it was a world destroyed, for he saw it destroyed. The boy who had knocked him on the head with the paddle, tied his legs securely and tossed him out on the beach ere he forgot him in the excitement of looting the *Arangi*.

With great shouting and song, the pretty teak-built yacht was towed in by the long canoes and beached close to where Jerry lay just beyond the confines of the coral-stone walls. Fires blazed on the beach, lanterns were lighted on board, and, amid a great feasting, the *Arangi* was gutted and stripped. Everything portable was taken ashore, from her pigs of iron ballast to her running gear and sails. No one in Somo slept that night. Even the tiniest of children toddled about the feasting fires or sprawled surfeited on the sands. At two in the morning, at Bashti's command, the shell of the boat was fired. And Jerry, thirsting for water, having whimpered and wailed himself to exhaustion, lying helpless, leg-tied, on his side, saw the floating world he had known so short a time go up in flame and smoke.

And by the light of her burning, old Bashti apportioned the loot. No one of the tribe was too mean to receive nothing. Even the wretched bush-slaves, who had trembled through all the time of their captivity from fear of being eaten, received each a clay pipe and several sticks of tobacco. The main bulk of the trade goods, which was not distributed, Bashti had carried up to his own large grass house. All the wealth of gear was stored in the several canoe houses. While in the devil devil houses the devil devil doctors set to work curing the many heads over slow smudges; for, along with the boat's crew there were a round dozen of No-ola return boys and several Malu boys which Van Horn had not yet delivered.

Not all these had been slain, however. Bashti had issued stern injunctions against wholesale slaughter. But this was not because his heart was kind. Rather was it because his head was shrewd. Slain they would all be in the end. Bashti had never seen ice, did not know it existed, and was unversed in the science of refrigeration. The only way he knew to keep meat was to keep it alive. And in the biggest canoe house, the club house of the stags, where no Mary might come under penalty of death by torture, the captives were stored.

Tied or trussed like fowls or pigs, they were tumbled on the hard-packed earthen floor, beneath which, shallowly buried, lay the remains of ancient chiefs, while, overhead, in wrappings of grass mats, swung all that was left of several of Bashti's immediate predecessors, his father latest among them and so swinging for two full generations. Here, too, since she was to be eaten and since the taboo had no bearing upon one condemned to be cooked, the thin little Mary from the lazarette was tumbled trussed upon the floor among the many blacks who had teased and mocked her for being fattened by Van Horn for the eating.

And to this canoe house Jerry was also brought to join the others on the floor. Agno, chief of the devil devil doctors, had stumbled across him on the beach, and, despite the protestations of the boy who claimed him as personal trove, had ordered him to the canoe house. Carried past the fires of the feasting, his keen nostrils had told him of what the feast consisted. And, new as the experience was, he had bristled and snarled and struggled against his bonds to be free. Likewise, at first, tossed down in the canoe house, he had bristled and snarled at his fellow captives, not realizing their plight, and, since always he had been trained to look upon niggers as the eternal enemy, considering them responsible for the catastrophe to the *Arangi* and to Skipper.

For Jerry was only a little dog, with a dog's limitations, and very young in the world. But not for long did he throat his rage at them. In vague ways it was borne in upon him that they, too, were not happy. Some had been cruelly wounded, and kept up a moaning and groaning. Without any clearness of concept, nevertheless Jerry had a realization that they were as painfully circumstanced as himself. And painful indeed was his own circumstance. He lay on his side, the cords that bound his legs so tight as to bite into his tender flesh and shut off the circulation. Also, he was perishing for water, and panted, dry-tongued, dry-mouthed, in the stagnant heat.

A dolorous place it was, this canoe house, filled with groans and sighs, corpses beneath the floor and composing the floor, creatures soon to be corpses upon the floor, corpses swinging in aerial sepulchre overhead, long black canoes, high-ended like beaked predatory monsters, dimly looming in the light of a slow fire where sat an ancient of the tribe of Somo at his interminable task of smoke-curing a bushman's head. He was withered, and blind, and senile, gibbering and mowing like some huge ape as ever he turned and twisted, and twisted back again, the suspended head in the pungent smoke, and handful by handful added rotten punk of wood to the smudge fire.

Sixty feet in the clear, the dim fire occasionally lighted, through shadowy cross-beams, the ridge-pole that was covered with sennit of coconut that was braided in barbaric designs of black and white and that was stained by the smoke of years almost to a monochrome of dirty brown. From the lofty cross-beams, on long sennit strings, hung the heads of enemies taken aforetime in jungle raid and sea foray. The place breathed the very atmosphere of decay and death, and the imbecile ancient, curing in the smoke the token of death, was himself palsiedly shaking into the disintegration of the grave.

Toward daylight, with great shouting and heaving and pull and haul, scores of Somo men brought in another of the big war canoes. They made way with foot and hand, kicking and thrusting dragging and shoving, the bound captives to either side of the space which the canoe was to occupy. They were anything but gentle to the meat with which they had been favoured by good fortune and the wisdom of Bashti.

For a time they sat about, all pulling at clay pipes and chirruping and laughing in queer thin falsettos at the events of the night and the previous afternoon. Now one and now another stretched out and slept without covering; for so, directly under the path of the sun, had they slept nakedly from the time they were born.

Remained awake, as dawn paled the dark, only the grievously wounded or the too-tightly bound, and the decrepit ancient who was not so old as Bashti. When the boy who had stunned Jerry with his paddle-blade and who claimed him as his own stole into the canoe house, the ancient did not hear him. Being blind, he did not see him. He continued gibbering and chuckling dementedly, to twist the bushman's head back and forth and to feed the smudge with punk-wood. This was no night-task for any man, nor even for him who had forgotten how to do aught else. But the excitement of cutting out the *Arangi* had been communicated to his addled brain, and, with vague reminiscent flashes of the strength of life triumphant, he shared deliriously in this triumph of Somo by applying himself to the curing of the head that was in itself the concrete expression of triumph.

But the twelve-year-old lad who stole in and cautiously stepped over the sleepers and threaded his way among the captives, did so with his heart in his mouth. He knew what taboos he was violating. Not old enough even to leave his father's grass roof and sleep in the youths' canoe house, much less to sleep with the young bachelors in their canoe house, he knew that he took his life, with all of its dimly guessed mysteries and arrogances, in his hand thus to trespass into the sacred precinct of the full-made, full-realized, full-statured men of Somo.

But he wanted Jerry and he got him. Only the lean little Mary, trussed for the cooking, staring through her wide eyes of fear, saw the boy pick Jerry up by his tied legs and carry him out and away from the booty of meat of which she was part. Jerry's heroic little heart of courage would have made him snarl and resent such treatment of handling had he not been too exhausted and had not his mouth and throat been too dry for sound. As it was, miserably and helplessly, not half himself, a puppet dreamer in a half-nightmare, he knew, as a restless sleeper awakening between vexing dreams, that he was being transported head-downward out of the canoe house that stank of death, through the village that was only less noisome, and up a path under lofty, wide-spreading trees that were beginning languidly to stir with the first breathings of the morning wind.

XIII

The boy's name, as Jerry was to learn, was Lamai, and to Lamai's house Jerry was carried. It was not much of a house, even as cannibal grass-houses go. On an earthen floor, hard-packed of the filth of years, lived Lamai's father and mother and a spawn of four younger brothers and sisters. A thatched roof that leaked in every heavy shower leaned to a wabbly ridge-pole over the floor. The walls were even more pervious to a driving rain. In fact, the house of Lamai, who was the father of Lumai, was the most miserable house in all Somo.

Lumai, the house-master and family head, unlike most Malaitans, was fat. And of his fatness it would seem had been begotten his good nature with its allied laziness. But as the fly in his ointment of jovial irresponsibility was his wife, Lenerengo—the prize shrew of Somo, who was as lean about the middle and all the rest of her as her husband was rotund; who was as remarkably sharp-spoken as he was soft-spoken; who was as ceaselessly energetic as he was unceasingly idle; and who had been born with a taste for the world as sour in her mouth as it was sweet in his.

The boy merely peered into the house as he passed around it to the rear, and he saw his father and mother, at opposite corners, sleeping without covering, and, in the middle of the floor, his four naked brothers and sisters curled together in a tangle like a litter of puppies. All about the house, which in truth was scarcely more than an animal lair, was an earthly paradise. The air was spicily and sweetly heavy with the scents of wild aromatic plants and gorgeous tropic blooms. Overhead three breadfruit trees interlaced their noble branches. Banana and plantain trees were burdened with great bunches of ripening fruit. And huge, golden melons of the papaia, ready for the eating, globuled directly from the slender-trunked trees not one-tenth the girth of the fruits they bore. And, for Jerry, most delightful of all, there was the gurgle and plash of a brooklet that pursued its invisible way over mossy stones under a garmenture of tender and delicate ferns. No conservatory of a king could compare with this wild wantonness of sun-generous vegetation.

Maddened by the sound of the water, Jerry had first to endure an embracing and hugging from the boy, who, squatted on his hams, rocked back and forth and mumbled a strange little crooning song. And

Jerry, lacking articulate speech, had no way of telling him of the thirst of which he was perishing.

Next, Lamai tied him securely with a sennit cord about the neck and untied the cords that bit into his legs. So numb was Jerry from lack of circulation, and so weak from lack of water through part of a tropic day and all of a tropic night, that he stood up, tottered and fell, and, time and again, essaying to stand, floundered and fell. And Lamai understood, or tentatively guessed. He caught up a coconut calabash attached to the end of a stick of bamboo, dipped into the greenery of ferns, and presented to Jerry the calabash brimming with the precious water.

Jerry lay on his side at first as he drank, until, with the moisture, life flowed back into the parched channels of him, so that, soon, still weak and shaky, he was up and braced on all his four wide-spread legs and still eagerly lapping. The boy chuckled and chirped his delight in the spectacle, and Jerry found surcease and easement sufficient to enable him to speak with his tongue after the heart-eloquent manner of dogs. He took his nose out of the calabash and with his rose-ribbon strip of tongue licked Lamai's hand. And Lamai, in ecstasy over this establishment of common speech, urged the calabash back under Jerry's nose, and Jerry drank again.

He continued to drink. He drank until his sun-shrunken sides stood out like the walls of a balloon, although longer were the intervals from the drinking in which, with his tongue of gratefulness, he spoke against the black skin of Lamai's hand. And all went well, and would have continued to go well, had not Lamai's mother, Lenerengo, just awakened, stepped across her black litter of progeny and raised her voice in shrill protest against her eldest born's introducing of one more mouth and much more nuisance into the household.

A squabble of human speech followed, of which Jerry knew no word but of which he sensed the significance. Lamai was with him and for him. Lamai's mother was against him. She shrilled and shrewed her firm conviction that her son was a fool and worse because he had neither the consideration nor the silly sense of a fool's solicitude for a hard-worked mother. She appealed to the sleeping Lumai, who awoke heavily and fatly, who muttered and mumbled easy terms of Somo dialect to the effect that it was a most decent world, that all puppy dogs and eldest-born sons were right delightful things to possess, that he had never yet starved to death, and that peace and sleep were the finest things that ever befell the lot of mortal man—and, in token thereof, back into the peace of sleep, he snuggled his nose into the biceps of his arm for a pillow and proceeded to snore.

But Lamai, eyes stubbornly sullen, with mutinous foot-stampings and a perfect knowledge that all was clear behind him to leap and flee away if his mother rushed upon him, persisted in retaining his puppy dog. In the end, after an harangue upon the worthlessness of Lamai's father, she went back to sleep.

Ideas beget ideas. Lamai had learned how astonishingly thirsty Jerry had been. This engendered the idea that he might be equally hungry. So he applied dry branches of wood to the smouldering coals he dug out of the ashes of the cooking-fire, and builded a large fire. Into this, as it gained strength, he placed many stones from a convenient pile, each fire-blackened in token that it had been similarly used many times. Next, hidden under the water of the brook in a netted hand-bag, he brought to light the carcass of a fat wood-pigeon he had snared the previous day. He wrapped the pigeon in green leaves, and, surrounding it with the hot stones from the fire, covered pigeon and stones with earth.

When, after a time, he removed the pigeon and stripped from it the scorched wrappings of leaves, it gave forth a scent so savoury as to prick up Jerry's ears and set his nostrils to quivering. When the boy had torn the steaming carcass across and cooled it, Jerry's meal began; nor did the meal cease till the last sliver of meat had been stripped and tongued from the bones and the bones crunched and crackled to fragments and swallowed. And throughout the meal Lamai made love to Jerry, crooning over and over his little song, and patting and caressing him.

On the other hand, refreshed by the water and the meat, Jerry did not reciprocate so heartily in the love-making. He was polite, and received his petting with soft-shining eyes, tail-waggings and the customary body-wrigglings; but he was restless, and continually listened to distant sounds and yearned away to be gone. This was not lost upon the boy, who, before he curled himself down to sleep, securely tied to a tree the end of the cord that was about Jerry's neck.

After straining against the cord for a time, Jerry surrendered and slept. But not for long. Skipper was too much with him. He knew, and yet he did not know, the irretrievable ultimate disaster to Skipper. So it was, after low whinings and whimperings, that he applied his sharp first-teeth to the sennit cord and chewed upon it till it parted.

Free, like a homing pigeon, he headed blindly and directly for the beach and the salt sea over which had floated the *Arangi*, on her deck Skipper in command. Somo was largely deserted, and those that were in it were sunk in sleep. So no one vexed him as he trotted through the winding pathways between the many houses and past the obscene kingposts of totemic heraldry, where the forms of men, carved from single tree trunks, were seated in the gaping jaws of carved sharks. For Somo, tracing back to Somo its founder, worshipped the shark-god and the salt-water deities as well as the deities of the bush and swamp and mountain.

Turning to the right until he was past the sea-wall, Jerry came on down to the beach. No *Arangi* was to be seen on the placid surface of the lagoon. All about him was the debris of the feast, and he scented the smouldering odours of dying fires and burnt meat. Many of the feasters had not troubled to return to their houses, but lay about on the sand, in the mid-morning sunshine, men, women, and children and entire families, wherever they had yielded to slumber.

Down by the water's edge, so close that his fore-feet rested in the water, Jerry sat down, his heart bursting for Skipper, thrust his nose heavenward at the sun, and wailed his woe as dogs have ever wailed since they came in from the wild woods to the fires of men.

And here Lamai found him, hushed his grief against his breast with cuddling arms, and carried him back to the grass house by the brook. Water he offered, but Jerry could drink no more. Love he offered, but Jerry could not forget his torment of desire for Skipper. In the end, disgusted with so unreasonable a puppy, Lamai forgot his love in his boyish savageness, clouted Jerry over the head, right side and left, and tied him as few whites men's dogs have ever been tied. For, in his way, Lamai was a genius. He had never seen the thing done with any dog, yet he devised, on the spur of the moment, the invention of tying Jerry with a stick. The stick was of bamboo, four feet long. One end he tied shortly to Jerry's neck, the other end, just as shortly to a tree. All that Jerry's teeth could reach was the stick, and dry and seasoned bamboo can defy the teeth of any dog.

XIV

For many days, tied by the stick, Jerry remained Lamai's prisoner. It was not a happy time, for the house of Lumai was a house of perpetual bickering and quarrelling. Lamai fought pitched battles with his brothers and sisters for teasing Jerry, and these battles invariably culminated in Lenerengo taking a hand and impartially punishing all her progeny.

After that, as a matter of course and on general principles, she would have it out with Lumai, whose soft voice always was for quiet and repose, and who always, at the end of a tongue-lashing, took himself off to the canoe house for a couple of days. Here, Lenerengo was helpless. Into the canoe house of the stags no Mary might venture. Lenerengo had never forgotten the fate of the last Mary who had broken the taboo. It had occurred many years before, when she was a girl, and the recollection was ever vivid of the unfortunate woman hanging up in the sun by one arm for all of a day, and for all of a second day by the other arm. After that she had been feasted upon by the stags of the canoe house, and for long afterward all women had talked softly before their husbands.

Jerry did discover liking for Lamai, but it was not strong nor passionate. Rather was it out of gratitude, for only Lamai saw to it that he received food and water. Yet this boy was no Skipper, no Mister Haggin. Nor was he even a Derby or a Bob. He was that inferior man-creature, a nigger, and Jerry had been thoroughly trained all his brief days to the law that the white men were the superior two-legged gods.

He did not fail to recognize, however, the intelligence and power that resided in the niggers. He did not reason it out. He accepted it. They had power of command over other objects, could propel sticks and stones through the air, could even tie him a prisoner to a stick that rendered him helpless. Inferior as they might be to the white-gods, still they were gods of a sort.

It was the first time in his life that Jerry had been tied up, and he did not like it. Vainly he hurt his teeth, some of which were loosening under the pressure of the second teeth rising underneath. The stick was stronger than he. Although he did not forget Skipper, the poignancy of his loss faded with the passage of time, until uppermost in his mind was the desire to be free.

But when the day came that he was freed, he failed to take advantage of it and scuttle away for the beach. It chanced that Lenerengo released him. She did it deliberately, desiring to be quit of him. But when she untied Jerry, he stopped to thank her, wagging his tail and smiling up at her with his hazel-brown eyes. She stamped her foot at him to be gone, and uttered a harsh and intimidating cry. This Jerry did not understand, and so unused was he to fear that he could not be frightened into running away. He ceased wagging his tail, and, though he continued to look up at her, his eyes no longer smiled. Her action and noise he identified as unfriendly, and he became alert and watchful, prepared for whatever hostile act she might next commit.

Again she cried out and stamped her foot. The only effect on Jerry was to make him transfer his watchfulness to the foot. This slowness in getting away, now that she had released him, was too much for her short temper. She launched the kick, and Jerry, avoiding it, slashed her ankle.

War broke on the instant, and that she might have killed Jerry in her rage was highly probable had not Lamai appeared on the scene. The stick untied from Jerry's neck told the tale of her perfidy and incensed Lamai, who sprang between and deflected the blow with a stone poi-pounder that might have brained Jerry.

Lamai was now the one in danger of grievous damage, and his mother had just knocked him down with a clout alongside the head when poor Lumai, roused from sleep by the uproar, ventured out to make peace. Lenerengo, as usual, forgot everything else in the fiercer pleasure of berating her spouse.

The conclusion of the affair was harmless enough. The children stopped their crying, Lamai retied Jerry with the stick, Lenerengo harangued herself breathless, and Lumai departed with hurt feelings for the canoe house where stags could sleep in peace and Marys pestered not.

That night, in the circle of his fellow stags, Lumai recited his sorrows and told the cause of them—the puppy dog which had come on the *Arangi*. It chanced that Agno, chief of the devil devil doctors, or high priest, heard the tale, and recollected that he had sent Jerry to the canoe house along with the rest of the captives. Half an hour later he was having it out with Lamai. Beyond doubt, the boy had broken the taboos, and privily he told him so, until Lamai trembled and wept and squirmed abjectly at his feet, for the penalty was death.

It was too good an opportunity to get a hold over the boy for Agno to misplay it. A dead boy was worth nothing to him, but a living boy whose life he carried in his hand would serve him well. Since no one else knew of the broken taboo, he could afford to keep quiet. So he ordered Lamai forthright down to live in the youths' canoe house, there to begin his novitiate in the long series of tasks, tests and ceremonies that would graduate him into the bachelors' canoe house and half way along toward being a recognized man.

In the morning, obeying the devil devil doctor's commands, Lenerengo tied Jerry's feet together, not without a struggle in which his head was banged about and her hands were scratched. Then she carried him down through the village on the way to deliver him at Agno's house. On the way, in the open centre of the village where stood the kingposts, she left him lying on the ground in order to join in the hilarity of the population.

Not only was old Bashti a stern law-giver, but he was a unique one. He had selected this day at the one time to administer punishment to two quarrelling women, to give a lesson to all other women, and to make all his subjects glad once again that they had him for ruler. Tiha and Wiwau, the two women, were squat and stout and young, and had long been a scandal because of their incessant quarrelling. Bashti had set them a race to run. But such a race. It was side-splitting. Men, women, and children, beholding, howled with delight. Even elderly matrons and greybeards with a foot in the grave screeched and shrilled their joy in the spectacle.

The half-mile course lay the length of the village, through its heart, from the beach where the *Arangi* had been burned to the beach at the other end of the sea-wall. It had to be covered once in each direction by Tiha and Wiwau, in each case one of them urging speed on the other and the other desiring speed that was unattainable.

Only the mind of Bashti could have devised the show. First, two round coral stones, weighing fully forty pounds each, were placed in Tiha's arms. She was compelled to clasp them tightly against her sides in order that they might not roll to the ground. Behind her, Bashti placed Wiwau, who was armed with a bristle of bamboo splints mounted on a light long shaft of bamboo. The splints were sharp as needles, being indeed the needles used in tattooing, and on the end of the pole they were intended to be applied to Tiha's back in the same way that men apply ox-goads to oxen. No serious damage, but much pain, could be inflicted, which was just what Bashti had intended.

Wiwau prodded with the goad, and Tiha stumbled and wabbled in gymnastic efforts to make speed. Since, when the farther beach had been reached, the positions would be reversed and Wiwau would carry the stones back while Tiha prodded, and since Wiwau knew that for what she gave Tiha would then try to give more, Wiwau exerted herself to give the utmost while yet she could. The perspiration ran down both their faces. Each had her partisans in the crowd, who encouraged and heaped ridicule with every prod.

Ludicrous as it was, behind it lay iron savage law. The two stones were to be carried the entire course. The woman who prodded must do so with conviction and dispatch. The woman who was prodded must not lose her temper and fight her tormentor. As they had been duly forewarned by Bashti, the penalty for infraction of the rules he had laid down was staking out on the reef at low tide to be eaten by the fish-sharks.

As the contestants came opposite where Bashti and Aora his prime minister stood, they redoubled their efforts, Wiwau goading enthusiastically, Tiha jumping with every thrust to the imminent danger of dropping the stones. At their heels trooped the children of the village and all the village dogs, whooping and yelping with excitement.

"Long time you fella Tiha no sit'm along canoe," Aora bawled to the victim and set Bashti cackling again.

At an unusually urgent prod, Tiha dropped a stone and was duly goaded while she sank to her knees and with one arm scooped it in against her side, regained her feet, and waddled on.

Once, in stark mutiny at so much pain, she deliberately stopped and addressed her tormentor.

"Me cross along you too much," she told Wiwau. "Bime by, close—"

But she never completed the threat. A warmly administered prod broke through her stoicism and started her tottering along.

The shouting of the rabble ebbed away as the queer race ran on toward the beach. But in a few minutes it could be heard flooding back, this time Wiwau panting with the weight of coral stone and Tiha, a-smart with what she had endured, trying more than to even the score.

Opposite Bashti, Wiwau lost one of the stones, and, in the effort to recover it, lost the other, which rolled a dozen feet away from the first. Tiha became a whirlwind of avenging fury. And all Somo went wild. Bashti held his lean sides with merriment while tears of purest joy ran down his prodigiously wrinkled cheeks.

And when all was over, quoth Bashti to his people: "Thus shall all women fight when they desire over much to fight."

Only he did not say it in this way. Nor did he say it in the Somo tongue. What he did say was in beche-de-mer, and his words were:

"Any fella Mary he like 'm fight, all fella Mary along Somo fight 'm this fella way."

XV

For some time after the conclusion of the race, Bashti stood talking with his head men, Agno among them. Lenerengo was similarly engaged with several old cronies. As Jerry lay off to one side where she had forgotten him, the wild-dog he had bullied on the *Arangi* came up and sniffed at him. At first he sniffed at a distance, ready for instant flight. Then he drew cautiously closer. Jerry watched him with smouldering eyes. At the moment wild-dog's nose touched him, he uttered a warning growl. Wild-dog sprang back and whirled away in headlong flight for a score of yards before he learned that he was not pursued.

Again he came back cautiously, as it was the instinct in him to stalk wild game, crouching so close to the ground that almost his belly touched. He lifted and dropped his feet with the lithe softness of a cat, and from time to time glanced to right and to left as if in apprehension of some flank attack. A noisy outburst of boys' laughter in the distance caused him to crouch suddenly down, his claws thrust into the ground for purchase, his muscles tense springs for the leap he knew not in what direction, from the danger he knew not what that might threaten him. Then he identified the noise, know that no harm impended, and resumed his stealthy advance on the Irish terrier.

What might have happened there is no telling, for at that moment Bashti's eyes chanced to rest on the golden puppy for the first time since the capture of the *Arangi*. In the rush of events Bashti had forgotten the puppy.

"What name that fella dog?" he cried out sharply, causing wild-dog to crouch down again and attracting Lenerengo's attention.

She cringed in fear to the ground before the terrible old chief and quavered a recital of the facts. Her good-for-nothing boy Lamai had picked the dog from the water. It had been the cause of much trouble in her house. But now Lamai had gone to live with the youths, and she was carrying the dog to Agno's house at Agno's express command.

"What name that dog stop along you?" Bashti demanded directly of Agno.

"Me kai-kai along him," came the answer. "Him fat fella dog. Him good fella dog kai-kai."

Into Bashti's alert old brain flashed an idea that had been long maturing.

"Him good fella dog too much," he announced. "Better you eat 'm bush fella dog," he advised, pointing at wild-dog.

Agno shook his head. "Bush fella dog no good kai-kai."

"Bush fella dog no good too much," was Bashti's judgment. "Bush fella dog too much fright. Plenty fella bush dog too much fright. White marster's dog no fright. Bush dog no fight. White marster's dog fight like hell. Bush dog run like hell. You look 'm eye belong you, you see."

Bashti stepped over to Jerry and cut the cords that tied his legs. And Jerry, upon his feet in a surge, was for once in too great haste to pause to give thanks. He hurled himself after wild-dog, caught him in mid-flight, and rolled him over and over in a cloud of dust. Ever wild-dog strove to escape, and ever Jerry cornered him, rolled him, and bit him, while Bashti applauded and called on his head men to behold.

By this time Jerry had become a raging little demon. Fired by all his wrongs, from the bloody day on the *Arangi* and the loss of Skipper down to this latest tying of his legs, he was avenging himself on wild-dog for everything. The owner of wild-dog, a return boy, made the mistake of trying to kick Jerry away. Jerry was upon him in a flash scratching his calves with his teeth, in the suddenness of his onslaught getting between the black's legs and tumbling him to the ground.

"What name!" Bashti cried in a rage at the offender, who lay fear-stricken where he had fallen, trembling for what next words might fall from his chief's lips.

But Bashti was already doubling with laughter at sight of wild-dog running for his life down the street with Jerry a hundred feet behind and tearing up the dust.

As they disappeared, Bashti expounded his idea. If men planted banana trees, it ran, what they would get would be bananas. If they planted yams, yams would be produced, not sweet potatoes or plantains, but yams, nothing but yams. The same with dogs. Since all black men's dogs were cowards, all the breeding of all black men's dogs would produce cowards. White men's dogs were courageous fighters. When they were bred they produced courageous fighters. Very well, and to the conclusion, namely, here was a white man's dog in their possession. The height of foolishness would be to eat it and to destroy for all time the courage that resided in it. The wise thing to do was to regard it as a seed dog, to keep it alive, so that in the coming generations of Somo dogs its courage would be repeated over and over and spread until all Somo dogs would be strong and brave.

Further, Bashti commanded his chief devil devil doctor to take charge of Jerry and guard him well. Also, he sent his word forth to all the tribe that Jerry was taboo. No man, woman, or child was to throw spear or stone at him, strike him with club or tomahawk, or hurt him in any way.

THENCEFORTH, AND UNTIL JERRY HIMSELF violated one of the greatest of taboos, he had a happy time in Agno's gloomy grass house. For Bashti, unlike most chiefs, ruled his devil devil doctors with an iron hand. Other chiefs, even Nau-hau of Langa-Langa, were ruled by their devil devil doctors. For that matter, the population of Somo believed that Bashti was so ruled. But the Somo folk did not know what went on behind the scenes, when Bashti, a sheer infidel, talked alone now with one doctor and now with another.

In these private talks he demonstrated that he knew their game as well as they did, and that he was no slave to the dark superstitions and gross impostures with which they kept the people in submission. Also, he exposited the theory, as ancient as priests and rulers, that priests and rulers must work together in the orderly governance of the people. He was content that the people should believe that the gods, and the priests who were the mouth-pieces of the gods, had the last word, but he would have the priests know that in private the last word was his. Little as they believed in their trickery, he told them, he believed less.

He knew taboo, and the truth behind taboo. He explained his personal taboos, and how they came to be. Never must he eat clam-meat, he told Agno. It was so selected by himself because he did not like clam-meat. It was old Nino, high priest before Agno, with an ear open to the voice of the shark-god, who had so laid the taboo. But, he, Bashti, had privily commanded Nino to lay the taboo against clam-meat upon him, because he, Bashti, did not like clam-meat and had never liked clam-meat.

Still further, since he had lived longer than the oldest priest of them, his had been the appointing of every one of them. He knew them, had made them, had placed them, and they lived by his pleasure. And they would continue to take program from him, as they had always taken it, or else they would swiftly and suddenly pass. He had but to remind them of the passing of Kori, the devil devil doctor who had believed himself stronger than his chief, and who, for his mistake, had screamed in pain for a week ere what composed him had ceased to scream and for ever ceased to scream.

IN AGNO'S LARGE GRASS HOUSE was little light and much mystery. There was no mystery there for Jerry, who merely knew things, or did not know things, and who never bothered about what he did not know. Dried heads and other cured and mouldy portions of human carcasses impressed him no more than the dried alligators and dried fish that contributed to the festooning of Agno's dark abode.

Jerry found himself well cared for. No children nor wives cluttered the devil devil doctor's house. Several old women, a fly-flapping girl of eleven, and two young men who had graduated from the canoe house of the youths and who were studying priestcraft under the master, composed the household and waited upon Jerry. Food of the choicest was his. After Agno had eaten first-cut of pig, Jerry was served second. Even the two acolytes and the fly-flapping maid ate after him, leaving the debris for the several old women. And, unlike the mere bush dogs, who stole shelter from the rain under overhanging eaves, Jerry was given a dry place under the roof where the heads of bushmen and of forgotten sandalwood traders hung down from above in the midst of a dusty confusion of dried viscera of sharks, crocodile skulls, and skeletons of Solomons rats that measured two-thirds of a yard in length from bone-tip of nose to bone-tip of tail.

A number of times, all freedom being his, Jerry stole away across the village to the house of Lumai. But never did he find Lamai, who, since Skipper, was the only human he had met that had placed a bid to his heart. Jerry never appeared openly, but from the thick fern of the brookside observed the house and scented out its occupants. No scent of Lamai did he ever obtain, and, after a time, he gave up his vain visits and accepted the devil devil doctor's house as his home and the devil devil doctor as his master.

But he bore no love for this master. Agno, who had ruled by fear so long in his house of mystery, did not know love. Nor was affection any part of him, nor was geniality. He had no sense of humour, and was as frostily cruel as an icicle. Next to Bashti he stood in power, and all his days had been embittered in that he was not first in power. He had no softness for Jerry. Because he feared Bashti he feared to harm Jerry.

The months passed, and Jerry got his firm, massive second teeth and increased in weight and size. He came as near to being spoiled as is possible for a dog. Himself taboo, he quickly learned to lord it over the Somo folk and to have his way and will in all matters. No one dared to dispute with him with stick or stone. Agno hated him—he knew that; but also he gleaned the knowledge that Agno feared him and would not dare to hurt him. But Agno was a chill-blooded philosopher and bided his time, being different from Jerry in that he possessed human prevision and could adjust his actions to remote ends.

From the edge of the lagoon, into the waters of which, remembering the crocodile taboo he had learned on Meringe, he never ventured, Jerry ranged to the outlying bush villages of Bashti's domain. All made way for him. All fed him when he desired food. For the taboo was upon him, and he might unchidden invade their sleeping-mats or food calabashes. He might bully as he pleased, and be arrogant beyond decency, and there was no one to say him nay. Even had Bashti's word gone forth that if Jerry were attacked by the full-grown bush dogs, it was the duty of the Somo folk to take his part and kick and stone and beat the bush dogs. And thus his own four-legged cousins came painfully to know that he was taboo.

And Jerry prospered. Fat to stupidity he might well have become, had it not been for his high-strung nerves and his insatiable, eager curiosity. With the freedom of all Somo his, he was ever a-foot over it, learning its metes and bounds and the ways of the wild creatures that inhabited its swamps and forests and that did not acknowledge his taboo.

Many were his adventures. He fought two battles with the wood-rats that were almost of his size, and that, being mature and wild and cornered, fought him as he had never been fought before. The first he had killed, unaware that it was an old and feeble rat. The second, in prime of vigour, had so punished him that he crawled back, weak and sick to the devil devil doctor's house, where, for a week, under the dried emblems of death, he licked his wounds and slowly came back to life and health.

He stole upon the dugong and joyed to stampede that silly timid creature by sudden ferocious onslaughts which he knew himself to be all sound and fury, but which tickled him and made him laugh with the consciousness of playing a successful joke. He chased the unmigratory tropi-ducks from their shrewd-hidden nests, walked circumspectly among the crocodiles hauled out of water for slumber, and crept under the jungle-roof and spied upon the snow-white saucy cockatoos, the fierce ospreys, the heavy-flighted buzzards, the lories and kingfishers, and the absurdly garrulous little pygmy parrots.

Thrice, beyond the boundaries of Somo, he encountered the little black bushmen who were more like ghosts than men, so noiseless and unperceivable were they, and who, guarding the wild-pig runways of the jungle, missed spearing him on the three memorable occasions. As the wood-rats had taught him discretion, so did these two-legged lurkers in the jungle twilight. He had not fought with them, although they tried to spear him. He quickly came to know that these were other folk than Somo folk, that his taboo did not extend to them, and that, even of a sort, they were two-legged gods who carried flying death in their hands that reached farther than their hands and bridged distance.

As he ran the jungle, so Jerry ran the village. No place was sacred to him. In the devil devil houses, where, before the face of mystery men and women crawled in fear and trembling, he walked stiff-legged and bristling; for fresh heads were suspended there—heads his eyes and keen nostrils identified as those of once living blacks he had known on board the *Arangi*. In the biggest devil devil house he encountered the head of Borckman, and snarled at it, without receiving response, in recollection of the fight he had fought with the schnapps-addled mate on the deck of the *Arangi*.

Once, however, in Bashti's house, he chanced upon all that remained on earth of Skipper. Bashti had lived very long, had lived most wisely and thought much, and was thoroughly aware that, having lived far beyond the span of man his own span was very short. And he was curious about it all—the meaning and purpose of life. He loved the world and life, into which he had been fortunately born, both as to constitution and to place, which latter, for him, had been the high place over hie priests and people. He was not afraid to die, but he wondered if he might live again. He discounted the silly views of the tricky priests, and he was very much alone in the chaos of the confusing problem.

For he had lived so long, and so luckily, that he had watched the waning to extinction of all the vigorous appetites and desires. He had known wives and children, and the keen-edge of youthful hunger. He had seen his children grow to manhood and womanhood and become fathers and grandfathers, mothers and grandmothers. But having known woman, and love, and fatherhood, and the belly-delights of eating, he had passed on beyond. Food? Scarcely did he know its meaning, so little did he eat. Hunger, that bit him like a spur when he was young and lusty, had long since ceased to stir and prod him. He ate out of a sense of necessity and duty, and cared little for what he ate, save for one thing: the eggs of the megapodes that were, in season, laid in his private, personal, strictly tabooed megapode laying-yard. Here was left to him his last lingering flesh thrill. As for the rest, he lived in his intellect, ruling his people, seeking out data from which to induce laws that would make his people stronger and rivet his people's clinch upon life.

But he realized clearly the difference between that abstract thing, the tribe, and that most concrete of things, the individual. The tribe persisted. Its members passed. The tribe was a memory of the history and habits of all previous members, which the living members carried on until they passed and became history and memory in the intangible sum that was the tribe. He, as a member, soon or late, and late was very near, must pass. But pass to what? There was the rub. And so it was, on occasion, that he ordered all forth from his big grass house, and, alone with his problem, lowered from the roof-beams the matting-wrapped parcels of heads of men he had once seen live and who had passed into the mysterious nothingness of death.

Not as a miser had he collected these heads, and not as a miser counting his secret hoard did he ponder these heads, unwrapped, held in his two hands or lying on his knees. He wanted to know. He wanted to know what he guessed they might know, now that they had long since gone into the darkness that rounds the end of life.

Various were the heads Bashti thus interrogated—in his hands, on his knees, in his dim-lighted grasshouse, while the overhead sun blazed down and the fading south-east sighed through the palm-fronds and breadfruit branches. There was the head of a Japanese—the only one he had ever seen or heard of. Before he was born it had been taken by his father. Ill-cured it was, and battered and marred with ancientness and rough usage. Yet he studied its features, decided that it had once had two lips as live as his own and a mouth as vocal and hungry as his had often been in the past. Two eyes and a nose it had, a thatched crown of roof, and a pair of ears like to his own. Two legs and a body it must once have had, and desires and lusts. Heats of wrath and of love, so he decided, had also been its once on a time when it never thought to die.

A head that amazed him much, whose history went back before his father's and grandfather's time, was the head of a Frenchman, although

Bashti knew it not. Nor did he know it was the head of La Perouse, the doughty old navigator, who had left his bones, the bones of his crews, and the bones of his two frigates, the *Astrolabe* and the *Boussole*, on the shores of the cannibal Solomons. Another head—for Bashti was a confirmed head-collector—went back two centuries before La Perouse to Alvaro de Mendana, the Spaniard. It was the head of one of Mendana's armourers, lost in a beach scrimmage to one of Bashti's remote ancestors.

Still another head, the history of which was vague, was a white woman's head. What wife of what navigator there was no telling. But earrings of gold and emerald still clung to the withered ears, and the hair, two-thirds of a fathom long, a shimmering silk of golden floss, flowed from the scalp that covered what had once been the wit and will of her that Bashti reasoned had in her ancient time been quick with love in the arms of man.

Ordinary heads, of bushmen and salt-water men, and even of schnapps-drinking white men like Borckman, he relegated to the canoe houses and devil devil houses. For he was a connoisseur in the matter of heads. There was a strange head of a German that lured him much. Red-bearded it was, and red-haired, but even in dried death there was an ironness of feature and a massive brow that hinted to him of mastery of secrets beyond his ken. No more than did he know it once had been a German, did he know it was a German professor's head, an astronomer's head, a head that in its time had carried within its content profound knowledge of the stars in the vasty heavens, of the way of star-directed ships upon the sea, and of the way of the earth on its starry course through space that was a myriad million times beyond the slight concept of space that he possessed.

Last of all, sharpest of bite in his thought, was the head of Van Horn. And it was the head of Van Horn that lay on his knees under his contemplation when Jerry, who possessed the freedom of Somo, trotted into Bashti's grass house, scented and identified the mortal remnant of Skipper, wailed first in woe over it, then bristled into rage.

Bashti did not notice at first, for he was deep in interrogation of Van Horn's head. Only short months before this head had been alive, he pondered, quick with wit, attached to a two-legged body that stood erect and that swaggered about, a loincloth and a belted automatic around its middle, more powerful, therefrom, than Bashti, but with less wit, for had not he, Bashti, with an ancient pistol, put darkness inside that skull where wit resided, and removed that skull from the soddenly relaxed framework of flesh and bone on which it had been supported to tread the earth and the deck of the *Arangi*?

What had become of that wit? Had that wit been all of the arrogant, upstanding Van Horn, and had it gone out as the flickering flame of a splinter of wood goes out when it is quite burnt to a powder-fluff of ash? Had all that made Van Horn passed like the flame of the splinter? Had he passed into the darkness for ever into which the beast passed, into which passed the speared crocodile, the hooked bonita, the netted mullet, the slain pig that was fat to eat? Was Van Horn's darkness as the darkness of the blue-bottle fly that his fly-flapping maid smashed and disrupted in mid-flight of the air?—as the darkness into which passed the mosquito that knew the secret of flying, and that, despite its perfectness of flight, with almost an unthought action, he squashed with the flat of his hand against the back of his neck when it bit him?

What was true of this white man's head, so recently alive and erectly dominant, Bashti knew was true of himself. What had happened to this white man, after going through the dark gate of death, would happen to him. Wherefore he questioned the head, as if its dumb lips might speak to him from out of the mystery and tell him the meaning of life, and the meaning of death that inevitably laid life by the heels.

Jerry's long-drawn howl of woe at sight and scent of all that was left of Skipper, roused Bashti from his reverie. He looked at the sturdy, golden-brown puppy, and immediately included it in his reverie. It was alive. It was like man. It knew hunger, and pain, anger and love. It had blood in its veins, like man, that a thrust of a knife could make redly gush forth and denude it to death. Like the race of man it loved its kind, and birthed and breast-nourished its young. And passed. Ay, it passed; for many a dog, as well as a human, had he, Bashti, devoured in his hey-dey of appetite and youth, when he knew only motion and strength, and fed motion and strength out of the calabashes of feasting.

But from woe Jerry went on into anger. He stalked stiff-legged, with a snarl writhen on his lips, and with recurrent waves of hair-bristling along his back and up his shoulders and neck. And he stalked not the head of Skipper, where rested his love, but Bashti, who held the head on his knees. As the wild wolf in the upland pasture stalks the mare mother with her newly delivered colt, so Jerry stalked Bashti. And Bashti, who had never feared death all his long life and who had laughed a joke with his forefinger blown off by the bursting flint-lock pistol, smiled gleefully to himself, for his glee was intellectual and in admiration of this half-grown puppy whom he rapped on the nose with a short, hardwood stick and compelled to keep distance. No matter how often and fiercely Jerry rushed him, he met the rush with the stick, and chuckled aloud, understanding the puppy's courage, marvelling at the stupidity of life that impelled him continually to thrust his nose to the hurt of the stick, and that drove him, by passion of remembrance of a dead man to dare the pain of the stick again and again.

This, too, was life, Bashti meditated, as he deftly rapped the screaming puppy away from him. Four-legged life it was, young and silly and hot, heart-prompted, that was like any young man making love to his woman in the twilight, or like any young man fighting to the death with any other young man over a matter of passion, hurt pride, or thwarted desire. As much as in the dead head of Van Horn or of any man, he realized that in this live puppy might reside the clue to existence, the solution of the riddle.

So he continued to rap Jerry on the nose away from him, and to marvel at the persistence of the vital something within him that impelled him to leap forward always to the stick that hurt him and made him recoil. The valour and motion, the strength and the unreasoning of youth he knew it to be, and he admired it sadly, and envied it, willing to exchange for it all his lean grey wisdom if only he could find the way.

"Some dog, that dog, sure some dog," he might have uttered in Van Horn's fashion of speech. Instead, in beche-de-mer, which was as habitual to him as his own Somo speech, he thought:

"My word, that fella dog no fright along me."

But age wearied sooner of the play, and Bashti put an end to it by rapping Jerry heavily behind the ear and stretching him out stunned. The spectacle of the puppy, so alive and raging the moment before, and, the moment after, lying as if dead, caught Bashti's speculative fancy. The stick, with a single sharp rap of it, had effected the change. Where had gone the anger and wit of the puppy? Was that all it was, the flame of the splinter that could be quenched by any chance gust of air? One instant Jerry had raged and suffered, snarled and leaped, willed and directed his actions. The next instant he lay limp and crumpled in the little death of unconsciousness. In a brief space, Bashti knew, consciousness, sensation, motion, and direction would flow back into the wilted little carcass. But where, in the meanwhile, at the impact of the stick, had gone all the consciousness, and sensitiveness, and will?

Bashti sighed wearily, and wearily wrapped the heads in their grass-mat coverings—all but Van Horn's; and hoisted them up in the air to hang from the roof-beams—to hang as he debated, long after he was dead and out if it, even as some of them had so hung from long before his father's and his grandfather's time. The head of Van Horn he left lying on the floor, while he stole out himself to peer in through a crack and see what next the puppy might do.

Jerry quivered at first, and in the matter of a minute struggled feebly to his feet where he stood swaying and dizzy; and thus Bashti, his eye to the crack, saw the miracle of life flow back through the channels of the inert body and stiffen the legs to upstanding, and saw consciousness, the mystery of mysteries, flood back inside the head of bone that was covered with hair, smoulder and glow in the opening eyes, and direct the lips to writhe away from the teeth and the throat to vibrate to the snarl that had been interrupted when the stick smashed him down into darkness.

And more Bashti saw. At first, Jerry looked about for his enemy, growling and bristling his neck hair. Next, in lieu of his enemy, he saw Skipper's head, and crept to it and loved it, kissing with his tongue the hard cheeks, the closed lids of the eyes that his love could not open, the immobile lips that would not utter one of the love-words they had been used to utter to the little dog.

Next, in profound desolation, Jerry set down before Skipper's head, pointed his nose toward the lofty ridge-pole, and howled mournfully and long. Finally, sick and subdued, he crept out of the house and away to the house of his devil devil master, where, for the round of twenty-four hours, he waked and slept and dreamed centuries of nightmares.

For ever after in Somo, Jerry feared that grass house of Bashti. He was not in fear of Bashti. His fear was indescribable and unthinkable. In that house was the nothingness of what once was Skipper. It was the token of the ultimate catastrophe to life that was wrapped and twisted into every fibre of his heredity. One step advanced beyond this, Jerry's uttermost, the folk of Somo, from the contemplation of death, had achieved concepts of the spirits of the dead still living in immaterial and supersensuous realms.

And thereafter Jerry hated Bashti intensely, as a lord of life who possessed and laid on his knees the nothingness of Skipper. Not that Jerry reasoned it out. All dim and vague it was, a sensation, an emotion, a feeling, an instinct, an intuition, name it mistily as one will in the misty nomenclature of speech wherein words cheat with the impression of definiteness and lie to the brain an understanding which the brain does not possess.

XVI

Three months more passed; the north-west monsoon, after its half-year of breath, had given way to the south-east trade; and Jerry still continued to live in the house of Agno and to have the run of the village. He had put on weight, increased in size, and, protected by the taboo, had become self-confident almost to lordliness. But he had found no master. Agno had never won a heart-throb from him. For that matter, Agno had never tried to win him. Nor, in his cold-blooded way, had he ever betrayed his hatred of Jerry.

Not even the several old women, the two acolytes, and the fly-flapping maid in Agno's house dreamed that the devil devil doctor hated Jerry. Nor did Jerry dream it. To him Agno was a neutral sort of person, a person who did not count. Those of the household Jerry recognized as slaves or servants to Agno, and he knew when they fed him that the food he ate proceeded from Agno and was Agno's food. Save himself, taboo protected, all of them feared Agno, and his house was truly a house of fear in which could bloom no love for a stray puppy dog. The eleven-years' maid might have placed a bid for Jerry's affection, had she not been deterred at the start by Agno, who reprimanded her sternly for presuming to touch or fondle a dog of such high taboo.

What delayed Agno's plot against Jerry for the half-year of the monsoon was the fact that the season of egg-laying for the megapodes in Bashti's private laying-yard did not begin until the period of the south-east trades. And Agno, having early conceived his plot, with the patience that was characteristic of him was content to wait the time.

Now the megapode of the Solomons is a distant cousin to the brush turkey of Australia. No larger than a large pigeon, it lays an egg the size of a domestic duck's. The megapode, with no sense of fear, is so silly that it would have been annihilated hundreds of centuries before had it not been preserved by the taboos of the chiefs and priests. As it was, the chiefs were compelled to keep cleared patches of sand for it, and to fence out the dogs. It buried its eggs two feet deep, depending on the heat of the sun for the hatching. And it would dig and lay, and continue to dig and lay, while a black dug out its eggs within two or three feet of it.

The laying-yard was Bashti's. During the season, he lived almost entirely on megapode eggs. On rare occasion he even had megapodes that were near to finishing their laying killed for his kai-kai. This was no more than a whim, however, prompted by pride in such exclusiveness of diet only possible to one in such high place. In truth, he cared no more for megapode meat than for any other meat. All meat tasted alike to him, for his taste for meat was one of the vanished pleasures in the limbo of memory.

But the eggs! He liked to eat them. They were the only article of food he liked to eat, They gave him reminiscent thrills of the ancient food-desires of his youth. Actually was he hungry when he had megapode eggs, and the well-nigh dried founts of saliva and of internal digestive juices were stimulated to flow again at contemplation of a megapode egg prepared for the eating. Wherefore, he alone of all Somo, barred rigidly by taboo, ate megapode eggs. And, since the taboo was essentially religious, to Agno was deputed the ecclesiastical task of guarding and cherishing and caring for the royal laying-yard.

But Agno was no longer young. The acid bite of belly desire had long since deserted him, and he, too, ate from a sense of duty, all meat tasting alike to him. Megapode eggs only stung his taste alive and stimulated the flow of his juices. Thus it was that he broke the taboos he imposed, and, privily, before the eyes of no man, woman, or child ate the eggs he stole from Bashti's private preserve.

So it was, as the laying season began, and when both Bashti and Agno were acutely egg-yearning after six months of abstinence, that Agno led Jerry along the taboo path through the mangroves, where they stepped from root to root above the muck that ever steamed and stank in the stagnant air where the wind never penetrated.

The path, which was not an ordinary path and which consisted, for a man, in wide strides from root to root, and for a dog in four-legged leaps and plunges, was new to Jerry. In all his ranging of Somo, because it was so unusual a path, he had never discovered it. The unbending of Agno, thus to lead him, was a surprise and a delight to Jerry, who, without reasoning about it, in a vague way felt the preliminary sensations that possibly Agno, in a small way, might prove the master which his dog's soul continually sought.

Emerging from the swamp of mangroves, abruptly they came upon a patch of sand, still so salt and inhospitable from the sea's deposit that no great trees rooted and interposed their branches between it and the sun's heat. A primitive gate gave entrance, but Agno did not take Jerry through it. Instead, with weird little chirrupings of encouragement and excitation, he persuaded Jerry to dig a tunnel beneath the rude palisade of fence. He helped with his own hands, dragging out the sand in quantities, but imposing on Jerry the leaving of the indubitable marks of a dog's paws and claws.

And, when Jerry was inside, Agno, passing through the gate, enticed and seduced him into digging out the eggs. But Jerry had no taste of the eggs. Eight of them Agno sucked raw, and two of them he tucked whole into his arm-pits to take back to his house of the devil devils. The shells of the eight he sucked he broke to fragments as a dog might break them, and, to build the picture he had long visioned, of the eighth egg he reserved a tiny portion which he spread, not on Jerry's jowls where his tongue could have erased it, but high up about his eyes and above them, where it would remain and stand witness against him according to the plot he had planned.

Even worse, in high priestly sacrilege, he encouraged Jerry to attack a megapode hen in the act of laying. And, while Jerry slew it, knowing that the lust of killing, once started, would lead him to continue killing the silly birds, Agno left the laying-yard to hot-foot it through the mangrove swamp and present to Bashti an ecclesiastical quandary. The taboo of the dog, as he expounded it, had prevented him from interfering with the taboo dog when it ate the taboo egg-layers. Which taboo might be the greater was beyond him. And Bashti, who had not tasted a megapode egg in half a year, and who was keen for the one recrudescent thrill of remote youth still left to him, led the way back across the mangrove swamp at so prodigious a pace as quite to wind his high priest who was many years younger than he.

And he arrived at the laying-yard and caught Jerry, red-pawed and red-mouthed, in the midst of his fourth kill of an egg-layer, the raw yellow yolk of the portion of one egg, plastered by Agno to represent many eggs, still about his eyes and above his eyes to the bulge of his forehead. In vain Bashti looked about for one egg, the six months' hunger stronger than ever upon him in the thick of the disaster. And Jerry, under the consent and encouragement of Agno, wagged his tail to Bashti in a bid for recognition, of prowess, and laughed with his red-dripping jowls and yellow plastered eyes.

Bashti did not rage as he would have done had he been alone. Before the eyes of his chief priest he disdained to lower himself to such commonness of humanity. Thus it is always with those in the high places, ever temporising with their natural desires, ever masking their ordinariness under a show of disinterest. So it was that Bashti displayed no vexation at the disappointment to his appetite. Agno was a shade less controlled, for he could not quite chase away the eager light in his eyes. Bashti glimpsed it and mistook it for simple curiosity of observation not guessing its real nature. Which goes to show two things of those in the high place: one, that they may fool those beneath them; the other, that they may be fooled by those beneath them.

Bashti regarded Jerry quizzically, as if the matter were a joke, and shot a careless side glance to note the disappointment in his priest's eyes. Ah, ha, thought Bashti; I have fooled him.

"Which is the high taboo?" Agno queried in the Somo tongue.

"As you should ask. Of a surety, the megapode."

"And the dog?" was Agno's next query.

"Must pay for breaking the taboo. It is a high taboo. It is my taboo. It was so placed by Somo, the ancient father and first ruler of all of us, and it has been ever since the taboo of the chiefs. The dog must die."

He paused and considered the matter, while Jerry returned to digging the sand where the scent was auspicious. Agno made to stop him, but Bashti interposed.

"Let be," he said. "Let the dog convict himself before my eyes."

And Jerry did, uncovering two eggs, breaking them and lapping that portion of their precious contents which was not spilled and wasted in the sand. Bashti's eyes were quite lack-lustre as he asked

"The feast of dogs for the men is to-day?"

"To-morrow, at midday," Agno answered. "Already are the dogs coming in. There will be at least fifty of them."

"Fifty and one," was Bashti's verdict, as he nodded at Jerry.

The priest made a quick movement of impulse to capture Jerry.

"Why now?" the chief demanded. "You will but have to carry him through the swamp. Let him trot back on his own legs, and when he is before the canoe house tie his legs there."

Across the swamp and approaching the canoe house, Jerry, trotting happily at the heels of the two men, heard the wailing and sorrowing of many dogs that spelt unmistakable woe and pain. He developed instant suspicion that was, however, without direct apprehension for himself. And at that moment, his ears cocked forward and his nose questing for further information in the matter, Bashti seized him by the nape of the neck and held him in the air while Agno proceeded to tie his legs.

No whimper, nor sound, nor sign of fear, came from Jerry—only choking growls of ferociousness, intermingled with snarls of anger, and a belligerent up-clawing of hind-legs. But a dog, clutched by the neck from the back, can never be a match for two men, gifted with the intelligence and deftness of men, each of them two-handed with four fingers and an opposable thumb to each hand.

His fore-legs and hind-legs tied lengthwise and crosswise, he was carried head-downward the short distance to the place of slaughter and cooking, and flung to the earth in the midst of the score or more of dogs similarly tied and helpless. Although it was mid-afternoon, a number of them had so lain since early morning in the hot sun. They were all bush dogs or wild-dogs, and so small was their courage that their thirst and physical pain from cords drawn too tight across veins and arteries, and their dim apprehension of the fate such treatment foreboded, led them to whimper and wail and howl their despair and suffering.

The next thirty hours were bad hours for Jerry. The word had gone forth immediately that the taboo on him had been removed, and of the men and boys none was so low as to do him reverence. About him, till night-fall, persisted a circle of teasers and tormenters. They harangued him for his fall, sneered and jeered at him, rooted him about contemptuously with their feet, made a hollow in the sand out of which he could not roll and desposited him in it on his back, his four tied legs sticking ignominiously in the air above him.

And all he could do was growl and rage his helplessness. For, unlike the other dogs, he would not howl or whimper his pain. A year old now, the last six months had gone far toward maturing him, and it was the nature of his breed to be fearless and stoical. And, much as he had been taught by his white masters to hate and despise niggers, he learned in the course of these thirty hours an especially bitter and undying hatred.

His torturers stopped at nothing. Even they brought wild-dog and set him upon Jerry. But it was contrary to wild-dog's nature to attack an enemy that could not move, even if the enemy was Jerry who had so often bullied him and rolled him on the deck. Had Jerry, with a broken leg or so, still retained power of movement, then he would have mauled him, perhaps to death. But this utter helplessness was different. So the expected show proved a failure. When Jerry snarled and growled, wild-dog snarled and growled back and strutted and bullied around him, him to persuasion of the blacks could induce but no sink his teeth into Jerry.

The killing-ground before the canoe house was a bedlam of horror. From time to time more bound dogs were brought in and flung down.

There was a continuous howling, especially contributed to by those which had lain in the sun since early morning and had no water. At times, all joined in, the control of the quietest breaking down before the wave of excitement and fear that swept spasmodically over all of them. This howling, rising and falling, but never ceasing, continued throughout the night, and by morning all were suffering from the intolerable thirst.

The sun blazing down upon them in the white sand and almost parboiling them, brought anything but relief. The circle of torturers formed about Jerry again, and again was wreaked upon him all abusive contempt for having lost his taboo. What drove Jerry the maddest were not the blows and physical torment, but the laughter. No dog enjoys being laughed at, and Jerry, least of all, could restrain his wrath when they jeered him and cackled close in his face.

Although he had not howled once, his snarling and growling, combined with his thirst, had hoarsened his throat and dried the mucous membranes of his mouth so that he was incapable, except under the sheerest provocation, of further sound. His tongue hung out of his mouth, and the eight o'clock sun began slowly to burn it.

It was at this time that one of the boys cruelly outraged him. He rolled Jerry out of the hollow in which he had lain all night on his back, turned him over on his side, and presented to him a small calabash filled with water. Jerry lapped it so fanatically that not for half a minute did he become aware that the boy had squeezed into it many hot seeds of ripe red peppers. The circle shrieked with glee, and what Jerry's thirst had been before was as nothing compared with this new thirst to which had been added the stinging agony of pepper.

Next in event, and a most important event it was to prove, came Nalasu. Nalasu was an old man of three-score years, and he was blind, walking with a large staff with which he prodded his path. In his free hand he carried a small pig by its tied legs.

"They say the white master's dog is to be eaten," he said in the Somo speech. "Where is the white master's dog? Show him to me."

Agno, who had just arrived, stood beside him as he bent over Jerry and examined him with his fingers. Nor did Jerry offer to snarl or bite, although the blind man's hands came within reach of his teeth more than once. For Jerry sensed no enmity in the fingers that passed so softly over him. Next, Nalasu felt over the pig, and several times, as if calculating, alternated between Jerry and the pig.

Nalasu stood up and voiced judgment:

"The pig is as small as the dog. They are of a size, but the pig has more meat on it for the eating. Take the pig and I shall take the dog."

"Nay," said Agno. "The white master's dog has broken the taboo. It must be eaten. Take any other dog and leave the pig. Take a big dog."

"I will have the white master's dog," Nalasu persisted. "Only the white master's dog and no other."

The matter was at a deadlock when Bashti chanced upon the scene and stood listening.

"Take the dog, Nalasu," he said finally. "It is a good pig, and I shall myself eat it."

"But he has broken the taboo, your great taboo of the laying-yard, and must go to the eating," Agno interposed quickly.

Too quickly, Bashti thought, while a vague suspicion arose in his mind of he knew not what.

"The taboo must be paid in blood and cooking," Agno continued.

"Very well," said Bashti. "I shall eat the small pig. Let its throat be cut and its body know the fire."

"I but speak the law of the taboo. Life must pay for the breaking."

"There is another law," Bashti grinned. "Long has it been since ever Somo built these walls that life may buy life."

"But of life of man and life of woman," Agno qualified.

"I know the law," Bashti held steadily on. "Somo made the law. Never has it been said that animal life may not buy animal life."

"It has never been practised," was the devil devil doctor's fling.

"And for reason enough," the old chief retorted. "Never before has a man been fool enough to give a pig for a dog. It is a young pig, and it is fat and tender. Take the dog, Nalasu. Take the dog now."

But the devil devil doctor was not satisfied.

"As you said, O Bashti, in your very great wisdom, he is the seed dog of strength and courage. Let him be slain. When he comes from the fire, his body shall be divided into many small pieces so that every man may eat of him and thereby get his portion of strength and courage. Better is it for Somo that its men be strong and brave rather than its dogs."

But Bashti held no anger against Jerry. He had lived too long and too philosophically to lay blame on a dog for breaking a taboo which it did not know. Of course, dogs often were slain for breaking the taboos. But he allowed this to be done because the dogs themselves in nowise interested him, and because their deaths emphasized the sacredness of the taboo. Further, Jerry had more than slightly interested him.

Often, since, Jerry had attacked him because of Van Horn's head, he had pondered the incident. Baffling as it was, as all manifestations of life were baffling, it had given him food for thought. Then there was his admiration for Jerry's courage and that inexplicable something in him that prevented him crying out from the pain of the stick. And, without thinking of it as beauty, the beauty of line and colour of Jerry had insensibly penetrated him with a sense of pleasantness. It was good to look upon.

There was another angle to Bashti's conduct. He wondered why his devil devil doctor so earnestly desired a mere dog's death. There were many dogs. Then why this particular dog? That the weight of something was on the other's mind was patent, although what it was Bashti could not gauge, guess—unless it might be revenge incubated the day he had prevented Agno from eating the dog. If such were the case, it was a state of mind he could not tolerate in any of his tribespeople. But whatever was the motive, guarding as he always did against the unknown, he thought it well to discipline his priest and demonstrate once again whose word was the last word in Somo. Wherefore Bashti replied:

"I have lived long and eaten many pigs. What man may dare say that the many pigs have entered into me and made me a pig?"

He paused and cast a challenging eye around the circle of his audience; but no man spoke. Instead, some men grinned sheepishly and were restless on their feet, while Agno's expression advertised sturdy unbelief that there was anything pig-like about his chief.

"I have eaten much fish," Bashti continued. "Never has one scale of a fish grown out on my skin. Never has a gill appeared on my throat. As you all know, by the looking, never have I sprouted one fin out of my backbone.—Nalasu, take the dog.—Aga, carry the pig to my house. I shall eat it to-day.—Agno, let the killing of the dogs begin so that the canoe-men shall eat at due time."

Then, as he turned to go, he lapsed into beche-de-mer English and flung sternly over his shoulder, "My word, you make 'm me cross along you."

JACK LONDON

XVII

As blind Nalasu slowly plodded away, with one hand tapping the path before him and with the other carrying Jerry head-downward suspended by his tied legs, Jerry heard a sudden increase in the wild howling of the dogs as the killing began and they realized that death was upon them.

But, unlike the boy Lamai, who had known no better, the old man did not carry Jerry all the way to his house. At the first stream pouring down between the low hills of the rising land, he paused and put Jerry down to drink. And Jerry knew only the delight of the wet coolness on his tongue, all about his mouth, and down his throat. Nevertheless, in his subconsciousness was being planted the impression that, kinder than Lamai, than Agno, than Bashti, this was the kindest black he had encountered in Somo.

When he had drunk till for the moment he could drink no more, he thanked Nalasu with his tongue—not warmly nor ecstatically as had it been Skipper's hand, but with due gratefulness for the life-giving draught. The old man chuckled in a pleased way, rolled Jerry's parched body into the water, and, keeping his head above the surface, rubbed the water into his dry skin and let him lie there for long blissful minutes.

From the stream to Nalasu's house, a goodly distance, Nalasu still carried him with bound legs, although not head-downward but clasped in one arm against his chest. His idea was to love the dog to him. For Nalasu, having sat in the lonely dark for many years, had thought far more about the world around him and knew it far better than had he been able to see it. For his own special purpose he had need of a dog. Several bush dogs he had tried, but they had shown little appreciation of his kindness and had invariably run away. The last had remained longest because he had treated it with the greatest kindness, but run away it had before he had trained it to his purpose. But the white master's dog, he had heard, was different. It never ran away in fear, while it was said to be more intelligent than the dogs of Somo.

The invention Lamai had made of tying Jerry with a stick had been noised abroad in the village, and by a stick, in Nalasu's house, Jerry found himself again tied. But with a difference. Never once was the blind man impatient, while he spent hours each day in squatting on his hams and petting Jerry. Yet, had he not done this, Jerry, who ate his food and who was growing accustomed to changing his masters, would have accepted Nalasu for master. Further, it was fairly definite in Jerry's mind, after the devil devil doctor's tying him and flinging him amongst the other helpless dogs on the killing-ground, that all mastership of Agno had ceased. And Jerry, who had never been without a master since his first days in the world, felt the imperative need of a master.

So it was, when the day came that the stick was untied from him, that Jerry remained, voluntarily in Nalasu's house. When the old man was satisfied there would be no running away, he began Jerry's training. By slow degrees he advanced the training until hours a day were devoted to it.

First of all Jerry learned a new name for himself, which was Bao, and he was taught to respond to it from an ever-increasing distance no matter how softly it was uttered, and Nalasu continued to utter it more softly until it no longer was a spoken word, but a whisper. Jerry's ears were keen, but Nalasu's, from long use, were almost as keen.

Further, Jerry's own hearing was trained to still greater acuteness. Hours at a time, sitting by Nalasu or standing apart from him, he was taught to catch the slightest sounds or rustlings from the bush. Still further, he was taught to differentiate between the bush noises and between the ways he growled warnings to Nalasu. If a rustle took place that Jerry identified as a pig or a chicken, he did not growl at all. If he did not identify the noise, he growled fairly softly. But if the noise were made by a man or boy who moved softly and therefore suspiciously, Jerry learned to growl loudly; if the noise were loud and careless, then Jerry's growl was soft.

It never entered Jerry's mind to question why he was taught all this. He merely did it because it was this latest master's desire that he should. All this, and much more, at a cost of interminable time and patience, Nalasu taught him, and much more he taught him, increasing his vocabulary so that, at a distance, they could hold quick and sharply definite conversations.

Thus, at fifty feet away, Jerry would "Whuff!" softly the information that there was a noise he did not know; and Nalasu, with different sibilances, would hiss to him to stand still, to whuff more softly, or to keep silent, or to come to him noiselessly, or to go into the bush and investigate the source of the strange noise, or, barking loudly, to rush and attack it.

Perhaps, if from the opposite direction Nalasu's sharp ears alone caught a strange sound, he would ask Jerry if he had heard it. And Jerry, alert to his toes to listen, by an alteration in the quantity or quality of his whuff, would tell Nalasu that he did not hear; next, that he did hear; and, perhaps finally, that it was a strange dog, or a wood-rat, or a man, or a boy—all in the softest of sounds that were scarcely more than breath-exhalations, all monosyllables, a veritable shorthand of speech.

Nalasu was a strange old man. He lived by himself in a small grass house on the edge of the village. The nearest house was quite a distance away, while his own stood in a clearing in the thick jungle which approached no where nearer than sixty feet. Also, this cleared space he kept continually free from the fast-growing vegetation. Apparently he had no friends. At least no visitors ever came to his dwelling. Years had passed since he discouraged the last. Further, he had no kindred. His wife was long since dead, and his three sons, not yet married, in a foray behind the bounds of Somo had lost their heads in the jungle runways of the higher hills and been devoured by their bushman slayers.

For a blind man he was very busy. He asked favour of no one and was self-supporting. In his house-clearing he grew yams, sweet potatoes, and taro. In another clearing—because it was his policy to have no trees close to his house—he had plantains, bananas, and half a dozen coconut palms. Fruits and vegetables he exchanged down in the village for meat and fish and tobacco.

He spent a good portion of his time on Jerry's education, and, on occasion, would make bows and arrows that were so esteemed by his tribespeople as to command a steady sale. Scarcely a day passed in which he did not himself practise with bow and arrow. He shot only by direction of sound; and whenever a noise or rustle was heard in the jungle, and when Jerry had informed him of its nature, he would shoot an arrow at it. Then it was Jerry's duty cautiously to retrieve the arrow had it missed the mark.

A curious thing about Nalasu was that he slept no more than three hours in the twenty-four, that he never slept at night, and that his brief daylight sleep never took place in the house. Hidden in the thickest part of the neighbouring jungle was a sort of nest to which led no path. He never entered nor left by the same way, so that the tropic growth on the rich soil, being so rarely trod upon, ever obliterated the slightest sign of his having passed that way. Whenever he slept, Jerry was trained to remain on guard and never to go to sleep.

Reason enough there was and to spare for Nalasu's infinite precaution. The oldest of his three sons had slain one, Ao, in a quarrel. Ao had been one of six brothers of the family of Anno which dwelt in one of the upper villages. According to Somo law, the Anno family was privileged to collect the blood-debt from the Nalasu family, but had been balked of it by the deaths of Nalasu's three sons in the bush. And, since the Somo code was a life for a life, and since Nalasu alone remained alive of his family, it was well known throughout the tribe that the Annos would never be content until they had taken the blind man's life.

But Nalasu had been famous as a great fighter, as well as having been the progenitor of three such warlike sons. Twice had the Annos sought to collect, the first time while Nalasu still retained his eyesight. Nalasu had discovered their trap, circled about it, and in the rear encountered and slain Anno himself, the father, thus doubling the blood-debt.

Then had come his accident. While refilling many-times used Snider cartridges, an explosion of black powder put out both his eyes. Immediately thereafter, while he sat nursing his wounds, the Annos had descended upon him—just what he had expected. And for which he had made due preparation. That night two uncles and another brother stepped on poisoned thorns and died horribly. Thus the sum of lives owing the Annos had increased to five, with only a blind man from whom to collect.

Thenceforth the Annos had feared the thorns too greatly to dare again, although ever their vindictiveness smouldered and they lived in hope of the day when Nalasu's head should adorn their ridgepole. In the meantime the state of affairs was not that of a truce but of a stalemate. The old man could not proceed against them, and they were afraid to proceed against him. Nor did the day come until after Jerry's adoption, when one of the Annos made an invention the like of which had never been known in all Malaita.

XVIII

M eanwhile the months slipped by, the south-east trade blew itself out, the monsoon had begun to breathe, and Jerry added to himself six months of time, weight, stature, and thickness of bone. An easy time his half-year with the blind man had been, despite the fact that Nalasu was a rigid disciplinarian who insisted on training Jerry for longer hours, day in and day out, than falls to the lot of most dogs. Never did Jerry receive from him a blow, never a harsh word. This man, who had slain four of the Annos, three of them after he had gone blind, who had slain still more men in his savage youth, never raised his voice in anger to Jerry and ruled him by nothing severer than the gentlest of chidings.

Mentally, the persistent education Jerry received, in this period of late puppyhood, fixed in him increased brain power for all his life. Possibly no dog in all the world had ever been so vocal as he, and for three reasons: his own intelligence, the genius for teaching that was Nalasu's, and the long hours devoted to the teaching.

His shorthand vocabulary, for a dog, was prodigious. Almost might it be said that he and the man could talk by the hour, although few and simple were the abstractions they could talk; very little of the immediate concrete past, and scarcely anything of the immediate concrete future, entered into their conversations. Jerry could no more tell him of Meringe, nor of the *Arangi*, than could he tell him of the great love he had borne Skipper, or of his reason for hating Bashti. By the same token, Nalasu could not tell Jerry of the blood-feud with the Annos, nor of how he had lost his eyesight.

Practically all their conversation was confined to the instant present, although they could compass a little of the very immediate past. Nalasu would give Jerry a series of instructions, such as, going on a scout by himself, to go to the nest, then circle about it widely, to continue to the other clearing where were the fruit trees, to cross the jungle to the main path, to proceed down the main path toward the village till he came to the great banyan tree, and then to return along the small path to Nalasu and Nalasu's house. All of which Jerry would carry out to the letter, and, arrived back, would make report. As, thus: at the nest nothing unusual save that a buzzard was near it; in the other clearing three coconuts had fallen to the ground—for Jerry could count unerringly up to five;

between the other clearing and the main path were four pigs; along the main path he had passed a dog, more than five women, and two children; and on the small path home he had noted a cockatoo and two boys.

But he could not tell Nalasu his states of mind and heart that prevented him from being fully contented in his present situation. For Nalasu was not a white-god, but only a mere nigger god. And Jerry hated and despised all niggers save for the two exceptions of Lamai and Nalasu. He tolerated them, and, for Nalasu, had even developed a placid and sweet affection. Love him he did not and could not.

At the best, they were only second-rate gods, and he could not forget the great white-gods such as Skipper and Mister Haggin, and, of the same breed, Derby and Bob. They were something else, something other, something better than all this black savagery in which he lived. They were above and beyond, in an unattainable paradise which he vividly remembered, for which he yearned, but to which he did not know the way, and which, dimly sensing the ending that comes to all things, might have passed into the ultimate nothingness which had already overtaken Skipper and the *Arangi*.

In vain did the old man play to gain Jerry's heart of love. He could not bid against Jerry's many reservations and memories, although he did win absolute faithfulness and loyalty. Not passionately, as he would have fought to the death for Skipper, but devotedly would he have fought to the death for Nalasu. And the old man never dreamed but what he had won all of Jerry's heart.

CAME THE DAY OF THE Annos, when one of them made the invention, which was thick-plaited sandals to armour the soles of their feet against the poisoned thorns with which Nalasu had taken three of their lives. The day, in truth, was the night, a black night, a night so black under a cloud-palled sky that a tree-trunk could not be seen an eighth of an inch beyond one's nose. And the Annos descended on Nalasu's clearing, a dozen of them, armed with Sniders, horse pistols, tomahawks and war clubs, walking gingerly, despite their thick sandals, because of fear of the thorns which Nalasu no longer planted.

Jerry, sitting between Nalasu's knees and nodding sleepily, gave the first warning to Nalasu, who sat outside his door, wide-eyed, ear-strung, as he had sat through all the nights of the many years. He listened still more tensely through long minutes in which he heard nothing, at the same time whispering to Jerry for information and commanding him to be soft-spoken; and Jerry, with whuffs and whiffs and all the short-hand breath-exhalations of speech he had been taught, told him that men approached, many men, more men than five.

Nalasu reached the bow beside him, strung an arrow, and waited. At last his own ears caught the slightest of rustlings, now here, now there, advancing upon him in the circle of the compass. Still speaking for softness, he demanded verification from Jerry, whose neck hair rose bristling under Nalasu's sensitive fingers, and who, by this time, was reading the night air with his nose as well as his ears. And Jerry, as softly as Nalasu, informed him again that it was men, many men, more men than five.

With the patience of age Nalasu sat on without movement, until, close at hand, on the very edge of the jungle, sixty feet away, he located a particular noise of a particular man. He stretched his bow, loosed the arrow, and was rewarded by a gasp and a groan strangely commingled. First he restrained Jerry from retrieving the arrow, which he knew had gone home; and next he fitted a fresh arrow to the bow string.

Fifteen minutes of silence passed, the blind man as if carven of stone, the dog, trembling with eagerness under the articulate touch of his fingers, obeying the bidding to make no sound. For Jerry, as well as Nalasu, knew that death rustled and lurked in the encircling dark. Again came a softness of movement, nearer than before; but the sped arrow missed. They heard its impact against a tree trunk beyond and a confusion of small sounds caused by the target's hasty retreat. Next, after a time of silence, Nalasu told Jerry silently to retrieve the arrow. He had been well trained and long trained, for with no sound even to Nalasu's ears keener than seeing men's ears, he followed the direction of the arrow's impact against the tree and brought the arrow back in his mouth.

Again Nalasu waited, until the rustlings of a fresh drawing-in of the circle could be heard, whereupon Nalasu, Jerry accompanying him, picked up all his arrows and moved soundlessly half-way around the circle. Even as they moved, a Snider exploded that was aimed in the general direction of the spot just vacated.

And the blind man and the dog, from midnight to dawn, successfully fought off twelve men equipped with the thunder of gunpowder and the wide-spreading, deep-penetrating, mushroom bullets of soft lead. And the blind man defended himself only with a bow and a hundred arrows.

He discharged many hundreds of arrows which Jerry retrieved for him and which he discharged over and over. But Jerry aided valiantly and well, adding to Nalasu's acute hearing his own acuter hearing, circling noiselessly about the house and reporting where the attack pressed closest.

Much of their precious powder the Annos wasted, for the affair was like a game of invisible ghosts. Never was anything seen save the flashes of the rifles. Never did they see Jerry, although they became quickly aware of his movements close to them as he searched out the arrows. Once, as one of them felt for an arrow which had narrowly missed him, he encountered Jerry's back with his hand and acknowledged the sharp slash of Jerry's teeth with a wild yell of terror. They tried firing at the twang of Nalasu's bowstring, but every time Nalasu fired he instantly changed position. Several times, warned of Jerry's nearness, they fired at him, and, once even, was his nose slightly powder burned.

When day broke, in the quick tropic grey that marks the leap from dark to sun, the Annos retreated, while Nalasu, withdrawn from the light into his house, still possessed eighty arrows, thanks to Jerry. The net result to Nalasu was one dead man and no telling how many arrow-pricked wounded men who dragged themselves away.

And half the day Nalasu crouched over Jerry, fondling and caressing him for what he had done. Then he went abroad, Jerry with him, and told of the battle. Bashti paid him a visit ere the day was done, and talked with him earnestly.

"As an old man to an old man, I talk," was Bashti's beginning. "I am older than you, O Nalasu; I have ever been unafraid. Yet never have I been braver than you. I would that every man of the tribe were as brave as you. Yet do you give me great sorrow. Of what worth are your courage and cunning, when you have no seed to make your courage and cunning live again?"

"I am an old man," Nalasu began.

"Not so old as I am," Bashti interrupted. "Not too old to marry so that your seed will add strength to the tribe."

"I was married, and long married, and I fathered three brave sons. But they are dead. I shall not live so long as you. I think of my young days as pleasant dreams remembered after sleep. More I think of death, and the end. Of marriage I think not at all. I am too old to marry. I am old enough to make ready to die, and a great curiousness have I about what will happen to me when I am dead. Will I be for ever dead? Will

I live again in a land of dreams—a shadow of a dream myself that will still remember the days when I lived in the warm world, the quick juices of hunger in my mouth, in the chest of the body of me the love of woman?"

Bashti shrugged his shoulders.

"I too, have thought much on the matter," he said. "Yet do I arrive nowhere. I do not know. You do not know. We will not know until we are dead, if it happens that we know anything when what we are we no longer are. But this we know, you and I: the tribe lives. The tribe never dies. Wherefore, if there be meaning at all to our living, we must make the tribe strong. Your work in the tribe is not done. You must marry so that your cunning and your courage live after you. I have a wife for you—nay, two wives, for your days are short and I shall surely live to see you hang with my fathers from the canoe-house ridgepole."

"I will not pay for a wife," Nalasu protested. "I will not pay for any wife. I would not pay a stick of tobacco or a cracked coconut for the best woman in Somo."

"Worry not," Bashti went on placidly. "I shall pay you for the price of the wife, of the two wives. There is Bubu. For half a case of tobacco shall I buy her for you. She is broad and square, round-legged, broad-hipped, with generous breasts of richness. There is Nena. Her father sets a stiff price upon her—a whole case of tobacco. I will buy her for you as well. Your time is short. We must hurry."

"I will not marry," the old blind man proclaimed hysterically.

"You will. I have spoken."

"No, I say, and say again, no, no, no, no. Wives are nuisances. They are young things, and their heads are filled with foolishness. Their tongues are loose with idleness of speech. I am old, I am quiet in my ways, the fires of life have departed from me, I prefer to sit alone in the dark and think. Chattering young things about me, with nothing but foam and spume in their heads, on their tongues, would drive me mad. Of a surety they would drive me mad—so mad that I will spit into every clam shell, make faces at the moon, and bite my veins and howl."

"And if you do, what of it? So long as your seed does not perish. I shall pay for the wives to their fathers and send them to you in three days."

"I will have nothing to do with them," Nalasu asserted wildly.

"You will," Bashti insisted calmly. "Because if you do not you will have to pay me. It will be a sore, hard debt. I will have every joint of you unhinged so that you will be like a jelly-fish, like a fat pig with the bones removed, and I will then stake you out in the midmost centre of the dog-killing ground to swell in pain under the sun. And what is left of you I shall fling to the dogs to eat. Your seed shall not perish out of Somo. I, Bashti, so tell you. In three days I shall send to you your two wives. . ."

He paused, and a long silence fell upon them.

"Well?" Bashti reiterated. "It is wives or staking out unhinged in the sun. You choose, but think well before you choose the unhinging."

"At my age, with all the vexations of youngness so far behind me!" Nalasu complained.

"Choose. You will find there is vexation, and liveliness and much of it, in the centre of the dog-killing yard when the sun cooks your sore joints till the grease of the leanness of you bubbles like the tender fat of a cooked sucking-pig."

"Then send me the wives," Nalasu managed to utter after a long pause. "But send them in three days, not in two, nor to-morrow."

"It is well," Bashti nodded gravely. "You have lived at all only because of those before you, now long in the dark, who worked so that the tribe might live and you might come to be. You are. They paid the price for you. It is your debt. You came into being with this debt upon you. You will pay the debt before you pass out of being. It is the law. It is very well."

XIX

And had Bashti hastened delivery of the wives by one day, or by even two days, Nalasu would have entered the feared, purgatory of matrimony. But Bashti kept his word, and on the third day was too busy, with a more momentous problem, to deliver Bubu and Nena to the blind old man who apprehensively waited their coming. For the morning of the third day all the summits of leeward Malaita smoked into speech. A warship was on the coast—so the tale ran; a big warship that was heading in through the reef islands at Langa-Langa. The tale grew. The warship was not stopping at Langa-Langa. The warship was not stopping at Binu. It was directing its course toward Somo.

Nalasu, blind, could not see this smoke speech written in the air. Because of the isolation of his house, no one came and told him. His first warning was when shrill voices of women, cries of children, and wailings of babes in nameless fear came to him from the main path that led from the village to the upland boundaries of Somo. He read only fear and panic from the sounds, deduced that the village was fleeing to its mountain fastnesses, but did not know the cause of the flight.

He called Jerry to him and instructed him to scout to the great banyan tree, where Nalasu's path and the main path joined, and to observe and report. And Jerry sat under the banyan tree and observed the flight of all Somo. Men, women, and children, the young and the aged, babes at breast and patriarchs leaning on sticks and staffs passed before his eyes, betraying the greatest haste and alarm. The village dogs were as frightened, whimpering and whining as they ran. And the contagion of terror was strong upon Jerry. He knew the prod of impulse to join in this rush away from some unthinkably catastrophic event that impended and that stirred his intuitive apprehensions of death. But he mastered the impulse with his sense of loyalty to the blind man who had fed him and caressed him for a long six months.

Back with Nalasu, sitting between his knees, he made his report. It was impossible for him to count more than five, although he knew the fleeing population numbered many times more than five. So he signified five men, and more; five women, and more five children, and more; five babies, and more; five dogs, and more—even of pigs did he announce five and more. Nalasu's ears told him that it was many, many times more, and he asked for names. Jerry know the names of Bashti, of

Agno, and of Lamai, and Lumai. He did not pronounce them with the slightest of resemblance to their customary soundings, but pronounced them in the whiff-whuff of shorthand speech that Nalasu had taught him.

Nalasu named over many other names that Jerry knew by ear but could not himself evoke in sound, and he answered yes to most of them by simultaneously nodding his head and advancing his right paw. To some names he remained without movement in token that he did not know them. And to other names, which he recognized, but the owners of which he had not seen, he answered no by advancing his left paw.

And Nalasu, beyond knowing that something terrible was impending—something horribly more terrible than any foray of neighbouring salt-water tribes, which Somo, behind her walls, could easily fend off, divined that it was the long-expected punitive man-of-war. Despite his three-score years, he had never experienced a village shelling. He had heard vague talk of what had happened in the matter of shell-fire in other villages, but he had no conception of it save that it must be, bullets on a larger scale than Snider bullets that could be fired correspondingly longer distances through the air.

But it was given to him to know shell-fire before he died. Bashti, who had long waited the cruiser that was to avenge the destruction of the *Arangi* and the taking of the heads of the two white men, and who had long calculated the damage to be wrought, had given the command to his people to flee to the mountains. First in the vanguard, borne by a dozen young men, went his mat-wrapped parcels of heads. The last slow trailers in the rear of the exodus were just passing, and Nalasu, his bow and his eighty arrows clutched to him, Jerry at his heels, made his first step to follow, when the air above him was rent by a prodigiousness of sound.

Nalasu sat down abruptly. It was his first shell, and it was a thousand times more terrible than he had imagined. It was a rip-snorting, sky-splitting sound as of a cosmic fabric being torn asunder between the hands of some powerful god. For all the world it was like the roughest tearing across of sheets that were thick as blankets, that were broad as the earth and wide as the sky.

Not only did he sit down just outside his door, but he crouched his head to his knees and shielded it with the arch of his arms. And Jerry, who had never heard shell-fire, much less imagined what it was like, was impressed with the awfulness of it. It was to him a natural catastrophe such as had happened to the *Arangi* when she was flung down reeling on her side by the shouting wind. But, true to his nature, he did not crouch down under the shriek of that first shell. On the contrary, he bristled his hair and snarled up with menacing teeth at whatever the thing was which was so enormously present and yet invisible to his eyes.

Nalasu crouched closer when the shell burst beyond, and Jerry snarled and rippled his hair afresh. Each repeated his actions with each fresh shell, for, while they screamed no more loudly, they burst in the jungle more closely. And Nalasu, who had lived a long life most bravely in the midst of perils he had known, was destined to die a coward out of his fear of the thing unknown, the chemically propelled missile of the white masters. As the dropping shells burst nearer and nearer, what final self-control he possessed left him. Such was his utter panic that he might well have bitten his veins and howled. With a lunatic scream, he sprang to his feet and rushed inside the house as if forsooth its grass thatch could protect his head from such huge projectiles. He collided with the door-jamb, and, ere Jerry could follow him, whirled around in a part circle into the centre of the floor just in time to receive the next shell squarely upon his head.

Jerry had just gained the doorway when the shell exploded. The house went into flying fragments, and Nalasu flew into fragments with it. Jerry, in the doorway, caught in the out-draught of the explosion, was flung a score of feet away. All in the same fraction of an instant, earthquake, tidal wave, volcanic eruption, the thunder of the heavens and the fire-flashing of an electric bolt from the sky smote him and smote consciousness out of him.

He had no conception of how long he lay. Five minutes passed before his legs made their first spasmodic movements, and, as he stumbled to his feet and rocked giddily, he had no thought of the passage of time. He had no thought about time at all. As a matter of course, his own idea, on which he proceeded to act without being aware of it, was that, a part of a second before, he had been struck a terrific blow magnified incalculable times beyond the blow of a stick at a nigger's hands.

His throat and lungs filled with the pungent stifling smoke of powder, his nostrils with earth and dust, he frantically wheezed and sneezed, leaping about, falling drunkenly, leaping into the air again, staggering on his hind-legs, dabbing with his forepaws at his nose head-downward between his forelegs, and even rubbing his nose into the ground. He had no thought for anything save to remove the biting pain from his nose and mouth, the suffocation from his lungs.

By a miracle he had escaped being struck by the flying splinters of iron, and, thanks to his strong heart, had escaped being killed by the shock of the explosion. Not until the end of five minutes of mad struggling, in which he behaved for all the world like a beheaded chicken, did he find life tolerable again. The maximum of stifling and of agony passed, and, although he was still weak and giddy, he tottered in the direction of the house and of Nalasu. And there was no house and no Nalasu—only a debris intermingled of both.

While the shells continued to shriek and explode, now near, now far, Jerry investigated the happening. As surely as the house was gone, just as surely was Nalasu gone. Upon both had descended the ultimate nothingness. All the immediate world seemed doomed to nothingness. Life promised only somewhere else, in the high hills and remote bush whither the tribe had already fled. Loyal he was to his salt, to the master whom he had obeyed so long, nigger that he was, who so long had fed him, and for whom he had entertained a true affection. But this master no longer was.

Retreat Jerry did, but he was not hasty in retreat. For a time he snarled at every shell-scream in the air and every shell-burst in the bush. But after a time, while the awareness of them continued uncomfortably with him, the hair on his neck remained laid down and he neither uttered a snarl nor bared his teeth.

And when he parted from what had been and which had ceased to be, not like the bush dogs did he whimper and run. Instead, he trotted along the path at a regular and dignified pace. When he emerged upon the main path, he found it deserted. The last refugee had passed. The path, always travelled from daylight to dark, and which he had so recently seen glutted with humans, now in its emptiness affected him profoundly with the impression of the endingness of all things in a perishing world. So it was that he did not sit down under the banyan tree, but trotted along at the far rear of the tribe.

With his nose he read the narrative of the flight. Only once did he encounter what advertised its terror. It was an entire group annihilated by a shell. There were: an old man of fifty, with a crutch because of the leg which had been slashed off by a shark when he was a young boy; a dead Mary with a dead babe at her breast and a dead child of three clutching her hand; and two dead pigs, huge and fat, which the woman had been herding to safety.

And Jerry's nose told him of how the stream of the fugitives had split and flooded past on each side and flowed together again beyond. Incidents of the flight he did encounter: a part-chewed joint of sugar-cane some child had dropped; a clay pipe, the stem short from successive breakages; a single feather from some young man's hair, and a calabash, full of cooked yams and sweet potatoes, deposited carefully beside the trail by some Mary for whom its weight had proved too great.

The shell-fire ceased as Jerry trotted along; next he heard the rifle-fire from the landing-party, as it shot down the domestic pigs on Somo's streets. He did not hear, however, the chopping down of the coconut trees, any more than did he ever return to behold what damage the axes had wrought.

For right here occurred with Jerry a wonderful thing that thinkers of the world have not explained. He manifested in his dog's brain the free agency of life, by which all the generations of metaphysicians have postulated God, and by which all the deterministic philosophers have been led by the nose despite their clear denouncement of it as sheer illusion. What Jerry did he did. He did not know how or why he did it any more than does the philosopher know how or why he decides on mush and cream for breakfast instead of two soft-boiled eggs.

What Jerry did was to yield in action to a brain impulse to do, not what seemed the easier and more usual thing, but to do what seemed the harder and more unusual thing. Since it is easier to endure the known than to fly to the unknown; since both misery and fear love company; the apparent easiest thing for Jerry to have done would have been to follow the tribe of Somo into its fastnesses. Yet what Jerry did was to diverge from the line of retreat and to start northward, across the bounds of Somo, and continue northward into a strange land of the unknown.

Had Nalasu not been struck down by the ultimate nothingness, Jerry would have remained. This is true, and this, perhaps, to the one who considers his action, might have been the way he reasoned. But he did not reason it, did not reason at all; he acted on impulse. He could count five objects, and pronounce them by name and number, but he was incapable of reasoning that he would remain in Somo if Nalasu lived, depart from Somo if Nalasu died. He merely departed from Somo because Nalasu was dead, and the terrible shell-fire passed quickly into the past of his consciousness, while the present became vivid after the way of the present. Almost on his toes did he tread the wild bushmen's trails, tense with apprehension of the lurking death he know infested such paths, his ears cocked alertly for jungle sounds, his eyes following his ears to discern what made the sounds.

No more doughty nor daring was Columbus, venturing all that he was to the unknown, than was Jerry in venturing this jungle-darkness of black Malaita. And this wonderful thing, this seeming great deed of free will, he performed in much the same way that the itching of feet and tickle of fancy have led the feet of men over all the earth.

Though Jerry never laid eyes on Somo again, Bashti returned with his tribe the same day, grinning and chuckling as he appraised the damage. Only a few grass houses had been damaged by the shells. Only a few coconuts had been chopped down. And as for the slain pigs, lest they spoil, he made of their carcasses a great feast. One shell had knocked a hole through his sea-wall. He enlarged it for a launching-ways, faced the sides of it with dry-fitted coral rock, and gave orders for the building of an additional canoe-house. The only vexation he suffered was the death of Nalasu and the disappearance of Jerry—his two experiments in primitive eugenics.

XX

A week Jerry spent in the bush, deterred always from penetrating to the mountains by the bushmen who ever guarded the runways. And it would have gone hard with him in the matter of food, had he not, on the second day, encountered a lone small pig, evidently lost from its litter. It was his first hunting adventure for a living, and it prevented him from travelling farther, for, true to his instinct, he remained by his kill until it was nearly devoured.

True, he ranged widely about the neighbourhood, finding no other food he could capture. But always, until it was gone, he returned to the slain pig. Yet he was not happy in his freedom. He was too domesticated, too civilized. Too many thousands of years had elapsed since his ancestors had run freely wild. He was lonely. He could not get along without man. Too long had he, and the generations before him, lived in intimate relationship with the two-legged gods. Too long had his kind loved man, served him for love, endured for love, died for love, and, in return, been partly appreciated, less understood, and roughly loved.

So great was Jerry's loneliness that even a two-legged black-god was desirable, since white-gods had long since faded into the limbo of the past. For all he might have known, had he been capable of conjecturing, the only white-gods in existence had perished. Acting on the assumption that a black-god was better than no god, when he had quite finished the little pig, he deflected his course to the left, down-hill, toward the sea. He did this, again without reasoning, merely because, in the subtle processes of his brain, experience worked. His experience had been to live always close by the sea; humans he had always encountered close by the sea; and down-hill had invariably led to the sea.

He came out upon the shore of the reef-sheltered lagoon where ruined grass houses told him men had lived. The jungle ran riot through the place. Six-inch trees, throated with rotten remnants of thatched roofs through which they had aspired toward the sun, rose about him. Quick-growing trees had shadowed the kingposts so that the idols and totems, seated in carved shark jaws, grinned greenly and monstrously at the futility of man through a rime of moss and mottled fungus. A poor little sea-wall, never much at its best, sprawled in ruin from the coconut roots to the placid sea. Bananas, plantains, and breadfruit lay rotting on the ground. Bones lay about, human bones, and Jerry nosed them out, knowing them for what they were, emblems of the nothingness of life. Skulls he did not encounter, for the skulls that belonged to the scattered bones ornamented the devil devil houses in the upland bush villages.

The salt tang of the sea gladdened his nostrils, and he snorted with the pleasure of the stench of the mangrove swamp. But, another Crusoe chancing upon the footprint of another man Friday, his nose, not his eyes, shocked him electrically alert as he smelled the fresh contact of a living man's foot with the ground. It was a nigger's foot, but it was alive, it was immediate; and, as he traced it a score of yards, he came upon another foot-scent, indubitably a white man's.

Had there been an onlooker, he would have thought Jerry had gone suddenly mad. He rushed frantically about, turning and twisting his course, now his nose to the ground, now up in the air, whining as frantically as he rushed, leaping abruptly at right angles as new scents reached him, scurrying here and there and everywhere as if in a game of tag with some invisible playfellow.

But he was reading the full report which many men had written on the ground. A white man had been there, he learned, and a number of blacks. Here a black had climbed a coconut tree and cast down the nuts. There a banana tree had been despoiled of its clustered fruit; and, beyond, it was evident that a similar event had happened to a breadfruit tree. One thing, however, puzzled him—a scent new to him that was neither black man's nor white man's. Had he had the necessary knowledge and the wit of eye-observance, he would have noted that the footprint was smaller than a man's and that the toeprints were different from a Mary's in that they were close together and did not press deeply into the earth. What bothered him in his smelling was his ignorance of talcum powder. Pungent it was in his nostrils, but never, since first he had smelled out the footprints of man, had he encountered such a scent. And with this were combined other and fainter scents that were equally strange to him.

Not long did he interest himself in such mystery. A white man's footprints he had smelled, and through the maze of all the other prints he followed the one print down through a breach of sea-wall to the sea-pounded coral sand lapped by the sea. Here the latest freshness of many feet drew together where the nose of a boat had rested on the beach and where men had disembarked and embarked again. He smelled up all the story, and, his forelegs in the water till it touched his shoulders, he gazed out across the lagoon where the disappearing trail was lost to his nose.

Had he been half an hour sooner he would have seen a boat, without oars, gasoline-propelled, shooting across the quiet water. What he did see was an *Arangi*. True, it was far larger than the *Arangi* he had known, but it was white, it was long, it had masts, and it floated on the surface of the sea. It had three masts, sky-lofty and all of a size; but his observation was not trained to note the difference between them and the one long and the one short mast of the *Arangi*. The one floating world he had known was the white-painted *Arangi*. And, since, without a quiver of doubt, this was the *Arangi*, then, on board, would be his beloved Skipper. If *Arangis* could resurrect, then could Skippers resurrect, and in utter faith that the head of nothingness he had last seen on Bashti's knees he would find again rejoined to its body and its two legs on the deck of the white-painted floating world, he waded out to his depth, and, swimming dared the sea.

He greatly dared, for in venturing the water he broke one of the greatest and earliest taboos he had learned. In his vocabulary was no word for "crocodile"; yet in his thought, as potent as any utterable word, was an image of dreadful import—an image of a log awash that was not a log and that was alive, that could swim upon the surface, under the surface, and haul out across the dry land, that was huge-toothed, mighty-mawed, and certain death to a swimming dog.

But he continued the breaking of the taboo without fear. Unlike a man who can be simultaneously conscious of two states of mind, and who, swimming, would have known both the fear and the high courage with which he overrode the fear, Jerry, as he swam, knew only one state of mind, which was that he was swimming to the *Arangi* and to Skipper. At the moment preceding the first stroke of his paws in the water out of his depth, he had known all the terribleness of the taboo he deliberately broke. But, launched out, the decision made, the line of least resistance taken, he knew, single-thoughted, single-hearted, only that he was going to Skipper.

Little practised as he was in swimming, he swam with all his strength, whimpering in a sort of chant his eager love for Skipper who indubitably must be aboard the white yacht half a mile away. His little song of love, fraught with keenness of anxiety, came to the ears of a man and woman lounging in deck-chairs under the awning; and it was the quick-eyed woman who first saw the golden head of Jerry and cried out what she saw.

"Lower a boat, Husband-Man," she commanded. "It's a little dog. He mustn't drown."

"Dogs don't drown that easily," was "Husband-Man's" reply. "He'll make it all right. But what under the sun a dog's doing out here. . ." He lifted his marine glasses to his eyes and stared a moment. "And a white man's dog at that!"

Jerry beat the water with his paws and moved steadily along, straining his eyes at the growing yacht until suddenly warned by a sensing of immediate danger. The taboo smote him. This that moved toward him was the log awash that was not a log but a live thing of peril. Part of it he saw above the surface moving sluggishly, and ere that projecting part sank, he had an awareness that somehow it was different from a log awash.

Next, something brushed past him, and he encountered it with a snarl and a splashing of his forepaws. He was half-whirled about in the vortex of the thing's passage caused by the alarmed flirt of its tail. Shark it was, and not crocodile, and not so timidly would it have sheered clear but for the fact that it was fairly full with a recent feed of a huge sea turtle too feeble with age to escape.

Although he could not see it, Jerry sensed that the thing, the instrument of nothingness, lurked about him. Nor did he see the dorsal fin break surface and approach him from the rear. From the yacht he heard rifle-shots in quick succession. From the rear a panic splash came to his ears. That was all. The peril passed and was forgotten. Nor did he connect the rifle-shots with the passing of the peril. He did not know, and he was never to know, that one, known to men as Harley Kennan, but known as "Husband-Man" by the woman he called "Wife-Woman," who owned the three-topmast schooner yacht *Ariel*, had saved his life by sending a thirty-thirty Marlin bullet through the base of a shark's fin.

But Jerry was to know Harley Kennan, and quickly, for it was Harley Kennan, a bowline around his body under his arm-pits, lowered by a couple of seamen down the generous freeboard of the *Ariel*, who gathered in by the nape of the neck the smooth-coated Irish terrier that, treading water perpendicularly, had no eyes for him so eagerly did he gaze at the line of faces along the rail in quest of the one face.

No pause for thanks did he make when he was dropped down upon the deck. Instead, shaking himself instinctively as he ran, he scurried along the deck for Skipper. The man and his wife laughed at the spectacle.

"He acts as if he were demented with delight at being rescued," Mrs. Kennan observed.

And Mr. Kennan: "It's not that. He must have a screw loose somewhere. Perhaps he's one of those creatures who've slipped the ratchet off the motion cog. Maybe he can't stop running till he runs down."

In the meantime Jerry continued to run, up port side and down starboard side, from stern to bow and back again, wagging his stump tail and laughing friendliness to the many two-legged gods he encountered. Had he been able to think to such abstraction he would have been astounded at the number of white-gods. Thirty there were at least of them, not counting other gods that were neither black nor white, but that still, two-legged, upright and garmented, were beyond all peradventure gods. Likewise, had he been capable of such generalization, he would have decided that the white-gods had not yet all of them passed into the nothingness. As it was, he realized all this without being aware that he realized it.

But there was no Skipper. He sniffed down the forecastle hatch, sniffed into the galley where two Chinese cooks jabbered unintelligibly to him, sniffed down the cabin companionway, sniffed down the engine-room skylight and for the first time knew gasoline and engine oil; but sniff as he would, wherever he ran, no scent did he catch of Skipper.

Aft, at the wheel, he would have sat down and howled his heartbreak of disappointment, had not a white-god, evidently of command, in gold-decorated white duck cap and uniform, spoken to him. Instantly, always a gentleman, Jerry smiled with flattened ears of courtesy, wagged his tail, and approached. The hand of this high god had almost caressed his head when the woman's voice came down the deck in speech that Jerry did not understand. The words and terms of it were beyond him. But he sensed power of command in it, which was verified by the quick withdrawal of the hand of the god in white and gold who had almost caressed him. This god, stiffened electrically and pointed Jerry along the deck, and, with mouth encouragements and urgings the import of which Jerry could only guess, directed him toward the one who so commanded by saying:

"Send him, please, along to me, Captain Winters."

Jerry wriggled his body in delight of obeying, and would loyally have presented his head to her outreaching caress of hand, had not the strangeness and difference of her deterred him. He broke off in mid-approach and with a show of teeth snarled himself back and away from the windblown skirt of her. The only human females he had known were naked Marys. This skirt, flapping in the wind like a sail, reminded him of the menacing mainsail of the *Arangi* when it had jarred and crashed and swooped above his head. The noises her mouth made were gentle and ingratiating, but the fearsome skirt still flapped in the breeze.

"You ridiculous dog!" she laughed. "I'm not going to bite you."

But her husband thrust out a rough, sure hand and drew Jerry in to him. And Jerry wriggled in ecstasy under the god's caress, kissing the hand with a red flicker of tongue. Next, Harley Kennan directed him toward the woman sitting up in the deck-chair and bending forward, with hovering hands of greeting. Jerry obeyed. He advanced with flattened ears and laughing mouth: but, just ere she could touch him, the wind fluttered the skirt again and he backed away with a snarl.

"It's not you that he's afraid of, Villa," he said. "But of your skirt. Perhaps he's never seen a skirt before."

"You mean," Villa Kennan challenged, "that these head-hunting cannibals ashore here keep records of pedigrees and maintain kennels; for surely this absurd adventurer of a dog is as proper an Irish terrier as the *Ariel* is an Oregon-pine-planked schooner."

Harley Kennan laughed in acknowledgment. Villa Kennan laughed too; and Jerry knew that these were a pair of happy gods, and himself laughed with them.

Of his own initiative, he approached the lady god again, attracted by the talcum powder and other minor fragrances he had already identified as the strange scents encountered on the beach. But the unfortunate trade wind again fluttered her skirt, and again he backed away—not so far, this time, with much less of a bristle of his neck and shoulder hair, and with no more of a snarl than a mere half-baring of his fangs.

"He's afraid of your skirt," Harley insisted. "Look at him! He wants to come to you, but the skirt keeps him away. Tuck it under you so that it won't flutter, and see what happens."

Villa Kennan carried out the suggestion, and Jerry came circumspectly, bent his head to her hand and writhed his back under it, the while he sniffed her feet, stocking-clad and shoe-covered, and knew them as the feet which had trod uncovered the ruined ways of the village ashore.

"No doubt of it," Harley agreed. "He's white-man selected, white-man bred and born. He has a history. He knows adventure from the ground-roots up. If he could tell his story, we'd sit listening entranced for days. Depend on it, he's not known blacks all his life. Let's try him on Johnny."

Johnny, whom Kennan beckoned up to him, was a loan from the Resident Commissioner of the British Solomons at Tulagi, who had come along as pilot and guide to Kennan rather than as philosopher and friend. Johnny approached grinning, and Jerry's demeanour immediately changed. His body stiffened under Villa Kennan's hand as he drew away from her and stalked stiff-legged to the black. Jerry's ears did not flatten, nor did he laugh fellowship with his mouth, as he inspected Johnny and smelt his calves for future reference. Cavalier he was to the extreme, and, after the briefest of inspection, he turned back to Villa Kennan.

"What did I say?" her husband exulted. "He knows the colour line. He's a white man's dog that has been trained to it."

"My word," spoke up Johnny. "Me know 'm that fella dog. Me know 'm papa and mamma belong along him. Big fella white marster Mister Haggin stop along Meringe, mamma and papa stop along him that fella place."

Harley Kennan uttered a sharp exclamation.

"Of course," he cried. "The Commissioner told me all about it. The *Arangi*, that the Somo people captured, sailed last from Meringe Plantation. Johnny recognizes the dog as the same breed as the pair Haggin, of Meringe, must possess. But that was a long time ago. He must have been a little puppy. Of course he's a white man's dog."

"And yet you've overlooked the crowning proof of it," Villa Kennan teased. "The dog carries the evidence around with him."

Harley looked Jerry over carefully.

"Indisputable evidence," she insisted.

After another prolonged scrutiny, Kennan shook his head.

"Blamed if I can see anything so indisputable as to leave conjecture out."

"The tail," his wife gurgled. "Surely the natives do not bob the tails of their dogs.—Do they, Johnny? Do black man stop along Malaita chop 'm off tail along dog."

"No chop 'm off," Johnny agreed. "Mister Haggin along Meringe he chop 'm off. My word, he chop 'm that fella tail, you bet."

"Then he's the sole survivor of the *Arangi*," Villa Kennan concluded. "Don't you agree, Mr. Sherlock Holmes Kennan?"

"I salute you, Mrs. S. Holmes," her husband acknowledged gallantly. "And all that remains is for you to lead me directly to the head of La

Perouse himself. The sailing directions record that he left it somewhere in these islands."

Little did they guess that Jerry had lived on intimate terms with one Bashti, not many miles away along the shore, who, in Somo, at that very moment, sat in his grass house pondering over a head on his withered knees that had once been the head of the great navigator, the history of which had been forgotten by the sons of the chief who had taken it.

XXI

The fine, three-topmast schooner *Ariel*, on a cruise around the world, had already been out a year from San Francisco when Jerry boarded her. As a world, and as a white-god world, she was to him beyond compare. She was not small like the *Arangi*, nor was she cluttered fore and aft, on deck and below, with a spawn of niggers. The only black Jerry found on her was Johnny; while her spaciousness was filled principally with two-legged white-gods.

He met them everywhere, at the wheel, on lookout, washing decks, polishing brass-work, running aloft, or tailing on to sheets and tackles half a dozen at a time. But there was a difference. There were gods and gods, and Jerry was not long in learning that in the hierarchy of the heaven of these white-gods on the *Ariel*, the sailorizing, ship-working ones were far beneath the captain and his two white-and-gold-clad officers. These, in turn, were less than Harley Kennan and Villa Kennan; for them, it came quickly to him, Harley Kennan commanded. Nevertheless, there was one thing he did not learn and was destined never to learn, namely, the supreme god over all on the *Ariel*. Although he never tried to know, being unable to think to such a distance, he never came to know whether it was Harley Kennan who commanded Villa, or Villa Kennan who commanded Harley. In a way, without vexing himself with the problem, he accepted their over-lordship of the world as dual. Neither out-ranked the other. They seemed to rule co-equal, while all others bowed before them.

It is not true that to feed a dog is to win a dog's heart. Never did Harley or Villa feed Jerry; yet it was to them he elected to belong, them he elected to love and serve rather than to the Japanese steward who regularly fed him. For that matter, Jerry, like any dog, was able to differentiate between the mere direct food-giver and the food source. That is, subconsciously, he was aware that not alone his own food, but the food of all on board found its source in the man and woman. They it was who fed all and ruled all. Captain Winters might give orders to the sailors, but Captain Winters took orders from Harley Kennan. Jerry knew this as indubitably as he acted upon it, although all the while it never entered his head as an item of conscious knowledge.

And, as he had been accustomed, all his life, as with Mister Haggin, Skipper, and even with Bashti and the chief devil devil doctor of

Somo, he attached himself to the high gods themselves, and from the gods under them received deference accordingly. As Skipper, on the *Arangi*, and Bashti in Somo, had promulgated taboos, so the man and the woman on the *Ariel* protected Jerry with taboos. From Sano, the Japanese steward, and from him alone, did Jerry receive food. Not from any sailor in whaleboat or launch could he accept, or would he be offered, a bit of biscuit or an invitation to go ashore for a run. Nor did they offer it. Nor were they permitted to become intimate, to the extent of romping and playing with him, nor even of whistling to him along the deck.

By nature a "one-man" dog, all this was very acceptable to Jerry. Differences of degree there were, of course; but no one more delicately and definitely knew those differences than did Jerry himself. Thus, it was permissible for the two officers to greet him with a "Hello," or a "Good morning," and even to touch a hand in a brief and friendly pat to his head. With Captain Winters, however, greater familiarity obtained. Captain Winters could rub his ears, shake hands with his, scratch his back, and even roughly catch him by the jowls. But Captain Winters invariably surrendered him up when the one man and the one woman appeared on deck.

When it came to liberties, delicious, wanton liberties, Jerry alone of all on board could take them with the man and woman, and, on the other hand, they were the only two to whom he permitted liberties. Any indignity that Villa Kennan chose to inflict upon him he was throbbingly glad to receive, such as doubling his ears inside out till they stuck, at the same time making him sit upright, with helpless forefeet paddling the air for equilibrium, while she blew roguishly in his face and nostrils. As bad was Harley Kennan's trick of catching him gloriously asleep on an edge of Villa's skirt and of tickling the hair between his toes and making him kick involuntarily in his sleep, until he kicked himself awake to hearing of gurgles and snickers of laughter at his expense.

In turn, at night on deck, wriggling her toes at him under a rug to simulate some strange and crawling creature of an invader, he would dare to simulate his own befoolment and quite disrupt Villa's bed with his frantic ferocious attack on the thing that he knew was only her toes. In gales of laughter, intermingled with half-genuine cries of alarm as almost his teeth caught her toes, she always concluded by gathering him into her arms and laughing the last of her laughter away into his flattened ears of joy and love. Who else, of all on board the *Ariel*, would have dared such devilishness with the lady-god's bed? This question it never entered his mind to ask himself; yet he was fully aware of how exclusively favoured he was.

Another of his deliberate tricks was one discovered by accident. Thrusting his muzzle to meet her in love, he chanced to encounter her face with his soft-hard little nose with such force as to make her recoil and cry out. When, another time, in all innocence this happened again, he became conscious of it and of its effect upon her; and thereafter, when she grew too wildly wild, too wantonly facetious in her teasing playful love of him, he would thrust his muzzle at her face and make her throw her head back to escape him. After a time, learning that if he persisted, she would settle the situation by gathering him into her arms and gurgling into his ears, he made it a point to act his part until such delectable surrender and joyful culmination were achieved.

Never, by accident, in this deliberate game, did he hurt her chin or cheek so severely as he hurt his own tender nose, but in the hurt itself he found more of delight than pain. All of fun it was, all through, and, in addition, it was fun. Such hurt was more than fun. Such pain was heart-pleasure.

All dogs are god-worshippers. More fortunate than most dogs, Jerry won to a pair of gods that, no matter how much they commanded, loved more. Although his nose might threaten grievously to hurt the cheek of his adored god, rather than have it really hurt he would have spilled out all the love-tide of his heart that constituted the life of him. He did not live for food, for shelter, for a comfortable place between the darknesses that rounded existence. He lived for love. And as surely as he gladly lived for love, would he have died gladly for love.

Not quickly, in Somo, had Jerry's memory of Skipper and Mister Haggin faded. Life in the cannibal village had been too unsatisfying. There had been too little love. Only love can erase the memory of love, or rather, the hurt of lost love. And on board the *Ariel* such erasement occurred quickly. Jerry did not forget Skipper and Mister Haggin. But at the moments he remembered them the yearning that accompanied the memory grew less pronounced and painful. The intervals between the moments widened, nor did Skipper and Mister Haggin take form and reality so frequently in his dreams; for, after the manner of dogs, he dreamed much and vividly.

XXII

Northward, along the leeward coast of Malaita, the *Ariel* worked her leisurely way, threading the colour-riotous lagoon that lay between the shore-reefs and outer-reefs, daring passages so narrow and coral-patched that Captain Winters averred each day added a thousand grey hairs to his head, and dropping anchor off every walled inlet of the outer reef and every mangrove swamp of the mainland that looked promising of cannibal life. For Harley and Villa Kennan were in no hurry. So long as the way was interesting, they dared not how long it proved from anywhere to anywhere.

During this time Jerry learned a new name for himself—or, rather, an entire series of names for himself. This was because of an aversion on Harley Kennan's part against renaming a named thing.

"A name he must have had," he argued to Villa. "Haggin must have named him before he sailed on the *Arangi*. Therefore, nameless he must be until we get back to Tulagi and find out his real name."

"What's in a name?" Villa had begun to tease.

"Everything," her husband retorted. "Think of yourself, shipwrecked, called by your rescuers 'Mrs. Riggs,' or 'Mademoiselle de Maupin,' or just plain 'Topsy.' And think of me being called 'Benedict Arnold,' or 'Judas,' or. . . or. . . 'Haman.' No, keep him nameless, until we find out his original name."

"Must call him something," she objected. "Can't think of him without thinking something."

"Then call him many names, but never the same name twice. Call him 'Dog' to-day, and 'Mister Dog' to-morrow, and the next day something else."

So it was, more by tone and emphasis and context of situation than by anything else, that Jerry came hazily to identify himself with names such as: Dog, Mister Dog, Adventurer, Strong Useful One, Sing Song Silly, Noname, and Quivering Love-Heart. These were a few of the many names lavished on him by Villa. Harley, in turn, addressed him as: Man-Dog, Incorruptible One, Brass Tacks, Then Some, Sin of Gold, South Sea Satrap, Nimrod, Young Nick, and Lion-Slayer. In brief, the man and woman competed with each other to name him most without naming him ever the same. And Jerry, less by sound and syllable than by what of their hearts vibrated in their throats, soon learned to know himself by any name they chose to address to him. He no longer thought of himself as Jerry, but, instead, as any sound that sounded nice or was love-sounded.

His great disappointment (if "disappointment" may be considered to describe an unconsciousness of failure to realize the expected) was in the matter of language. No one on board, not even Harley and Villa, talked Nalasu's talk. All Jerry's large vocabulary, all his proficiency in the use of it, which would have set him apart as a marvel beyond all other dogs in the mastery of speech, was wasted on those of the *Ariel*. They did not speak, much less guess, the existence of the whiff-whuff shorthand language which Nalasu had taught him, and which, Nalasu dead, Jerry alone knew of all living creatures in the world.

In vain Jerry tried it on the lady-god. Sitting squatted on his haunches, his head bowed forward and held between her hands, he would talk and talk and elicit never a responsive word from her. With tiny whines and thin whimperings, with whiffs and whuffs and growly sorts of noises down in his throat, he would try to tell her somewhat of his tale. She was all meltingness of sympathy; she would hold her ear so near to the articulate mouth of him as almost to drown him in the flowing fragrance of her hair; and yet her brain told her nothing of what he uttered, although her heart surely sensed his intent.

"Bless me, Husband-Man!" she would cry out. "The Dog is talking. I know he is talking. He is telling me all about himself. The story of his life is mine, could I but understand. It's right here pouring into my miserable inadequate ears, only I can't catch it."

Harley was sceptical, but her woman's intuition guessed aright.

"I know it!" she would assure her husband. "I tell you he could tell the tale of all his adventures if only we had understanding. No other dog has ever talked this way to me. There's a tale there. I feel its touches. Sometimes almost do I know he is telling of joy, of love, of high elation, and combat. Again, it is indignation, hurt of outrage, despair and sadness."

"Naturally," Harley agreed quietly. "A white man's dog, adrift among the anthropophagi of Malaita, would experience all such sensations and, just as naturally, a white man's woman, a Wife-Woman, a dear, delightful Villa Kennan woman, can of herself imagine such a dog's experiences and deem his silly noises a recital of them, failing to recognize them as projections of her own delicious, sensitive, sympathetic self. The song of the sea from the lips of the shell—Pshaw! The song oneself makes of the sea and puts into the shell."

"Just the same—"

"Always the same," he gallantly cut her off. "Always right, especially when most wrong. Not in navigation, of course, nor in affairs such as the multiplication table, where the brass tacks of reality stud the way of one's ship among the rocks and shoals of the sea; but right, truth beyond truth to truth higher than truth, namely, intuitional truth."

"Now you are laughing at me with your superior man-wisdom," she retorted. "But I know—" she paused for the strength of words she needed, and words forsook her, so that her quick sweeping gesture of hand-touch to heart named authority that overrode all speech.

"We agree—I salute," he laughed gaily. "It was just precisely what I was saying. Our hearts can talk our heads down almost any time, and, best all, our hearts are always right despite the statistic that they are mostly wrong."

Harley Kennan did not believe, and never did believe, his wife's report of the tales Jerry told. And through all his days to the last one of them, he considered the whole matter a pleasant fancy, all poesy of sentiment, on Villa's part.

But Jerry, four-legged, smooth-coated, Irish terrier that he was, had the gift of tongues. If he could not teach languages, at least he could learn languages. Without effort, and quickly, practically with no teaching, he began picking up the language of the *Ariel*. Unfortunately, it was not a whiff-whuff, dog-possible language such as Nalasu had invented. While Jerry came to understand much that was spoken on the *Ariel*, he could speak none of it. Three names, at least, he had for the lady-god: "Villa," "Wife-Woman," "Missis Kennan," for so he heard her variously called. But he could not so call her. This was god-language entire, which only gods could talk. It was unlike the language of Nalasu's devising, which had been a compromise between god-talk and dog-talk, so that a god and a dog could talk in the common medium.

In the same way he learned many names for the one-man god: "Mister Kennan," "Harley," "Captain Kennan," and "Skipper." Only in the intimacy of the three of them alone did Jerry hear him called: "Husband-Man," "My Man," "Patient One," "Dear Man," "Lover," and "This Woman's Delight." But in no way could Jerry utter these names in address of the one-man nor the many names in address of the one-woman. Yet on a quiet night with no wind among the trees, often and often had he whispered to Nalasu, by whiff-whuff of name, from a hundred feet away.

One day, bending over him, her hair (drying from a salt-water swim) flying about him, the one-woman, her two hands holding his head and jowls so that his ribbon of kissing tongue just missed her nose in the empty air, sang to him: "'Don't know what to call him, but he's mighty lak' a rose!'"

On another day she repeated this, at the same time singing most of the song to him softly in his ear. In the midst of it Jerry surprised her. Equally true might be the statement that he surprised himself. Never, had he consciously done such a thing before. And he did it without volition. He never intended to do it. For that matter, the very thing he did was what mastered him into doing it. No more than could he refrain from shaking the water from his back after a swim, or from kicking in his sleep when his feet were tickled, could he have avoided doing this imperative thing.

As her voice, in the song, made soft vibrations in his ears, it seemed to him that she grew dim and vague before him, and that somehow, under the soft searching prod of her song, he was otherwhere. So much was he otherwhere that he did the surprising thing. He sat down abruptly, almost cataleptically, drew his head away from the clutch of her hands and out of the entanglement of her hair, and, his nose thrust upward at an angle of forty-five degrees, he began to quiver and to breathe audibly in rhythm to the rhythm of her singing. With a quick jerk, cataleptically, his nose pointed to the zenith, his mouth opened, and a flood of sound poured forth, running swiftly upward in crescendo and slowly falling as it died away.

This howl was the beginning, and it led to the calling him "Sing Song Silly." For Villa Kennan was quick to seize upon the howling her singing induced and to develop it. Never did he hang back when she sat down, extended her welcoming hands to him, and invited: "Come on, Sing Song Silly." He would come to her, sit down with the loved fragrance of her hair in his nostrils, lay the side of his head against hers, point his nose past her ear, and almost immediately follow her when she began her low singing. Minor strains were especially provocative in getting him started, and, once started, he would sing with her as long as she wished.

Singing it truly was. Apt in all ways of speech, he quickly learned to soften and subdue his howl till it was mellow and golden. Even could he manage it to die away almost to a whisper, and to rise and fall, accelerate and retard, in obedience to her own voice and in accord with it.

Jerry enjoyed the singing much in the same way the opium eater enjoys his dreams. For dream he did, vaguely and indistinctly, eyes wide open and awake, the lady-god's hair in a faint-scented cloud about him, her voice mourning with his, his consciousness drowning in the dreams of otherwhereness that came to him of the singing and that was the singing. Memories of pain were his, but of pain so long forgotten that it was no longer pain. Rather did it permeate him with a delicious sadness, and lift him away and out of the *Ariel* (lying at anchor in some coral lagoon) to that unreal place of Otherwhere.

For visions were his at such times. In the cold bleakness of night, it would seem he sat on a bare hill and raised his howl to the stars, while out of the dark, from far away, would drift to him an answering howl. And other howls, near and far, would drift along until the night was vocal with his kind. His kind it was. Without knowing it he *knew* it, this camaraderie of the land of Otherwhere.

Nalasu, in teaching him the whiff-whuff language, deliberately had gone into the intelligence of him; but Villa, unwitting of what she was doing, went into the heart of him, and into the heart of his heredity, touching the profoundest chords of ancient memories and making them respond.

As instance: dim shapes and shadowy forms would sometimes appear to him out of the night, and as they flitted spectrally past he would hear, as in a dream, the hunting cries of the pack; and, as his pulse quickened, his own hunting instinct would rouse until his controlled soft-howling in the song broke into eager whinings. His head would lower out of the entanglement of the woman's hair; his feet would begin making restless, spasmodic movements as if running; and Presto, in a flash, he would be out and away, across the face of time, out of reality and into the dream, himself running in the midst of those shadowy forms in the hunting fellowship of the pack.

And as men have ever desired the dust of the poppy and the juice of the hemp, so Jerry desired the joys that were his when Villa Kennan opened her arms to him, embraced him with her hair, and sang him across time and space into the dream of his ancient kind.

Not always, however, were such experiences his when they sang together. Usually, unaccompanied by visions, he knew no more than vaguenesses of sensations, sadly sweet, ghosts of memories that they were. At other times, incited by such sadness, images of Skipper and Mister Haggin would throng his mind; images, too, of Terrence, and

Biddy, and Michael, and the rest of the long-vanished life at Meringe Plantation.

"My dear," Harley said to Villa at the conclusion of one such singing, "it's fortunate for him that you are not an animal trainer, or, rather, I suppose, it would be better called 'trained animal show-woman'; for you'd be topping the bill in all the music-halls and vaudeville houses of the world."

"If I did," she replied, "I know he'd just love to do it with me—"

"Which would make it a very unusual turn," Harley caught her up.

"You mean. . . ?"

"That in about one turn in a hundred does the animal love its work or is the animal loved by its trainer."

"I thought all the cruelty had been done away with long ago," she contended.

"So the audience thinks, and the audience is ninety-nine times wrong."

Villa heaved a great sigh of renunciation as she said, "Then I suppose I must abandon such promising and lucrative career right now in the very moment you have discovered it for me. Just the same the billboards would look splendid with my name in the hugest letters—"

"Villa Kennan the Thrush-throated Songstress, and Sing Song Silly the Irish-Terrier Tenor," her husband pictured the head-lines for her.

And with dancing eyes and lolling tongue Jerry joined in the laughter, not because he knew what it was about, but because it tokened they were happy and his love prompted him to be happy with them.

For Jerry had found, and in the uttermost, what his nature craved— the love of a god. Recognizing the duality of their lordship over the *Ariel*, he loved the pair of them; yet, somehow, perhaps because she had penetrated deepest into his heart with her magic voice that transported him to the land of Otherwhere, he loved the lady-god beyond all love he had ever known, not even excluding his love for Skipper.

XXIII

One thing Jerry learned early on the *Ariel*, namely, that nigger-chasing was not permitted. Eager to please and serve his new gods, he took advantage of the first opportunity to worry a canoe-load of blacks who came visiting on board. The quick chiding of Villa and the command of Harley made him pause in amazement. Fully believing he had been mistaken, he resumed his ragging of the particular black he had picked upon. This time Harley's voice was peremptory, and Jerry came to him, his wagging tail and wriggling body all eagerness of apology, as was his rose-strip of tongue that kissed the hand of forgiveness with which Harley patted him.

Next, Villa called him to her. Holding him close to her with her hands on his jowls, eye to eye and nose to nose, she talked to him earnestly about the sin of nigger-chasing. She told him that he was no common bush-dog, but a blooded Irish gentleman, and that no dog that was a gentleman ever did such things as chase unoffending black men. To all of which he listened with unblinking serious eyes, understanding little of what she said, yet comprehending all. "Naughty" was a word in the *Ariel* language he had already learned, and she used it several times. "Naughty," to him, meant "must not," and was by way of expressing a taboo.

Since it was their way and their will, who was he, he might well have asked himself, to disobey their rule or question it? If niggers were not to be chased, then chase them he would not, despite the fact that Skipper had encouraged him to chase them. Not in such set terms did Jerry consider the matter; but in his own way he accepted the conclusions.

Love of a god, with him, implied service. It pleased him to please with service. And the foundation-stone of service, in his case, was obedience. Yet it strained him sore for a time to refrain from snarl and snap when the legs of strange and presumptuous blacks passed near him along the *Ariel's* white deck.

But there were times and times, as he was to learn, and the time came when Villa Kennan wanted a bath, a real bath in fresh, rain-descended, running water, and when Johnny, the black pilot from Tulagi, made a mistake. The chart showed a mile of the Suli river where it emptied into the sea. Why it showed only a mile was because no white man had ever explored it farther. When Villa proposed the bath, her husband advised with Johnny. Johnny shook his head.

"No fella boy stop 'm along that place," he said. "No make 'm trouble along you. Bush fella boy stop 'm long way too much."

So it was that the launch went ashore, and, while its crew lolled in the shade of the beach coconuts, Villa, Harley, and Jerry followed the river inland a quarter of a mile to the first likely pool.

"One can never be too sure," Harley said, taking his automatic pistol from its holster and placing it on top his heap of clothes. "A stray bunch of blacks might just happen to surprise us."

Villa stepped into the water to her knees, looked up at the dark jungle roof high overhead through which only occasional shafts of sunlight penetrated, and shuddered.

"An appropriate setting for a dark deed," she smiled, then scooped a handful of chill water against her husband, who plunged in in pursuit.

For a time Jerry sat by their clothes and watched the frolic. Then the drifting shadow of a huge butterfly attracted his attention, and soon he was nosing through the jungle on the trail of a wood-rat. It was not a very fresh trail. He knew that well enough; but in the deeps of him were all his instincts of ancient training—instincts to hunt, to prowl, to pursue living things, in short, to play the game of getting his own meat though for ages man had got the meat for him and his kind.

So it was, exercising faculties that were no longer necessary, but that were still alive in him and clamorous for exercise, he followed the long-since passed wood-rat with all the soft-footed crouching craft of the meat-pursuer and with utmost fineness of reading the scent. The trail crossed a fresh trail, a trail very fresh, very immediately fresh. As if a rope had been attached to it, his head was jerked abruptly to right angles with his body. The unmistakable smell of a black was in his nostrils. Further, it was a strange black, for he did not identify it with the many he possessed filed away in the pigeon-holes of his brain.

Forgotten was the stale wood-rat as he followed the new trail. Curiosity and play impelled him. He had no thought of apprehension for Villa and Harley—not even when he reached the spot where the black, evidently startled by bearing their voices, had stood and debated, and so left a very strong scent. From this point the trail swerved off toward the pool. Nervously alert, strung to extreme tension, but without alarm, still playing at the game of tracking, Jerry followed.

From the pool came occasional cries and laughter, and each time they reached his ears Jerry experienced glad little thrills. Had he been asked, and had he been able to express the sensations of emotion in terms of thought, he would have said that the sweetest sound in the world was any sound of Villa Kennan's voice, and that, next sweetest, was any sound of Harley Kennan's voice. Their voices thrilled him, always, reminding him of his love for them and that he was beloved of them.

With the first sight of the strange black, which occurred close to the pool, Jerry's suspicions were aroused. He was not conducting himself as an ordinary black, not on evil intent, should conduct himself. Instead, he betrayed all the actions of one who lurked in the perpetration of harm. He crouched on the jungle floor, peering around a great root of a board tree. Jerry bristled and himself crouched as he watched.

Once, the black raised his rifle half-way to his shoulder; but, with an outburst of splashing and laughter, his unconscious victims evidently removed themselves from his field of vision. His rifle was no old-fashioned Snider, but a modern, repeating Winchester; and he showed habituation to firing it from his shoulder rather than from the hip after the manner of most Malaitans.

Not satisfied with his position by the board tree, he lowered his gun to his side and crept closer to the pool. Jerry crouched low and followed. So low did he crouch that his head, extended horizontally forward, was much lower than his shoulders which were humped up queerly and composed the highest part of him. When the black paused, Jerry paused, as if instantly frozen. When the black moved, he moved, but more swiftly, cutting down the distance between them. And all the while the hair of his neck and shoulders bristled in recurrent waves of ferocity and wrath. No golden dog this, ears flattened and tongue laughing in the arms of the lady-god, no Sing Song Silly chanting ancient memories in the cloud-entanglement of her hair; but a four-legged creature of battle, a fanged killer ripe to rend and destroy.

Jerry intended to attack as soon as he had crept sufficiently near. He was unaware of the *Ariel* taboo against nigger-chasing. At that moment it had no place in his consciousness. All he knew was that harm threatened the man and woman and that this nigger intended this harm.

So much had Jerry gained on his quarry, that when again the black squatted for his shot, Jerry deemed he was near enough to rush. The rifle was coming to shoulder when he sprang forward. Swiftly as he sprang, he made no sound, and his victim's first warning was when Jerry's body, launched like a projectile, smote the black squarely between the shoulders. At the same moment his teeth entered the back of the neck, but too near the base in the lumpy shoulder muscles to permit the fangs to penetrate to the spinal cord.

In the first fright of surprise, the black's finger pulled the trigger and his throat loosed an unearthly yell. Knocked forward on his face, he rolled over and grappled with Jerry, who slashed cheek-bone and cheek and ribboned an ear; for it is the way of an Irish terrier to bite repeatedly and quickly rather than to hold a bulldog grip.

When Harley Kennan, automatic in hand and naked as Adam, reached the spot, he found dog and man locked together and tearing up the forest mould in their struggle. The black, his face streaming blood, was throttling Jerry with both hands around his neck; and Jerry, snorting, choking, snarling, was scratching for dear life with the claws of his hind feet. No puppy claws were they, but the stout claws of a mature dog that were stiffened by a backing of hard muscles. And they ripped naked chest and abdomen full length again and again until the whole front of the man was streaming red. Harley Kennan did not dare chance a shot, so closely were the combatants locked. Instead, stepping in close; he smashed down the butt of his automatic upon the side of the man's head. Released by the relaxing of the stunned black's hands, Jerry flung himself in a flash upon the exposed throat, and only Harley's hand on his neck and Harley's sharp command made him cease and stand clear. He trembled with rage and continued to snarl ferociously, although he would desist long enough to glance up with his eyes, flatten his ears, and wag his tail each time Harley uttered "Good boy."

"Good boy" he knew for praise; and he knew beyond any doubt, by Harley's repetition of it, that he had served him and served him well.

"Do you know the beggar intended to bush-whack us," Harley told Villa, who, half-dressed and still dressing, had joined him. "It wasn't fifty feet and he couldn't have missed. Look at the Winchester. No old smooth bore. And a fellow with a gun like that would know how to use it."

"But why didn't he?" she queried.

Her husband pointed to Jerry.

Villa's eyes brightened with quick comprehension. "You mean. . . ?" she began.

He nodded. "Just that. Sing Song Silly beat him to it." He bent, rolled the man over, and discovered the lacerated back of the neck. "That's where he landed on him first, and he must have had his finger on the trigger, drawing down on you and me, most likely me first, when Sing Song Silly broke up his calculations."

Villa was only half hearing, for she had Jerry in her arms and was calling him "Blessed Dog," the while she stilled his snarling and soothed down the last bristling hair.

But Jerry snarled again and was for leaping upon the black when he stirred restlessly and dizzily sat up. Harley removed a knife from between the bare skin and a belt.

"What name belong you?" he demanded.

But the black had eyes only for Jerry, staring at him in wondering amaze until he pieced the situation together in his growing clarity of brain and realized that such a small chunky animal had spoiled his game.

"My word," he grinned to Harley, "that fella dog put 'm crimp along me any amount."

He felt out the wounds of his neck and face, while his eyes embraced the fact that the white master was in possession of his rifle.

"You give 'm musket belong me," he said impudently.

"I give 'm you bang alongside head," was Harley's answer.

"He doesn't seem to me to be a regular Malaitan," he told Villa. "In the first place, where would he get a rifle like that? Then think of his nerve. He must have seen us drop anchor, and he must have known our launch was on the beach. Yet he played to take our heads and get away with them back into the bush—"

"What name belong you?" he again demanded.

But not until Johnny and the launch crew arrived breathless from their run, did he learn. Johnny's eyes gloated when he beheld the prisoner, and he addressed Kennan in evident excitement.

"You give 'm me that fella boy," he begged. "Eh? You give 'm me that fella boy."

"What name you want 'm?"

Not for some time would Johnny answer this question, and then only when Kennan told him that there was no harm done and that he intended to let the black go. At this Johnny protested vehemently.

"Maybe you fetch 'm that fella boy along Government House, Tulagi, Government House give 'm you twenty pounds. Him plenty bad fella boy too much. Makawao he name stop along him. Bad fella boy too much. Him Queensland boy—"

"What name Queensland?" Kennan interrupted. "He belong that fella place?"

Johnny shook his head.

"Him belong along Malaita first time. Long time before too much he recruit 'm along schooner go work along Queensland."

"He's a return Queenslander," Harley interpreted to Villa. "You know, when Australia went 'all white,' the Queensland plantations had to send all the black birds back. This Makawao is evidently one of them, and a hard case as well, if there's anything in Johnny's gammon about twenty pounds reward for him. That's a big price for a black."

Johnny continued his explanation which, reduced to flat and sober English, was to the effect that Makawao had always borne a bad character. In Queensland he had served a total of four years in jail for thefts, robberies, and attempted murder. Returned to the Solomons by the Australian government, he had recruited on Buli Plantation for the purpose—as was afterwards proved—of getting arms and ammunition. For an attempt to kill the manager he had received fifty lashes at Tulagi and served a year. Returned to Buli Plantation to finish his labour service, he had contrived to kill the owner in the manager's absence and to escape in a whaleboat.

In the whaleboat with him he had taken all the weapons and ammunition of the plantation, the owner's head, ten Malaita recruits, and two recruits from San Cristobal—the two last because they were salt-water men and could handle the whaleboat. Himself and the ten Malaitans, being bushmen, were too ignorant of the sea to dare the long passage from Guadalcanar.

On the way, he had raided the little islet of Ugi, sacked the store, and taken the head of the solitary trader, a gentle-souled half-caste from Norfolk Island who traced back directly to a Pitcairn ancestry straight from the loins of McCoy of the Bounty. Arrived safely at Malaita, he and his fellows, no longer having any use for the two San Cristobal boys, had taken their heads and eaten their bodies.

"My word, him bad fella boy any amount," Johnny finished his tale. "Government House, Tulagi, damn glad give 'm twenty pounds along that fella."

"You blessed Sing Song Silly," Villa, murmured in Jerry's ears. "If it hadn't been for you—"

"Your head and mine would even now be galumping through the bush as Makawao hit the high places for home," Harley concluded for her. "My word, some fella dog that, any amount," he added lightly.

"And I gave him merry Ned just the other day for nigger-chasing, and he knew his business better than I did all the time."

"If anybody tries to claim him—" Villa threatened.

Harley confirmed her muttered sentiment with a nod.

"Any way," he said, with a smile, "there would have been one consolation if your head had gone up into the bush."

"Consolation!" she cried, throaty with indignation.

"Why, yes; because in that case my head would have gone along."

"You dear and blessed Husband-Man," she murmured, a quick cloudiness of moisture in her eyes, as with her eyes she embraced him, her arms still around Jerry, who, sensing the ecstasy of the moment, kissed her fragrant cheek with his ribbon-tongue of love.

XXIV

When the *Ariel* cleared from Malu, on the north-west coast of Malaita, Malaita sank down beneath the sea-rim astern and, so far as Jerry's life was concerned, remained sunk for ever—another vanished world, that, in his consciousness, partook of the ultimate nothingness that had befallen Skipper. For all Jerry might have known, though he pondered it not, Malaita was a universe, beheaded and resting on the knees of some brooding lesser god, himself vastly mightier than Bashti whose knees bore the brooding weight of Skipper's sun-dried, smoke-cured head, this lesser god vexed and questing, feeling and guessing at the dual twin-mysteries of time and space and of motion and matter, above, beneath, around, and beyond him.

Only, in Jerry's case, there was no pondering of the problem, no awareness of the existence of such mysteries. He merely accepted Malaita as another world that had ceased to be. He remembered it as he remembered dreams. Himself a live thing, solid and substantial, possessed of weight and dimension, a reality incontrovertible, he moved through the space and place of being, concrete, hard, quick, convincing, an absoluteness of something surrounded by the shades and shadows of the fluxing phantasmagoria of nothing.

He took his worlds one by one. One by one his worlds evaporated, rose beyond his vision as vapours in the hot alembic of the sun, sank for ever beneath sea-levels, themselves unreal and passing as the phantoms of a dream. The totality of the minute, simple world of the humans, microscopic and negligible as it was in the siderial universe, was as far beyond his guessing as is the siderial universe beyond the starriest guesses and most abysmal imaginings of man.

Jerry was never to see the dark island of savagery again, although often in his sleeping dreams it was to return to him in vivid illusion, as he relived his days upon it, from the destruction of the *Arangi* and the man-eating orgy on the beach to his flight from the shell-scattered house and flesh of Nalasu. These dream episodes constituted for him another land of Otherwhere, mysterious, unreal, and evanescent as clouds drifting across the sky or bubbles taking iridescent form and bursting on the surface of the sea. Froth and foam it was, quick-vanishing as he awoke, non-existent as Skipper, Skipper's head on the withered knees of Bashti in the lofty grass house. Malaita the real,

Malaita the concrete and ponderable, vanished and vanished for ever, as Meringe had vanished, as Skipper had vanished, into the nothingness.

From Malaita the *Ariel* steered west of north to Ongtong Java and to Tasman—great atolls that sweltered under the Line not quite awash in the vast waste of the West South Pacific. After Tasman was another wide sea-stretch to the high island of Bougainville. Thence, bearing generally south-east and making slow progress in the dead beat to windward, the *Ariel* dropped anchor in nearly every harbour of the Solomons, from Choiseul and Ronongo islands, to the islands of Kulambangra, Vangunu, Pavuvu, and New Georgia. Even did she ride to anchor, desolately lonely, in the Bay of a Thousand Ships.

Last of all, so far as concerned the Solomons, her anchor rumbled down and bit into the coral-sanded bottom of the harbour of Tulagi, where, ashore on Florida Island, lived and ruled the Resident Commissioner.

To the Commissioner, Harley Kennan duly turned over Makawao, who was committed to a grass-house jail, well guarded, to sit in leg-irons against the time of trial for his many crimes. And Johnny, the pilot, ere he returned to the service of the Commissioner, received a fair portion of the twenty pounds of head money that Kennan divided among the members of the launch crew who had raced through the jungle to the rescue the day Jerry had taken Makawao by the back of the neck and startled him into pulling the trigger of his unaimed rifle.

"I'll tell you his name," the Commissioner said, as they sat on the wide veranda of his bungalow. "It's one of Haggin's terriers—Haggin of Meringe Lagoon. The dog's father is Terrence, the mother is Biddy. The dog's own name is Jerry, for I was present at the christening before ever his eyes were open. Better yet, I'll show you his brother. His brother's name is Michael. He's nigger-chaser on the *Eugenie*, the two-topmast schooner that rides abreast of you. Captain Kellar is the skipper. I'll have him bring Michael ashore. Beyond all doubt, this Jerry is the sole survivor of the *Arangi*."

"When I get the time, and a sufficient margin of funds, I shall pay a visit to Chief Bashti—oh, no British cruiser program. I'll charter a couple of trading ketches, take my own black police force and as many white men as I cannot prevent from volunteering. There won't be any shelling of grass houses. I'll land my shore party down the coast and cut in and come down upon Somo from the rear, timing my vessels to arrive on Somo's sea-front at the same time."

"You will answer slaughter with slaughter?" Villa Kennan objected.

"I will answer slaughter with law," the Commissioner replied. "I will teach Somo law. I hope that no accidents will occur. I hope that no life will be lost on either side. I know, however, that I shall recover Captain Van Horn's head, and his mate Borckman's, and bring them back to Tulagi for Christian burial. I know that I shall get old Bashti by the scruff of the neck and sit him down while I pump law and square-dealing into him. Of course. . ."

The Commissioner, ascetic-looking, an Oxford graduate, narrow-shouldered and elderly, tired-eyed and bespectacled like the scholar he was, like the scientist he was, shrugged his shoulders. "Of course, if they are not amenable to reason, there may be trouble, and some of them and some of us will get hurt. But, one way or the other, the conclusion will be the same. Old Bashti will learn that it is expedient to maintain white men's heads on their shoulders."

"But how will he learn?" Villa Kennan asked. "If he is shrewd enough not to fight you, and merely sits and listens to your English law, it will be no more than a huge joke to him. He will no more than pay the price of listening to a lecture for any atrocity he commits."

"On the contrary, my dear Mrs. Kennan. If he listens peaceably to the lecture, I shall fine him only a hundred thousand coconuts, five tons of ivory nut, one hundred fathoms of shell money, and twenty fat pigs. If he refuses to listen to the lecture and goes on the war path, then, unpleasantly for me, I assure you, I shall be compelled to thrash him and his village, first: and, next, I shall triple the fine he must pay and lecture the law into him a trifle more compendiously."

"Suppose he doesn't fight, stops his ears to the lecture, and declines to pay?" Villa Kennan persisted.

"Then he shall be my guest, here in Tulagi, until he changes his mind and heart, and does pay, and listens to an entire course of lectures."

So it was that Jerry came to hear his old-time name on the lips of Villa and Harley, and saw once again his full-brother Michael.

"Say nothing," Harley muttered to Villa, as they made out, peering over the bow of the shore-coming whaleboat, the rough coat, red-wheaten in colour, of Michael. "We won't know anything about anything, and we won't even let on we're watching what they do."

Jerry, feigning interest in digging a hole in the sand as if he were on a fresh scent, was unaware of Michael's nearness. In fact, so well had

Jerry feigned that he had forgotten it was all a game, and his interest was very real as he sniffed and snorted joyously in the bottom of the hole he had dug. So deep was it, that all he showed of himself was his hind-legs, his rump, and an intelligent and stiffly erect stump of a tail.

Little wonder that he and Michael failed to see each other. And Michael, spilling over with unused vitality from the cramped space of the *Eugenie's* deck, scampered down the beach in a hurly-burly of joy, scenting a thousand intimate land-scents as he ran, and describing a jerky and eccentric course as he made short dashes and good-natured snaps at the coconut crabs that scuttled across his path to the safety of the water or reared up and menaced him with formidable claws and a spluttering and foaming of the shell-lids of their mouths.

The beach was only so long. The end of it reached where rose the rugged wall of a headland, and while the Commissioner introduced Captain Kellar to Mr. and Mrs. Kennan, Michael came tearing back across the wet-hard sand. So interested was he in everything that he failed to notice the small rear-end portion of Jerry that was visible above the level surface of the beach. Jerry's ears had given him warning, and, the precise instant that he backed hurriedly up and out of the hole, Michael collided with him. As Jerry was rolled, and as Michael fell clear over him, both erupted into ferocious snarls and growls. They regained their legs, bristled and showed teeth at each other, and stalked stiff-leggedly, in a stately and dignified sort of way, as they drew intimidating semi-circles about each other.

But they were fooling all the while, and were more than a trifle embarrassed. For in each of their brains were bright identification pictures of the plantation house and compound and beach of Meringe. They knew, but they were reticent of recognition. No longer puppies, vaguely proud of the sedateness of maturity, they strove to be proud and sedate while all their impulse was to rush together in a frantic ecstasy.

Michael it was, less travelled in the world than Jerry, by nature not so self-controlled, who threw the play-acting of dignity to the wind, and, with shrill whinings of emotion, with body-wrigglings of delight, flashed out his tongue of love and shouldered his brother roughly in eagerness to get near to him.

Jerry responded as eagerly with kiss of tongue and contact of shoulder; then both, springing apart, looked at each other, alert and querying, almost in half challenge, Jerry's ears pricked into living interrogations, Michael's one good ear similarly questioning, his withered ear retaining its permanent queer and crinkly cock in the tip of it. As one, they sprang away in a wild scurry down the beach, side by side, laughing to each other and occasionally striking their shoulders together as they ran.

"No doubt of it," said the Commissioner. "The very way their father and mother run. I have watched them often."

BUT, AFTER TEN DAYS OF comradeship, came the parting. It was Michael's first visit on the *Ariel*, and he and Jerry had spent a frolicking half-hour on her white deck amid the sound and commotion of hoisting in boats, making sail, and heaving out anchor. As the *Ariel* began to move through the water and heeled to the filling of her canvas by the brisk trade-wind, the Commissioner and Captain Kellar shook last farewells and scrambled down the gang-plank to their waiting whaleboats. At the last moment Captain Kellar had caught Michael up, tucked him under an arm, and with him dropped into the, sternsheets of his whaleboat.

Painters were cast off, and in the sternsheets of each boat solitary white men were standing up, heads bared in graciousness of conduct to the furnace-stab of the tropic sun, as they waved additional and final farewells. And Michael, swept by the contagion of excitement, barked and barked again, as if it were a festival of the gods being celebrated.

"Say good-bye to your brother, Jerry," Villa Kennan prompted in Jerry's ear, as she held him, his quivering flanks between her two palms, on the rail where she had lifted him.

And Jerry, not understanding her speech, torn about with conflicting desires, acknowledged her speech with wriggling body, a quick back-toss of head, and a red flash of kissing tongue, and, the next moment, his head over the rail and lowered to see the swiftly diminishing Michael, was mouthing grief and woe very much akin to the grief and woe his mother, Biddy, had mouthed in the long ago, on the beach of Meringe, when he had sailed away with Skipper.

For Jerry had learned partings, and beyond all peradventure this was a parting, though little he dreamed that he would again meet Michael across the years and across the world, in a fabled valley of far California, where they would live out their days in the hearts and arms of the beloved gods.

Michael, his forefeet on the gunwale, barked to him in a puzzled, questioning sort of way, and Jerry whimpered back incommunicable understanding. The lady-god pressed his two flanks together reassuringly, and he turned to her, his cool nose touched questioningly to her cheek. She gathered his body close against her breast in one encircling arm, her free hand resting on the rail, half-closed, a pink-and-white heart of flower, fragrant and seducing. Jerry's nose quested the way of it. The aperture invited. With snuggling, budging, and nudging-movements he spread the fingers slightly wider as his nose penetrated into the sheer delight and loveliness of her hand.

He came to rest, his golden muzzle soft-enfolded to the eyes, and was very still, all forgetful of the *Ariel* showing her copper to the sun under the press of the wind, all forgetful of Michael growing small in the distance as the whaleboat grew small astern. No less still was Villa. Both were playing the game, although to her it was new.

As long as he could possibly contain himself, Jerry maintained his stiffness. And then, his love bursting beyond the control of him, he gave a sniff—as prodigious a one as he had sniffed into the tunnel of Skipper's hand in the long ago on the deck of the *Arangi*. And, as Skipper had relaxed into the laughter of love, so did the lady-god now. She gurgled gleefully. Her fingers tightened, in a caress that almost hurt, on Jerry's muzzle. Her other hand and arm crushed him against her till he gasped. Yet all the while his stump of tail valiantly bobbed back and forth, and, when released from such blissful contact, his silky ears flattened back and down as, with first a scarlet slash of tongue to cheek, he seized her hand between his teeth and dented the soft skin with a love bite that did not hurt.

And so, for Jerry, vanished Tulagi, its Commissioner's bungalow on top of the hill, its vessels riding to anchor in the harbour, and Michael, his full blood-brother. He had grown accustomed to such vanishments. In such way had vanished as in the mirage of a dream, Meringe, Somo, and the *Arangi*. In such way had vanished all the worlds and harbours and roadsteads and atoll lagoons where the *Ariel* had lifted her laid anchor and gone on across and over the erasing sea-rim.

A Note About the Author

Jack London (1876–1916) was an American novelist and journalist. Born in San Francisco to Florence Wellman, a spiritualist, and William Chaney, an astrologer, London was raised by his mother and her husband, John London, in Oakland. An intelligent boy, Jack went on to study at the University of California, Berkeley before leaving school to join the Klondike Gold Rush. His experiences in the Klondike—hard labor, life in a hostile environment, and bouts of scurvy—both shaped his sociopolitical outlook and served as powerful material for such works as "To Build a Fire" (1902), *The Call of the Wild* (1903), and *White Fang* (1906). When he returned to Oakland, London embarked on a career as a professional writer, finding success with novels and short fiction. In 1904, London worked as a war correspondent covering the Russo-Japanese War and was arrested several times by Japanese authorities. Upon returning to California, he joined the famous Bohemian Club, befriending such members as Ambrose Bierce and John Muir. London married Charmian Kittredge in 1905, the same year he purchased the thousand-acre Beauty Ranch in Sonoma County, California. London, who suffered from numerous illnesses throughout his life, died on his ranch at the age of 40. A lifelong advocate for socialism and animal rights, London is recognized as a pioneer of science fiction and an important figure in twentieth century American literature.

A Note from the Publisher

Spanning many genres, from non-fiction essays to literature classics to children's books and lyric poetry, Mint Edition books showcase the master works of our time in a modern new package. The text is freshly typeset, is clean and easy to read, and features a new note about the author in each volume. Many books also include exclusive new introductory material. Every book boasts a striking new cover, which makes it as appropriate for collecting as it is for gift giving. Mint Edition books are only printed when a reader orders them, so natural resources are not wasted. We're proud that our books are never manufactured in excess and exist only in the exact quantity they need to be read and enjoyed.

Discover more of your favorite classics with Bookfinity™.

- Track your reading with custom book lists.
- Get great book recommendations for your personalized Reader Type.
- Add reviews for your favorite books.
- AND MUCH MORE!

Visit **bookfinity.com** and take the fun Reader Type quiz to get started.

Enjoy our classic and modern companion pairings!